Southern Haunts

Spirits That Walk Among Us

Southern Haunts

Spirits That
Walk Among Us

edited by
Alexander S. Brown
&
J.L. Mulvihill

SEVENTH STAR PRESS

Cover art and design: Enggar Adirasa
Cover art in this book copyright © 2013 Enggar Adirasa & Seventh Star Press, LLC.

Interior Illustrations: Robert K
Interior artwork ©2013 Robert K. & Seventh Star Press

Editors: Alexander S. Brown and J.L. Mulvihill

Published by Seventh Star Press, LLC.

ISBN Number 9781937929121

Library of Congress Control Number: 2013934969

Seventh Star Press
www.seventhstarpress.com
info@seventhstarpress.com

Printed in the United States of America

First Edition

Copyright Acknowledgements

Dedication:

J.L. Mulvihill and Alexander S. Brown would like to dedicate this anthology to all departed loved ones connected to the authors, editors, artists, and publishers of this project. We would like to give special thanks to our assistant editor Louise Myers for her suggestions and hauntingly keen eye, Seventh Star Press for the publication of this anthology, artist Robert K for his interior art, and artist Enggar Adirasa for his cover art.

Table of Contents

Introduction

It was October 2010 when author, J.L. Mulvihill, and myself visited Hot Springs, AR. Our trip regarded participation with an event by Imagicopter known as, "The Zombie Dance," which consisted of a gathering of authors that read to the public. Once parting from the event, we explored the city with wonder as the night fell. In our roaming about, J.L. and myself spoke of subjects such as writing and how to entertain contemporary crowds with the art of literature.

While in brainstorming, we found a paranormal tour that began near the witching hour. After brief debate, we decided to break from business to join this crowd of believers and skeptics. Once the tour ended, both, J.L. and myself, felt inspired. We then visited a nearby pub to drink a few spirits and enjoy a late night meal. Upon entering this establishment, we felt as if we had stepped into a wonderland as this pub was elaborately decorated in the spirit of Halloween. In the background, fitting music played, such as, I Put A Spell on You, Bad Moon Rising, etc.

While enjoying the atmosphere, one of us, I can't remember which one, brought up ghost stories and folk tales. We discussed stories that were inspired by true events and stories that were nothing more than urban myth. While speaking of ghosts and hauntings, I realized then that she and I were on the same decayed page of being infatuated by the afterlife.

Then simply, we decided it would be fun to gather a collection of ghost stories from authors we had met at conventions as well as online acquaintances. Therefore on that cold, October night of 2010 where steam arose from the streets like some unsettled soul, we created the anthology that you now hold in your hands.

For us, we have always admired the ghost story, may it be fictional or nonfictional. Therefore, we asked each of our authors to provide us with a story that was loosely based on a factual subject and then fictionalize it. Actually, isn't that what most ghost stories are? Fact and fiction?

Since ancient civilization to modern times, it seems the paranormal has always been a part of life, may it be non-fictional or fictional. The timeline for spiritual documentation is as follows: The Ancient Near East/Egypt, Classical Greece, European Renaissance, and the time span throughout the 1800's known as, The Spiritual Movement. Near the turn of the century, the paranormal craze began to die out where scientific skepticism and alternative explanations debunked many superstitions or paranormal experiences.

In modern times, investigations and belief in the supernatural continue to haunt and amaze us. Reasonably, time is now somewhat repeating itself as for the last few decades, The Spiritual Movement, has been resurrected. Examples are seen in our theaters where the audience is

Introduction

introduced to angels, demons, vengeful ghosts, and helpful spirits. Books continue forward with the classic ghost tale, inspiring new nightmares and the possibility that maybe we aren't alone.

Outside of entertainment, almost every county in the USA has one or sometimes two paranormal groups, active in that area. Finally, we have haunted, historical lodgings to consider such as: bed and breakfasts, inns and plantation homes, most which advertise themselves as being haunted. This advertising is becoming a focal point because most innkeepers understand that hauntings draw in vacationers, who hope to experience something unnatural.

Now, I come to you ghost story lover. May you be a believer or a skeptic; you are in for a treat. In the following pages, I invite you to pull the curtains and dim the lights. You are soon to be introduced to the spirits that walk among us.

Sincerely, Yours,
Alexander S. Brown

Interview for a Ghost Hunter
by:
Windsong Levitch

Wanted!
(Southern Hunters of Paranormal Phenomena.)
We are currently looking for a new team member.
Someone with good self-esteem, works well with
Others, is strong mentally and emotionally. Has a good
Sense of humor and interested in the paranormal.
Send résumé and picture to www.shopp.com

"Hi! Good to meet you, come on in. My name is Stormy McCloud and my husband is Rain McCloud. Yeah…I know; pretty bad. Our parents were hippies. If you don't know what that is, look it up on the Internet. We're kind of the Mutt and Jeff of our team. Why? Well, I am four feet, nine and half inches tall and weigh eighty pounds soaking wet, and my husband is six feet, two inches tall, and two-hundred eighty pounds."

"Would you like some coffee, water or a coke?" I point to the fridge and counter as I guide the interviewee through the house.

"You want coffee; do you want cream and sugar or just black?" I stop, grab a mug, and pour some coffee.

"Black?" I hand her the mug. "As for me, I like my coffee with lots of sugar and cream. We all drink lots of coffee around here. You know the coffee joke don't you? For every one cup you drink, you pee four. It's a wonder any ghost hunting gets done."

I lead her back to the office. "Have a seat and let me tell you a little about our group. Then, we can get to talking about you joining the team. Well, my nickname is Wrath. It would seem some people think I have a bit of a temper, but I don't, so don't be worried, it's just a dumb joke."

I sit in my well-worn chair with the hand-knitted afghan draped over the back and pick up my own mug of coffee. "My job is to set up all the hunts, talk to the clients and do research. I also listen to some of the E.V.P.'s and review the video and pictures, which is something you would be helping me with. You would also be helping with set up at the sites. How does that sound to you?"

She nods as she sips her coffee. "Good. I don't mind helping any way I can."

I smile and pick a pen, twirling it as I lean back in my chair. "Okay! So let me tell you about the team. Crash, my husband, is the team leader. He is the one who tells everyone where to go and what to do. He's good at directing because he's a cop. Why do we call him Crash? Well, he is a bit clumsy at times. You notice you are drinking out of a plastic cup? Well, that is because if it were glass it would be broken." She laughs and I continue.

"Then there's Lurch. He's my husband's brother. Why Lurch? Well, he is about 6 feet, 9 ½ inches tall. He doesn't talk much but he has a wicked sense of humor. He's a cop, too. That crazy son-of-a-bitch used to make me nuts when he first joined us on hunts."

"Why?"

I shake my head, remembering. "Because every time he thought he saw or heard something he would yell, 'Police! Freeze! Put your hands on your head and turn around slowly!' The first couple of times it was funny, but after ten or twelve times, you just want to kill him, you know?"

She laughs until her cheeks turn ruddy. When she gets her breath, she asks, "How did you stop him?"

"You would be amazed what bad habits can be cured with a stun gun." Her jaw drops and I say, "I'm just kidding! As you can see, if you want to run with this bunch of misfits you must have a good sense of humor. When it gets scary, you need to laugh."

She nods and smiles.

"Now that brings us to Master and Blaster. They're the tech team. I don't think there is an electronic gadget on earth that they can't fix. And if it doesn't exist, they'll make it! Why do we call them Master and Blaster? They both work at the same computer store, and they're roommates. Well, they're a couple; do you follow me?"

"Yeah."

"Master is a bit tall and thin as a rail, and Blaster is kind of short and almost as wide as he is tall. They're a lot of fun to be with, nothing rattles them, and Blaster makes the best brownies in the world! You can't hunt ghosts without brownies and coffee. Master drives a mobile home. Yeah, real road warriors, those two!"

"Nice."

"Yep. Now, we come to Twitch, she is our resident sensitive. She is very professional on the job and a hoot when we're just goofing. If you ever need someone to talk to, she's the one. Twitch works best in the dark, pardon the pun, but she does not want to know anything. She likes to pick up things on her own, and she is damn good at it too."

"Last is my sis, Sandy. She's twelve years older than me and can she tell you some stories that would curl your hair. She's handicapped now and can't leave her home. She helps with E.V.P.s and runs the S.H.O.P.P. chat room. Sometimes when we do a hunt live on the web, she will run the open chat. She never misses a thing- I love it! Even though she can't come with us, she still has our back. Her husband Gorge is a real jerk; doesn't believe in the paranormal, and loves riding our butts about it. He thinks it's funny to say 'the only thing I believe in is the life insurance I have on her, and how I can hardly wait to collect it.' I got so annoyed with him; I warned him that he could be our next hunt."

She snickers as she sets her empty mug on the edge of my desk.

I pick up her résumé and scan the highlights. "I see you

are a Marine. That's great. How many tours did you do?"

"Two."

"Same as our girls, well young ladies I should say, but to us they will always be our girls. At least I know you have courage and won't run when spooked. By the way, thank you for serving our country."

She dips her head in a gracious nod.

"Well, like I was saying, it looks like you know all the terms and lingo. You have a very good understanding of how to use the equipment; who knows, you might show us a thing or two. Plus, I can tell you have a good head on your shoulders." I set the résumé down and look her in the eye. "Are you ready to join our team, or better yet, our happy little family? Of course you would be on a trial period at first, no big thing really. Do you have any questions?"

"Well, I'd like to know why you need a new team member."

"Why? No biggie; you know people move on, need a change that kind of thing. Trip just got to a point in life where he wants something different. That's all."

"I read the paper."

I wave a dismissive hand. "Look, papers write a lot of flashy things. That's what they do! They make incidents sound a lot worse than they are."

"Really? So there was nothing to the story?"

"Trip's a really nice guy. OK?"

"Getting a bit defensive?"

"No! I am not getting defensive. It's just that we all love

Trip a lot and we're going to miss him." I take a deep breath and stop tapping my pen against the desk. "The paper did not say where we were but you have to admit the, headline *'Ghost Hunter Permanently Traumatized!!!'* makes a good eye-catcher. The truth is nothing bad ever happened. Trip just got the begeezers scared out of him and to be honest with you, I am surprised it didn't happen sooner."

"Was he not suited for the job?"

I shrug one shoulder. "Trip is a good guy. He's sometimes not all there. You know what I mean?"

"Is that why you call him Trip?"

"What? Nah, that's his real name. I guess even his folks knew he would be a klutz when he was born. He is a sweet guy that cannot do a dang thing right to save his soul. He was always tipping things over, dropping things, forgetting equipment, you name it."

"So why did you keep him on for so long?"

"We kept hoping he would 'get it', but on our last hunt, well, let's just say he finally pissed the ghost off so much it reached out and touched him, as in grabbed a good bit of him. To tell the truth I didn't think a ghost could get so annoyed with a person, but I have to admit that it was funny- scary funny."

"Not so funny for Trip, I bet."

I sigh. "Yeah, I guess you're right, it wasn't funny to Trip." I fold my arms across my chest and frown. "Thanks for making me feel like a jerk for laughing about it." I pause and consider before erasing my frown and saying, "If you want to be a part of the team you have a right to know what happened."

"I wouldn't be here if I wasn't interested in the job. So what happened?"

I lean back and stare up at the cuckoo clock as I think back. "Last August, we, the team, went up to Old South Pittsburg Hospital. It was our fourth trip up there."

"And Trip's last trip?"

"Yes. You might say that was the straw that broke the camel's back. I think the best way for you to get the story right is to just play the E.V.P.'s for you. First, I want to tell you that we literally hit the ground running. From the time we get to a site until we leave, we have our digital recorders on. Crash, Lurch, and I do the walk through with the client. It's amazing what you catch doing a walk through."

I turn and pull up the recording on the computer. I look over my shoulder before I hit the play icon. "So here is the first E.V.P. from the first time we went through the hospital. You will hear Crash and Trip on the third floor."

I click the little arrow and sit back, reliving it as I listen to the recording.

Crash says, "Hand me the tripod."

Trip responds, "What tripod?"

"Trip! The tripod I told you to get out of the van."

I picture Trip shrugging as he responds, "I didn't know you wanted it now." A long deep sigh answers at the same time Crash says "Trip, what part of set up do you NOT get?"

Trips asks, "So you want me to go get it?"

A male voice belonging to none of our team, exclaims, "Oh God!"

I lean forward and click on the next recording, "This is two hours later. Lurch and Trip are on the first floor." I click play and a loud crash blares through the speakers. Lurch asks, "Did you hear that?"

Trip says, "All I heard was a loud crash. Do you think that was something?"

The same unexplained male voice, clearly an E.V.P., responds, "DUH!" Then another very loud, long sigh resonates through the recording.

Minutes later Lurch asks, "Did you see the door open?"

Trip asks, "Did you do that?"

Lurch yells, "Dude, I am standing right next to you! The door is ten feet away!" The E.V.P. exclaims, "Shoot Him!"

I look over at my interviewee. "Many strange occurrences where recorded that night, but as you can see the male E.V.P was not impressed with Trip." I scroll through the list of recordings to the next one I want. "Now here are some of the E.V.P. recordings from the second time we went into the hospital. As we walked into the place, my digital recorder caught this. I click, "play."

A female E.V.P. says in a sing-song voice, "He's back!!"

A male E.V.P responds, "Oh SHIT!"

The interviewee cocks one eyebrow, but says nothing.

"This one is four hours in to the investigation," I explain.

My voice echoes through the speakers, "My batteries just went dead"

Trip says, "Mine too! What do you think we should do?"

The male E.V.P. yells, "YOU DIE TOO!!"

My voice retorts, "Gee, I don't know. Put fresh ones in maybe?"

Trip asks, "Do you have fresh batteries?"

I respond, "How many times do I say make sure you have extras?"

The E.V.P. answers, "A thousand times!" and then howling laughter spills from the speakers.

I try not to laugh as I pull up the next recording. "Now this is from the last time we went up there. First, we'll listen to some of the E.V.P. recordings. Then, I will show you the video. Now, I am going to tell you to go on and laugh. It is hard for me not to."

She frowns, as if maybe she thinks I'm pulling her leg, but I keep talking. "The first thing that happened when we got there is we tried to unlock the door; I already have my digital recorder on."

The E.V.P. female voice initiates the recording, saying, "Don't let him in!!"

I narrate, "It took us five minutes, and that damn door wouldn't open."

The male E.V.P. says over the racket of the crew trying to open the door, "Make him go away!"

"Now understand, at this point we have not listened to the tape yet. We don't hear the voices, you know? Anyhow, as you can hear, we're still trying to get the door open, but

I had a hunch." I turn the volume up and my voice says to Trip, "Go sit in the van." Trip's footsteps fade away and moments later I get the door open.

"Now, I have Crash and Lurch hold the door and tell Trip to run as fast as he can inside."

The interviewee laughs.

"Go on and laugh. I am!" I scroll down and click the next recording. "Now this is the E.V.P. we got as Trip ran inside."

"Damn he's in!" the same male voice complains.

I explain, "Crash and Trip are in the hallway and Trip is in the lead. There's a classic car parked inside on display and Trip is about ten feet away from the car."

The E.V.P. male voice yells, "GO BACK!!"

Trip whines, "Someone just hit me in the head!"

Crash says, "I think you need to stay away from the car, Trip."

I pull up another file. "Now, watch the video."

The wobbly footage plays on the flash player. "You see how close Trip is to the car?"

She nods as she watches the video. Caught up in the story, she's scooted to the edge of her seat. Her jaw drops. "Oh my God, it looked like he got pushed back!"

I nod. "Yep. Now listen to the tape from about three hours later. Trip and Crash are on the third floor."

Crash exclaims, "Wow! Did you see the shadow? It looked just like a person. Please tell me you got that on video."

Trip responds, "I thought you had the video camera. I have the thermal cam and the digital record."

Crash groans. "Please tell me you got the thermal on!"

"Uh, I forgot to turn it on."

An E.V.P. sighs loudly and a moment later adds, "Oh, God! Let me do it!!"

I hit the pause button and explain, "After that we all decided to take a break. We went to the mobile home for some coffee and brownies, and to chill a bit. This is where I feel bad, because Trip said he'd had it for the night." I shake my head. "He wanted to just stay in the mobile home and help Master and Blaster. Instead, I talked him into going back in." I shrug. "Oh well. You know what they say?"

"If hindsight were foresight we would all be rich!"

I nod. "What's done is done and now we need a new team member, but to tell the truth I think this has been coming for a long time." I gesture to the computer to get her focus back on the recordings.

"So now it is about one in the morning. Crash, Lurch and Trip are back by the car. Trip loves cars, so he starts to go over to get a better look at it."

Lurch's voice says, "Trip, stay away from the car. The guy's ghost doesn't like it if anyone gets too close to his car."

The male E.V.P. booms, "THAT'S IT!!"

Crash asks, "Did you hear that?"

"Ya, it sounded like someone yelling," Lurch responds.

Crash's voice says, "Oh SHIT! Trip! Trip!"

"OH MY GOD!" Lurch says. "Grab him, Crash!"

"I'm trying!"

I pause the recording. She's leaning forward on her elbows and stares at the sudden stop. "So now this is when I think you need to see the video." As I pull up the file, I ask, "By the way, do you know the expression 'the bum's rush'?" She scowls and shakes her head. "It is when someone is grabbed by the back of the pants and the back of their shirt collar and quite literally run out of a place-- as down the hall and out the door." Her eyes go wide as I explain. I grin. "Well, you are about to see it right now, up close and personal. Sorry it's just this makes me laugh every time, so here is the video."

I narrate, pointing out the bits we just listened to, "Crash, Lurch, and Trip are all in the hallway with the car. Lurch is telling Trip to stay away from the car. The E.V.P. male voice yells, and see, all the guys are yelling. Now, wait for it...wait for it... and, *now* look at that!"

"Oh-my-god! Oh-my-god! He looks like he is flying down the hall!!!"

I shake my head as I laugh. "Ya, it does, but not really. That, my dear, is a man being given the bum's rush by a ghost!" I gesture to the video. "Just keep watching. It's not over yet."

"Jeeze! The door, did it just open up by its self? Did it?"

"Ghost, dear." I smile and point at the video. "And out the door goes Trip and the door shuts." I pull up the voice recordings. "This is the last one."

The male E.V.P. says, "Don't Come Back!"

16

Interview for a Ghost Hunter

A female voice adds, "Don't let door hit your as-" and muted laughter echoes until I click the stop button. "And that is why we now need a new team member." I lean over and yank a Kleenex from the box on the desk. "Here is a tissue to wipe your eyes."

She's laughing so hard she can barely catch her breath. I laugh some too and say, "It's okay. I'll wait for you to stop. Are you okay now?" She nods. "Good. So do you what to join our team? Please say yes!" I set my hands flat on the desk. "Look, the lady that was in here before you claimed to be a vampire! She could not promise that she would not suck the blood out of us if she got hungry on a hunt. The guy before her, well he was a werewolf, and can't work on a full moon!"

She hiccups with more laughter.

"Please say you what the job, and please don't be a whack job!"

She catches her breath and nods. "Yes. Yes I'll take the job- on one condition."

"Sure, what is it?"

"You've got to play that last bit for me again."

I grin. "No problem. By the way your name, Belladonna, do you have a nickname?"

"Yeah. Call me Boo."

"Well, Boo, welcome to the team. Where would you like your first hunt to be?"

"Are you kidding? Old South Pittsburg Hospital! Where else?"

THE END

This story is based on E.V.P.'s and video taken by a real group of very brave people. Names have been changed to protect the not always so innocent (LOL), but always professionals in what they do. They work with both the living and the living on the other side.

Thank you, TRIPS for your love and support. Good Hunting!

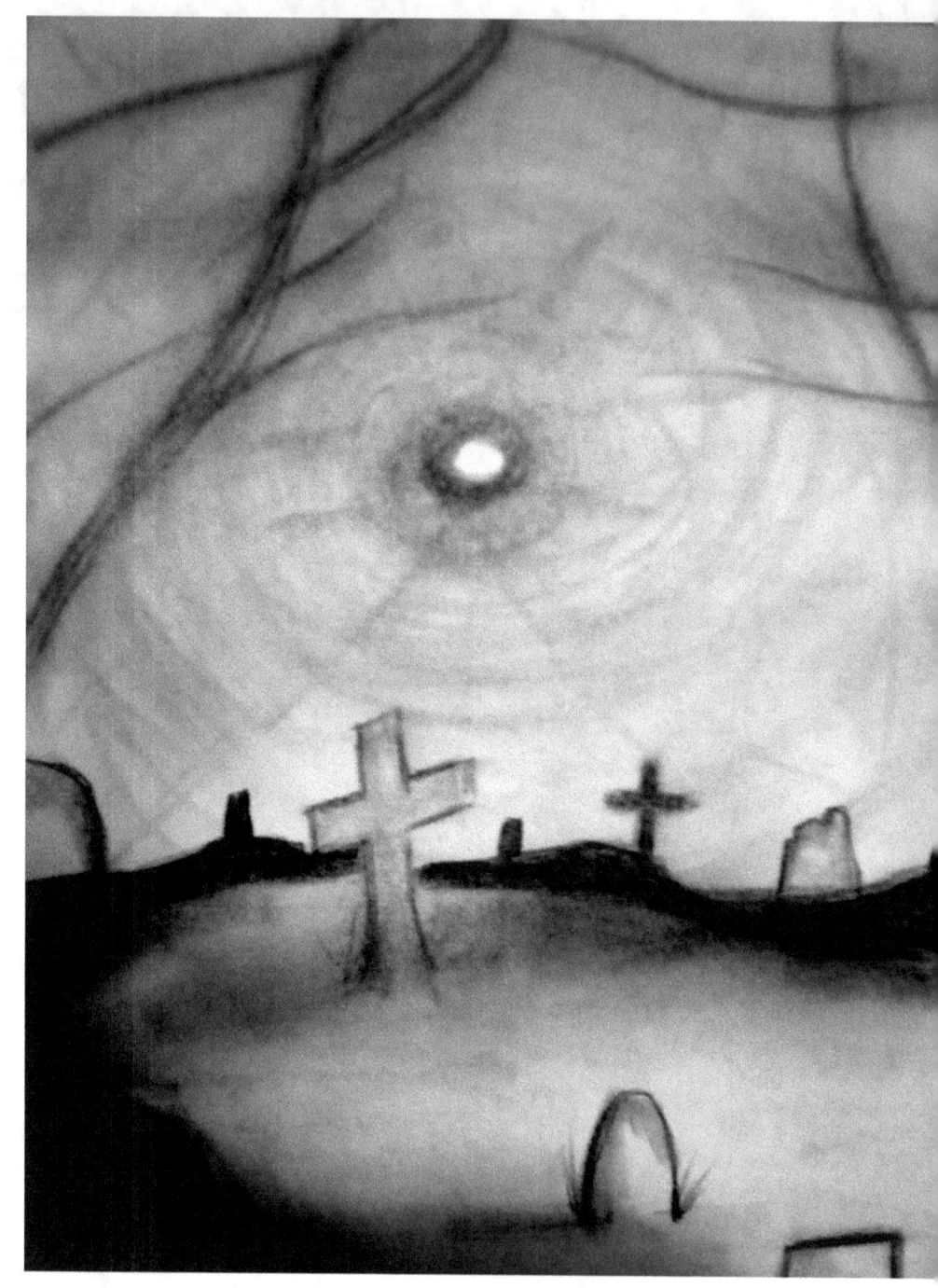

An Eclipse over Elmwood
by:
H. David Blalock

Maybe they got bored, just lying there in Elmwood Cemetery for more than a century, covered in that cold, unmarked graveyard earth. Side by side, head to toe, more than a thousand of them, they lie quiet and obedient to death until the night of the lunar eclipse.

Now, a lunar eclipse is nothing special. There are two or three every year. But, this one was different. It wasn't supposed to happen. And it definitely wasn't supposed to happen four nights in a row.

The scientists went crazy trying to explain it: cosmic dust, atmospheric anomaly, volcanic cloud, high altitude electric discharge. They fought constantly, but nobody really cared, not in Memphis, until the first night the apparitions began.

Some people said they saw carnival floats filled with masked phantoms, the ghost of that Cotton Festival held in defiance of the yellow fever. Mixed in with the faded music of calliope and trumpet was the creaking of the funeral trains that filled the streets those fateful summer months of 1878. Five thousand and more dead, the gutters filled with sewage, dead rats, and vermin unidentifiable for the rot.

The second night of the eclipse a man ran screaming down Beale Street, pale as death and bellowing in German a prayer for salvation from what paced behind him – a parade of ghastly vision: Nuns in full habit, priests and ministers of the faith walking soundlessly along the cobbled street. The garish lights of Beale dimming respectfully as they progressed toward the river front, tourists scattering like leaves in a high wind before them.

I arrived the third day of the eclipse, landing at Memphis International about noon after spending an interminable layover in Atlanta. Compared to the immensity that was Hartsfield, the Memphis airport seemed downright homey.

As I stood watching the flight baggage travel around its racetrack, hoping that once again I had dodged the bullet of lost luggage, someone tapped me on the shoulder. I turned to find myself confronted by a large black man in an expensive business suit, grinning at me under his salt-and-pepper hair.

"Father Joseph Bertrand?" he asked.

"Yes?"

He stuck out a meaty hand. "Anderson's the name. Charles Anderson. Welcome to Memphis."

I took his hand and tried not to wince when he shook it vigorously.

"Pleased to meet you," I said through the pain.

"We're so glad you came," he went on. "You have no

idea how glad."

"Well. I..."

"We have you put up in a hotel. Hope you don't mind. It's just that the church has been full since it all began. The homeless, you know. They don't want to sleep outside with everything going on. And the mission houses are full, too."

"No, no, that's quite..."

"It's been a mixed blessing, you know. Scary, of course, but it has brought people into the fold that... Is that your bag? Let me get that for you."

He reached down and lifted my case with the air of a man dusting a fly off his shoulder. I couldn't help but be impressed. I could never lift it without effort and usually set it down to run on its wheels. He stood with it at his side, smiling, and motioned me to follow.

"We'll get you situated and give you a chance to freshen up before we get started," he said as he led me outside. "No hurry. I mean, after all, if it stops tonight, it wouldn't break any hearts, would it?"

I followed him to a late model Japanese sedan and waited while he loaded the bag into the trunk. He kept up a constant chatter the whole time discussing the weather, the local sights and politics. I nodded and smiled at the appropriate cues, making the right noises to encourage him when he took a breath. It dawned on me he was talking to cover his fear, in spite of his imposing appearance. This was my first sign of how significant the impact of the apparitions had been on Memphis.

We rolled out of the airport and onto the highway toward downtown. The lack of traffic on the divided six-lane was striking. We drove for miles and met perhaps a couple dozen other cars. Even when the six-lane gave way to the narrower Riverside Drive, the traffic remained light. We paralleled the Mississippi to our left and the bluffs on the right while Anderson kept up a running monologue. After the first few miles, he seemed to have forgotten I was even there.

At last, we turned away from the river and climbed the hill into downtown, crossing railroad tracks to enter the city proper. Here, the traffic was non-existent. The streets were entirely empty in the early afternoon sun. There should have been people going to and from lunch, traffic filling the streets on early September business. Instead, the city cowered within itself, holding its breath in fear of the coming night and what it might bring.

We pulled up in front of the Peabody Hotel. Anderson flashed me that grin of his.

"Here we are," he said. "Your home for the duration."

I got out and stood, stretching my cramped frame. Only then did it strike me how quiet the place really was. The avenue practically echoed it was so empty. A shiver ran up my spine. I had spent the last two days rattling across the rutted roads of the Kenyan countryside, fighting the crowded airports of Nairobi, Rome, New York and Atlanta to get here. It was eerie to find the same kind of silence in a city the size of Memphis as I had found in the open plains of the African savannah.

An Eclipse Over Elmwood

The hotel lobby was just as empty, the burbling of the fountain where the famous Peabody ducks floated loud in that silence. It seemed almost sacrilegious for Anderson to stride across that lobby with his non-stop monologue toward the elevators.

The room was much more than I had expected. A Catholic priest seldom gets time in a luxury hotel. It was too bad I couldn't take the time to enjoy it. Anderson's phone rang as he dropped my bag on the bed.

"Hello? Yes. Yes, we'll be right there." He hung up and shrugged at me with that maddening grin. "Sorry, Father. It seems they're starting early today."

I looked at my watch. 12:45.

My assignment had begun early.

***

The church was standing room only and smelled like the losers' locker room after a long game. People bustled from the anteroom to the sanctuary, where a soup line was set up for the homeless who sought shelter from the night haunts. The sights and sounds reminded me of the mission in Kenya from which I had been called for this job. To find the poverty I had only seen in the third world here in a major American city were startling to say the least. I was touched to the heart at the misery around me and appalled at my own ignorance. I resolved to speak to the monsignor at the earliest opportunity about this.

"Father Bertrand," said one of the women standing behind the nearest soup tureen. She wiped her hands on the stained apron she wore and stepped forward, untying the garment. "Thank you for coming."

I smiled at her. She was middle-aged, with a care-worn face. Her graying hair was pulled into a tight bun, putting more years on her than she deserved, but her smile was genuine and reached into her eyes.

"I hope I can help," I said.

"We need more than the help of one man, Father," she replied, then offered her hand. "Stephanie Fulton."

"Pleased to meet you," I told her.

"Has anyone briefed you yet on what's to be done?" she asked, hanging the apron on a small hook beside the tureen.

"No, but I believe I have a fair idea what's wanted."

"Good."

I held up my hand. "However, the Holy See has instructed me to first verify the event."

I don't know exactly how I expected her to react. I do know I never expected her to laugh.

"Verify?" she said, finally. "The eyewitness testimony of over a thousand tourists, dozens of policemen, news reporters and local citizens not enough, eh?"

I blushed at that, why, I don't know. It wasn't my call. I was just following the directions given me by the Holy See, but for some reason I was embarrassed, as if I had personally questioned her word.

"It's okay, Father," she allowed when she realized my

distress. "I know how it must sound to an outsider." She looked around, scanning the crowded church. "Father James is here somewhere. He can take you out to Elmwood. Let's see." Her gaze locked onto someone behind me. "Ah, here he is."

Making his way toward us was a portly fellow in his mid-thirties, flushed complexion and receding hairline. He walked with a slight limp and I noticed the glitter of metal on the side of his left leg.

"Father James, Father Bertrand," Ms. Fulton said as he pulled up alongside.

"Father."

"Father," I responded.

"Thanks for coming," he said, though he knew as well as I it had not been my doing.

"Charles brought him early because it's started already," Ms. Fulton told him.

He scowled. "So soon? Lord help us. Let's hope it's not getting worse." He turned to me. "I suppose you want to see the cemetery."

"If you like," I said.

He nodded grimly. "May as well. Follow me, please."

He shouldered his way through the crowd with me in tow until we came to an exit, where he paused and took a small keyring from a hook by the door. He pushed the bar, opening the door out into a small parking lot. An old bus painted red and white with the church name on its side in fading black letters sat slowly dripping oil in a far spot.

"We figured out fairly quickly there was a connection between Elmwood and the sightings downtown," Father James said, shaking the keyring and unlocking the bus.

"Wait up!"

A blonde girl of about twenty years dressed in jeans and a colored shirt advertising a band I didn't recognize ran up to my host.

"Going to the cemetery?" she asked.

"Yes, but only for a few minutes," Father James answered. "Just going to show Father Bertrand here..."

She spun on me. "You're the exorcist."

"I am a priest," I corrected her.

"But, you're here to put down the ghosts, aren't you?"

"Now, Jessie, leave him alone," Father James interrupted. He gripped her by the shoulders and pointed her at the church. "Go help Stephanie. She's swamped."

She shook him off. "I already asked her if she could spare me," she said, irritated. "She said it was okay."

It was obvious this wasn't the first time they'd had this kind of argument. I leaned against the bus and listened to them fight until Father James gave in. She clambered into the back seat as we got in, Father James still shaking his head and mumbling to himself.

The ride to Elmwood was brief. I was amazed at how big the cemetery actually was, and how well-kept. From the stories I'd heard about recent events, I expected to find a graveyard overrun with kudzu, monuments weathered and askew, graffiti covering what few older crypts still stood.

Instead, I found myself in a literal park, with tree-lined lanes and manicured grass. The monuments stood proud and beautiful. Columned crypts, angelic statues, crosses, stars, plates, obelisks, every conceivable marker dating back nearly two hundred years testified to the memories of thousands. Walking there, nearing the marker announcing "No Man's Land," I was struck speechless by the tension in the air.

"You feel that?" Jessie asked.

I nodded, not breaking stride. An invisible miasma swirled around me. I could feel it not on my skin, but underneath, down where the nerves crawled, sending phantom insects scurrying along my arms and up my spine to tickle the hairs on my neck. I could hear Father James muttering a prayer under his breath and was sorely tempted to join him.

There is a section of Elmwood where nearly two thousand people were buried in hastily dug trench graves at the height of the yellow fever epidemic in 1878. The closer we got to that, the heavier the air got until it was thick enough to taste the corruption in the back of my throat. At first, I thought I was imagining it, but when Jessie said:

"Why is it so dark here?"

I knew it was true. Not only had the air grown dense, but the light around us was dimmer. I looked up; expecting to see at least a cloud overhead, but the sky was unbroken. I looked out over the grounds and caught movement.

"My God," Father James breathed.

They had been people once, vital, with dreams and

goals, never considering their own ends. They laughed and cried, argued and agreed, sang, ran, bled, loved, until the fever came with its suffering. Maybe they had unfinished business. How many of us die fully prepared for the end? The fever came for them and took what they had, what they would have, and what they might have. Perhaps they were simply protesting the injustice of it all. Everyone should have a fullness of years to make their mistakes and have the chance to fix them before the curtain falls. Maybe all they had was the bitter memories of their mistakes. Maybe that was the thickness in the air, the rot I tasted and that clung to me wetly in a gathering mist.

I stopped. Just ahead a group of figures was forming in the mist. At first not much more than an outline, multi-headed, multi-limbed, it slowly coalesced into the shadows of five men in clerical garb. They drifted closer to us and I fancied I could make out more details as they neared: The flash of spectacles on one, the glitter of a crucifix on the leader. They paused before us and I got the feeling they were aware of our presence, although I knew that shouldn't be the case.

Spirits typically were like recordings, endlessly replaying a specific set of motions without regard for their surroundings. They were echoes of events long gone, unaffected by changing times. Their invulnerability to the evolving environs allowed them to walk through walls and float across open spaces, remaining true to the strictures they suffered in life. Seldom, if ever, did they interact with the present, not as phantoms, anyway. Poltergeists often did, but they were increasingly suspected of not being true hauntings, as they were statistically associated with living adolescent children.

I gazed at the central figure that hovered before me, half a body's shade. Although the image was vague, I got the impression I faced a man about my age and size, with a shock of red hair. The crucifix around his neck was his clearest bit. The other forms wavered behind him.

"Hello," I said, then bit my tongue at the inanity of that greeting. What was I thinking? That the spirit would respond in kind? Shove out a ghostly hand for me to shake?

Still, there was something in the way the specter hung before me, as if expectantly awaiting an action on my part. I glanced at my companions, realizing they felt it, too, as they met my look. I cleared my throat.

"My name is Joseph Bertrand," I managed. "Can you communicate your name to me?"

There was a long moment when I thought nothing would happen. I don't know what I expected in response, but it certainly wasn't what I got, although in retrospect I shouldn't have been surprised.

The chill that settled around us so suddenly hit all the way to the bone. It lanced even to the soul, a spear thrust into our very being. Simultaneously, Jessie began to speak. Her voice was normal in tone and volume, but something lay behind it, something not quite right, slightly unnatural, just enough of wrong to be felt down where that chill settled.

"We have names," it said.

31

The statement confused me. I hesitated to even move; afraid any motion would cause the apparition to vanish.

"We have names!" it repeated more forcefully.

Then, as quickly as it came, the chill dissipated, carrying the phantoms with it. We found ourselves standing once again in the cemetery's quiet green, blinking in the returning sunlight.

"I feel sick," Jessie said, weakly. "I wanna throw up."

***

"Whatever we saw in Elmwood is definitely connected," Father James said. He reached into a drawer of his desk and produced two small glasses and a bottle of wine.

"Why do you say that?" I asked.

He poured me a glass and passed it across the desk to me. I took it and thanked him, but set it in my lap without sipping.

"The apparition with the cross around its neck," he answered. He pushed a folder toward me, pouring himself a drink as I took the folder.

Opening it, I again was looking into the face I knew so well. I could almost see the red in his hair, though the picture was little more than a faded sepia-toned portrait.

"Father Bartholomew Lane," Father James said. "Dispatched to Memphis in late September 1878. He treated dozens and officiated at the burials of hundreds."

"Is he buried at Elmwood?" I had to ask.

"No one knows. There are a lot of unknowns there. He very well could be one of them."

I frowned. "I don't understand. Weren't those people buried in hallowed ground?"

"Oh, it's hallowed now."

I shot him a puzzled look. "What does that mean?"

"The cemetery was expanded from the original forty acres to eighty shortly after the Civil War," he told me, "but the epidemics of 1872 and 1878 caused... an overflow." He stood and walked to a nearby bookshelf. Taking down an old volume, he opened it to a marker about one-third way through. "Listen to this:

"It will be well to remember how the dead daily encumbered the graveyard, and how a hundred coffins lay around Elmwood daily waiting internment, which had to be postponed for days, sometimes, owing to the scarcity of grave-diggers, the terrible death rate, and the sickness of those in charge of the cemetery during the gloomy days of September, when the fever pest gathered in two hundred victims a day."

"My God," I said.

"That's from 'A History of the Yellow Fever', an account written by J. M. Keating in 1879. He worked at the Appeal during the epidemic. The account isn't well-known today, but you might find it interesting."

I put the folder back on his desk and took the book from him. I turned it to the table of contents. A heading caught my eye: "The Dead of 1878." I gasped.

"There are over fifty pages of names here," I said.

Father James nodded. "Keating included the names from Tennessee, Mississippi, Arkansas, Alabama, Louisiana, and Kentucky."

I opened it to that section. A note at the bottom of the page assured the reader "Under this head will be found authenticated lists of all who died of yellow fever during the epidemic of 1878."

"I never realized how extensive that epidemic was," I admitted. Thumbing through the lists, I was appalled at the numbers. Men, women, and children died, entire families killed by the indiscriminate and merciless disease. I paged back into the descriptions of the horrors of life in Memphis in those months between August and October 1878. I couldn't read long without becoming ill at the brutal descriptions of the effects of the yellow fever: black vomit from digested internal bleeding, yellow eyes, high fever, delirium and death. The suffering of these people was beyond my ability to grasp and I now understood, a least a little, the need they might have to break away from that anonymous darkness of history's forgetfulness. They remembered their lives, but that memory was shared only with the other dead. There was no immortality for them like there was for those who survived. They left no one to carry on their memory, to visit even the unmarked trench that enclosed their mortal remains. Their names were forever gone, a casualty of the epidemic as much as their bodies.

It was the ultimate insult heaped on the ultimate injury:

namelessness after death.

No one had mourned them. Fear of the fever kept even the grave-diggers away. Their belongings were reduced to ash, the evidence of their presence purged by carbolic acid, bleach and fire. They had been abandoned to their fate, many dying alone in tortuous agony and despair.

I couldn't hold back the tears.

Father James sat back down and sighed. "I know how you feel."

I nodded and wiped my eyes. "It's not just this. I came from Kenya, Father James. Before that, I was in three other African countries. These accounts, the ones Keating writes about, could have been written yesterday over there. The heroics, the villainy, they still..." I shook my head. "At least here, I think, we have a way to set things right."

"How do you mean?" he asked.

I held up the book.

"We will make sure they know they are remembered."

***

Elmwood was just as beautiful as I remembered it, but this time the heaviness that nagged at the edges of my consciousness held a note of anticipation. Father James, young Jessie, Ms. Fulton, and Charles Anderson had volunteered to help me with the task ahead. We stood beside the "No Man's Land" marker as the sun dipped toward the Mississippi. I faced the gathering dark, putting the reddening horizon behind me.

"We are here to pay homage to those who died during the terrible yellow fever outbreak of 1878," I began. "This is not the first memorial held for those lost then, but it will be the first in which each person who died will be named." I looked at each of my company. "This will take some time, but I believe that no one should ever be completely forgotten, as we are all children of God." I opened the book to the list. "Let us begin."

Under an improvised reading light, I began reading the names one at a time, the others intoning "Benedicto Domine" and making the sign of the Cross after each. We went on for nearly three hours without pause, my voice the only sound in the thick silence. The sunlight faded into night and the moon rose to creep slowly toward zenith, casting gray light across the monuments glowing silvery in response. Overhead, the stars listened, blinking in the growing moonlight until we realized the eclipse was beginning.

I have seen many lunar eclipses in my life, partial and total, but none like this. There was no well-defined edge to this shadow. It was more a mist that crept slowly across the moon's face, translucent and a gangrenous color.

As the names went on, I tried to ignore the ghoulish reflections on the monuments, the nearly solid shadows they cast, and I could have if not for the fact those shadows began moving, rising to form wraiths in the chill air. With each name pronounced, another apparition rose to join the growing host. They hovered as if awaiting instruction after a summons.

An Eclipse Over Elmwood

The final name rang out and the team intoned the benediction. Silence settled again over Elmwood, but this silence was not empty. It was a silence full of expectation and long-forgotten hope.

The half-torso form I now identified as Father Bartholomew floated toward me out of the murk and hung a few feet away. I had the feeling he was waiting for me to do or say something, but had no idea what.

Suddenly, the Cross around his neck glowed star-white bright against the ghastly green of the surrounding dark. Voices, as from far off, were raised in the familiar lilt of an ancient hymn. As the moonlight disappeared, as the final moonbeam was consumed by that shadow, I felt a movement in my chest, a swelling of grief, and a great need to feel a connection with those who stood before me. I wanted to give them relief, to give them comfort from their pain, and there was only one way I knew to do that.

The words of the Latin Mass, learned but never before given, poured out of me, but the really disturbing part of that service was the responses that echoed from the spectral ranks.

I had presided over many Masses, in America and overseas. I had heard the voices of men, women and children raised in song so beautiful it touched my heart. I had felt the presence of God in those voices.

At least, I thought I had.

The Mass neared its end and the apparitions seemed to close in on us, reaching with invisible hands in our direction.

"Deo Gratias," the chorus rang out, and there was a rush of air, the aroma of blood and wine, the sighing of many hearts relieved from long suffering.

The night went still. We blinked at each other in the full moonlight.

***

The eclipse did not return after that night, nor were any phantoms seen to haunt the Memphis streets. I, however, had one last encounter to experience before taking my leave and returning to the relative sanity of Kenya.

As I was packing to leave, I unrolled the cassock I had worn that night and a Cross fell out of the folds. As I held it up to the light, I thought, just for a moment, I caught the figure of a red-haired priest out of the corner of my eye.

Sidney's Cotton
by:
Richard Parks

Transformation was the order of the day in Jackson's old warehouse district. In the stretch of vintage industrial buildings between Capitol Street and the train tracks, a former coldstorage facility, complete with the original meat hooks, had now become an upscale restaurant and nightclub. And Sidney's Cotton, one of the hottest new nightspots downtown Jackson had seen since the days of Miss Maggie LeCroix's House of Delight, was once a cotton warehouse.

"But not, it seems, an empty one," said David Summer, the actual owner of Sidney's Cotton so named appropriately after John Michael Sidney, a cotton baron and gunrunner of local repute. David never tired of telling the story, especially to a listener as charming as this one.

"No?"

The young woman at the bar seemed politely interested in the story, and David, more than politely interested in her. Though the hour was late and the crowd thinning, she seemed in no hurry as she sipped her Margarita. She was a

41

honey, with a pretty smile and hair so black he suspected a New Orleans connection.

"No," Davis said, pausing to sip his Manhattan for dramatic effect. "You see, there were bodies."

"What sort of bodies?"

"Dead bodies," said David. "Dead for a very long time. No wonder they say this place is haunted. Even I've even heard things I can't explain."

She smiled again. "Of course the warehouse is haunted. Any place or any person with any history is haunted by something. And Jackson has more than its share of history."

David smiled too. "Then I must have a history because you're definitely beginning to haunt me."

"How gallant Sir, and truer than you realize." She took a lick of salt on the edge of her glass in a way that sent shivers up and down David's spine. "Tell me more."

"This building was a cotton warehouse since before the Civil War. After that it was a *mostly* empty warehouse, until we bought it and started renovations"

"War Between the States," she corrected primly. Her accent poured out like liquid honey, but David did believe she may have been laying it on a little thick now for his benefit, "Or, more properly, the War of Northern Aggression. I knew you weren't from around here."

David raised his hands in mock surrender. "You've found me out, Ma'am. I'm a Union spy originally from Doylestown, Pennsylvania, here to ply you with drink and learn your secrets. Will I be shot at dawn?"

She laughed. "You're lucky the war is over. If one of my ancestors had caught you, then you wouldn't have lasted until dawn. Please continue."

"Where...oh, yeah. Renovation. Our contractor had been checking the flooring in the main warehouse when they found a false floor. It wasn't on any of the blueprints, including the originals in the state archive. He thinks it might've been added just before the war."

David didn't bother to say which war. There might have been two World Wars in the meantime, but he knew from experience when people in Jackson or most anywhere else in the South said 'The War,' it could only mean one particular war, on the exact terminology of which he'd just been fastidiously reprimanded.

"You wonder about that, don't you," she said. "Why a war that's been over for nearly one hundred and forty years still informs so much of our culture here? I can see it on your face."

"Are you a mind-reader?" he asked, after a moment.

She shrugged. "I'm a woman, and reading men is a survival skill." She grinned impishly. "Aren't I simply fascinating? The right answer is 'yes,' in case you were wondering."

"Yes," David said. "You are. It would help me remember that if I knew your name."

"It's Margaret. You may finish your story now."

"There's not much else to it. We opened the floor and found a secret room underneath. Ole Sidney apparently used his warehouse to smuggle weapons; we found a case of almost perfectly preserved Springfields. They went to the Battlefield Museum at Vicksburg, except one we kept for display." Dave pointed to the ancient rifle mounted behind the bar. "It was in all the papers, the TV news..."

"I was away," Margaret said. "I missed it. What about the bodies?"

"A man and a woman," David said. "We have no idea who the woman was, but there's little doubt that the male skeleton was John Michael Sidney. They were behind some empty crates on the side nearest the old rail yard, and they'd clearly been there a very long time. There was another exit tunnel there, though it had been filled in, apparently since the war. One of our workers found a CSA uniform button in the debris."

Margaret finished her drink. "I want to see it. Local history is one of my passions, David. I'd be really, really grateful."

It wasn't an implied promise, or even a hint, but David didn't need too much goading. "How can I refuse a Lady?"

She smiled. "If you're a gentleman, you can't. You do want to be a Gentleman, don't you?"

"You know, I think I do."

Margaret allowed David to take her arm like a belle being guided to the dance floor. They left the dwindling crowd at the main room and moved past the bar, past the restrooms, down a narrow corridor that seemed to go nowhere except into the darkness. David found a light switch. "Through here," he said. David opened a door in the north wall and they stepped out into an echoing emptiness.

"This was the main warehouse," Margaret said. It wasn't a question, nor needed to be. The room appeared huge, with massive wooden timbers. Some timbers had clearly been replaced over the years, some patched with laminated pieces from a much later time, but the original structure remained intact. Hanging lights had been installed in the forties when the warehouse had been used as a temporary armory, but now the ones that still worked only dispelled the darkness within their little circles. The moonlight streaming through dusty windows did more good, but not much. The dormers opened to the night chilling the room despite the heat of the previous day.

"We're probably going to turn this part into a concert hall, hire local bands, bring in outside acts now and then. We haven't decided yet." His voice echoed a little louder than he expected. He dropped it down to a whisper, though he wasn't sure why. Making noise just seemed...well, wrong.

"I like to dance." Margaret shivered and she didn't protest when David put his arm around her. For a moment she leaned against him as if grateful for his warmth, and then she pulled away and walked toward the northwestern corner of the building. "Is this it?"

"I'm surprised you could see it." David followed along behind her. There a patch of greater darkness on the floor could be seen; the original trap door followed the lines of planking and joints on the floor making it hard to see, but now the door swung wide and held open by a pair of ropes.

Margaret clearly wasn't listening. She peered down into the absolute blackness revealed by the open trapdoor. "It's big, isn't it?"

"Sidney apparently had a big operation. There appears to be plenty of room for a lot of contraband."

"What do you know about that?" she asked. "You're not from here, remember."

"I read about it after the find," David said. "That's why we named the bar Sidney's Cotton in the first place; sort of a pun, really. He had the warehouse for cotton, but made most of his money on guncotton and munitions. He disappeared just before the war ended. People thought he took his gold and went north, but clearly that's not what happened."

"Clever," Margaret said, though she didn't sound as if she really meant it. "Too clever for his own good."

"You're not talking about me, are you?"

Margaret looked up. "No, silly. John Michael Sidney. The rumor was that he made a deal with the local Federal commander. They didn't burn the warehouse, though most of the rest of the city wasn't so lucky. But even after Grant's army took Jackson on their way to Vicksburg there were still units of Pemberton's men operating independently in the countryside."

"Wasn't the war pretty much over by then?"

"Not quite. The Union still had to take Vicksburg to control the river and cut our supply lines. These units were fighting a guerrilla action against the troops besieging Vicksburg."

"With supplies from Sidney," David said. An educated guess on David's part, but Margaret's smile told him it was the right one. "So Sidney had played both sides. That might explain how he turned up dead in his own warehouse."

"Maybe." Margaret looked around. "Is there a light?"

"You mean you want to go down there? It's filthy, and the people from the State Archives went over it pretty thoroughly. I doubt you'll find any souvenirs."

"I'm not looking for souvenirs," she said. "Is there a light or not?"

"No... But I think there's a lamp here somewhere." David rummaged around in the corner, came up with a nine-volt lantern. "The workmen were using this earlier." He turned on the lamp and shone the light down the hole. There wasn't much to see except debris and the steps leading down. "What are you looking for, by the way?"

"It's a secret. Let's go."

David hesitated. "Margaret, you just met me. I'm a decent guy but there's no way you could know that yet. Isn't it a little risky going down into a hole in the ground with someone you barely know?"

She smiled at him. "I'm not afraid of you, David. Are you afraid of me?"

"No," he said, but he wondered if that were really true.

"Come on then. Lead or follow, but hold the light steady. These stairs look tricky."

Margaret put her right foot down carefully on the top step. David took her hand to steady her and together they very carefully descended the rickety stairway into the hidden room.

The air smelled thick with the scent of things long buried. The light receding above gave David the distinct feeling that he was walking down into a grave, a pit, a bottomless void that would swallow him forever. Then, they set foot on packed earth and the feeling eased a bit. Some daylight still crept in, albeit weak, from the door hole in the floor overhead. David shone his lantern about, marking the distance of the four walls from where he stood and the feeling that the walls were closing in on him faded a bit.

Margaret just stood there; looking around with an expression David couldn't see clearly and couldn't interpret in any case.

"Here we are. Cozy, isn't it?"

She ignored that. "They were over there, weren't they?"

David nodded, "Side by side near the corner there. I'm surprised no one found them earlier."

"It was war, David. People disappeared all the time."

Not for the first time, David had the sense of matters that were beyond him, or at least, perhaps, beyond anything he really wished to know. "There. You've seen it. I think we should go now."

"Not yet," she said. "I'm not finished."

"There's nothing to see down here, just dust and a few boxes."

"I said this wasn't about souvenirs."

"What then?"

Margaret sighed. "Redemption."

"You're not making any sense."

She smiled then. David saw it as a flash of white in the darkness, like a small bit of lightning. "I'm about to make even less. David, I need to ask you something, something very important. I need a favor."

"What sort of favor?"

"I want you to kill me."

David couldn't answer for several long moments. "I don't know what kind of joke you're playing, but it's not funny."

"It certainly isn't . . . wasn't meant to be," she said very clearly and calmly. "And no, I'm not crazy. Or, at least no more than you'd expect under the circumstances. Don't worry David--you can't hurt me. Just think of it as a play, a scene from some bad melodrama. All you have to do is what you can't help doing."

"Margaret, I don't understand any of this." It was getting harder to see by the moment; the light from the battery-powered lantern started to fade. David gave it a few good raps on the side but the beam didn't so much as flicker. It merely kept fading. "Damn...we're losing the light. We have to go now before we break a leg or something."

"Do you ever have bad dreams?" she asked, as if she hadn't heard a word he said.

The question stunned him into answering it straight out without hedging, without dismissing it, without even thinking about it. "All my life," he said.

I've never told that to anyone before, he thought.

"What about?"

"I dream that I killed someone…that I keep killing someone…." David blinked. He hadn't made the connection, at least, not until Margaret made it for him. "Oh my God, it's you."

"Yes, David," she said. "It's me. And you weren't dreaming."

"But…that's impossible! Who are you?!"

"Margaret. I told you that. My family name is LeCroix. Margaret LeCroix."

For a moment or two David just stared at her, and she saw the recognition in his eyes.

"You understand now, David. You even think you remember, but there's something missing, something you've forgotten. I need you to remember all of it. And the light's not fading. We are. For what happens next, I'm going to have to ask you to trust me."

"Trust—"

***

"--you?"

"Keep your voice down, Sergeant."

The captain hissed the order at him. David closed his mouth. He looked down the line; Everett and Jimson were following, spaced about three strides apart. He could see Captain Harlsy three strides ahead, keeping low. Off to the north they could see the faint glimmer of a campfire; Grant's division had set their pickets barely a quarter of a mile from the warehouse. The garrison Pemberton had sent from Vicksburg was broken and trying to regroup near the Yazoo. The only reason the rest of Jackson hadn't already fallen could be attributed to the mere fact that the Federals had run out of daylight. David found it strange that the warehouse hadn't been burned already; he could still see the glow from burning houses further north.

Harlsy slipped into the shadow of the train depot; three months of dodging Grant's and Sherman's men had taught them all to move like shadows at need. David looked right at his Captain, only knowing his position because he'd seen him move in. David followed, faint footfalls behind told him that Everett and Jimson kept close. Their faces were blackened with soot; their pistol barrels muffled. No one really thought the wadding would help keep the noise down if it came down to that, but they had to try.

They stood in the darkness, the depot building between themselves and the Federal sentries. They waited until the signal appeared: one flash from a hooded lantern. Harlsy went first, with David close behind. They were the first to descend the stairs that suddenly opened in front of them, barely lit from the glow of a candle. David glanced toward the Federal lines again, but saw nothing unusual. Then, he put his head down and emerged into the cellar of the warehouse.

David recognized Sidney at once; a well-dressed man

looking every inch the gentleman he wasn't, not by a long shot. Miss Maggie, who despite her profession, appeared every bit a lady, stood behind Sidney.

What is this woman doing here? David thought the question just as the Captain asked it.

Sidney took hold of Miss Maggie's hand. "That's not your concern. Concluding our business is."

"We've come for the rifles and supplies. Let's get this done," Harlsy said. "We've got your blood money."

"As long as you have it in gold," Sidney said.

Harlsy glared at him. "That was not our agreement, Sir."

Maggie frowned. "John, you told me you had this arranged."

"Be quiet, Maggie. I know what I'm doing."

But Sidney did not. He proceeded to make that even clearer. "It's gold or nothing. I know you have part of the city's stash. The Confederate Notes are worthless now and we both know it."

The Captain tried reason. "We don't have time to argue, Mr. Sidney. What gold remained was moved to Vicksburg before the encirclement. And even if we had it, I'd certainly not bring it with me."

Sidney looked grim. "Then I guess we have a problem."

"Take what we have, Mr. Sidney. That's my advice."

"It won't be any use where we're going!" Sidney's facade of calm now rapidly crumbling. "Maggie and I are leaving tonight; we took a big risk waiting this long."

"We're getting married," Maggie said, a little wistfully. "At least, I thought so."

"We are, that's why we need payment in gold," Sidney repeated, as if he hadn't heard a word Harlsy said. Everett and Jimson had their hands on their pistols by the entrance, confusion and anger on their faces. Harlsy nodded to them. "Get the ammunition first. Then, we'll take as many of the rifles as we can carry."

"I won't let you-"

Sidney grabbed for the pistol at his belt and Captain Harlsy shot him dead. The pistol fairly burst and Harlsy dropped it, grabbing his hand in pain. Acrid smoke on the air stung David's eyes. Maggie looked at the fallen man. Her eyes were watering, but that could have been the smoke. She didn't faint or scream or anything David expected. She only looked tragically sad, as if she hadn't really expected things to turn out any differently. As if the world she knew could not have been expected to treat her otherwise. Jimson and Everett hesitated only a moment then started carrying out their captain's orders.

Harlsy calmly picked up the singed wadding from his pistol and used it to wrap a bandage about his right hand. David stepped forward to help but Harlsy waved him off. "My pistol's ruined, Sergeant. You'll have to do it."

"Do what, Sir?"

Harlsy nodded at Maggie. David, to his horror, understood. Clearly, so did Maggie.

"Is that how it has to be then?" she asked softly.

"Captain, you're not thinking clear--" David began.

"My thoughts, damn you, have never been clearer, Sergeant." Harlsy made himself look at the woman. "You were going North with this man, weren't you?" She nodded, and he sighed. "We can't take you with us and we can't leave you here to alert the Federals of our presence. I won't risk my men that way. I'm sorry."

She shrugged her face hard and expressionless. "I could give you my word as a lady, Captain, but we both know what that's worth."

"Carry out your orders, Sergeant."

"I can't, Sir." David said.

Harlsy's tone sounded as flat and cold as death itself. "Who would you prefer then? Everett? Jimson? Which one of your friends would you hand this duty off to?"

David felt the pistol in his hand; he didn't remember how it got there. There was something wrong with the lantern. David could no longer see his companions clearly. Had they already left? No, there were flickers of movement in the shadows, no more than shadows themselves, as if they were nothing more than apparitions cast by the fading lantern.

Carry out your orders, Sergeant.

***

David didn't hear the voice now. Only inside his mind it echoed and it would not leave. It repeated over and over again. How many times? Once? Twice? Three times? Or had he heard it a thousand times, over and over again. When he was awake, and when he dreamed. It wouldn't stop. He wanted to make it stop. The world and all he knew shrank down to two people: David Lee McAllen and Miss Maggie LeCroix. His friends were gone, his commander was gone. Alone in the darkness with Maggie, and she was all he could see. She seemed perfectly solid, unlike the fading shadows around him, but she shone with an inner light.

David held his hand in front of his face, and through his closed fingers he still saw Miss Maggie LeCroix. She was the same woman, but she didn't look the same. Her dress looked different, even her hair. But, the eyes were the same. He would never forget her eyes, no, not in a hundred years. David was very sure of that.

"You had to do it," Maggie said.

Had? "I don't understand."

"It happened long ago, David, but part of you never left. A part of you has been haunting this cellar ever since. You never could forgive yourself."

"It's happening now..." David said, and he tightened his hand on the pistol.

Maggie nodded, sadly. "For you, it's always happening. It never stops. Don't you think it's time it did?"

"I didn't want to."

Didn't? Damn, now she had him doing it. The woman had gone crazy with fear, that was all. Knowing it would be best to end it quickly David raised the pistol. "I'm sorry."

"It wasn't your fault."

The words were like barbs of ice, freezing him in place. Maggie went on quickly. "I trusted John Sidney. I believed him when he said he had a plan to get us away; that we could go north and live well. I was just a big enough fool to believe in him, and I think my share of the blame is bigger than yours. Yet, your guilt and your sorrow brings you back to this moment time and again, and you bring me with you. I'm tired of being dead in this cellar, David. I know you are too."

"It wasn't my...fault?" The words sank in. David didn't want to hope, didn't *dare* to hope, but he could not keep the words out of his mind. Like the order that would not be shut out, only now it was. The order, though still there, seemed much fainter. The lights were coming up, as if it were the end of a play. He could see the cobwebs, and the decay in the cellar. He saw the strange clothes Maggie wore; he looked down and saw the strange clothes that he appeared to be wearing. David held an empty hand pointed at Miss Maggie LeCroix.

The words echoed, *Carry out your orders Sergeant,* so faint, so far away within his mind. He could barely hear it now.

Maggie nodded, as if she had heard the order clearly. "One more time David Lee McAllen. Do what you have to do. And let it be the last time."

David squeezed a trigger of empty air, and the shot went out, lost in eternity.

Sydney's Cotton

***

David came to on the floor of the cellar near Margaret's crumpled form. The smell of damp earth permeated his nostrils. Though a little dazed, David remembered it all: the uniform, the pistol and his comrades. And the name he had born in a different time, David Lee McAllen. It was as if he had watched the whole thing, powerless to move or intervene, the David that was now subsumed, for a while, by the David that had been. He felt what the man had felt, knew what he knew. The memories faded a bit, as a dream would, but parts of it would never leave. They were the things he needed to remember.

David crawled over to the fallen woman. "Margaret? Are you all right?"

Margaret's eyelids fluttered open, and she smiled at him. "I am now."

"You're Maggie LeCroix, aren't you?"

She smiled again. "I wish I'd met you under better circumstances…give or take a hundred years…." Her eyes closed, and she let out one breath like a parting sigh. David shook her. "Margaret!"

Her eyes opened again, and David suddenly realized that he did not know the woman looking back at him, nor she him. She screamed and lashed out at him. David pinned her flailing arms down to avoid either one of them being injured.

"Will you please stop that? I'm not going to hurt you.

You're safe."

She sat up. "Who are you? What am I doing here?" She looked down at herself. "And what am I doing in this dress? I look like a tramp!"

"I'm David Summers, don't you remember? You were dressed like that when you came to the bar, Margaret."

"In the first place, my name is Louise and I don't go to bars! Look, Mister, I don't know what you're trying to pull, but I warn you..."

David backed away. "Miss, there's been a misunderstanding and I think we need to talk. Let's go upstairs."

The woman's last name did turn out to be LeCroix. David wasn't too surprised. Nor had he been surprised that she acted more than a little offended when he mentioned her notorious relative. It was, apparently, a subject her family did not discuss. She had no memory of coming to the bar, no memories at all since that morning. David supplied some of the background of the evening, but left most of it out. Then he suggested she have a medical checkup, and Miss LeCroix primly admitted that this seemed a sensible precaution, and that he would hear from the police if anything of a criminal nature should be revealed. She gathered her dignity and took it out the door. Jackson wasn't that large of a city, but David never saw her again.

The next day David visited the State Archives and identified the woman whose skeleton had been found in the cellar along with John Sidney's. The historian had been a bit skeptical until David got him to produce one of the two known glass plate photographs of Maggie LeCroix. The dress in the second was a perfect match to the remnants of the one still clinging to the skeleton. The historian asked how David knew. David called it a hunch.

Later, he talked his partner into changing the name of the bar to "Maggie's Place."

"Much more interesting than that Sidney fellow, don't you think?"

His partner agreed, whatever he thought; David had the larger share. They took the rifle down and sent it to the museum in Vicksburg where it belonged. In its place over the bar David put up a large oil portrait of Miss Maggie LeCroix in her full glory. The artist worked at least partly from a print of the photograph; the rest of the details David supplied from someone else's memory. He only had to look at Maggie's painted smile to know he had gotten it right.

Ghost Road
by:
Jason Hughes

A Vulgar *Display* blasted loudly as a thick cloud of smoke rolled from the car's windows. The full moon glowed in full radiance from the sky above and illuminated fragments of the road through the draping trees. Soda and beer cans hung from some of the tree branches facing the road. The cool October air dominated the Texas sky of Saratoga. A slight chill crawled down the spines of every eager passenger in the car. No one would mention the ominously eerie feeling that gripped their bodies, but it was surely present. They all knew it, as their parents and grandparents had spoken of the same sensation while seeking out the local legend in which they were searching.

Stuart Waters had been to the long stretch of dark road several times prior to this trip. It was almost a family ritual for the Waters tribe. "I remember a while back when this road used to be called *Bragg* Road. Nothing has changed, except for the name," Stuart said. He had a little bit of history on the road, due to the constantly rambled stories from his elder family members. His cousins, aunts, uncles, grandparents and parents all claimed to have seen the mysterious light that dwelled the mile long road, once the sky grew dark. Stuart had taken a few trips on his own, just to feel as though he was a part of his family's traditional eye witnessing party of the local legend known since the early nineteen - hundreds as the ghost of Bragg road.

Stacy Pearl, Bobby Mounts and Diane Morrow looked at him in a silent daze. "I don't really think I want to be out here. I shouldn't have come," Stacy said as her head turned slowly, examining the walls of thicket that enclosed the cruising vehicle. Stacy could feel her left leg twitching in nervousness without the ability to calm herself from the atmosphere that engulfed the group. Even though the music was blasting and all seemed content with being together, a creepy cloud of dread lingered directly above the car. Claustrophobia was beginning to eat away at Stacy's mind and well-being.

"So, why is this guy headless and wandering around this road again? Wasn't it because he was decapitated by an angry farmer or something?" Diane asked in an aura of curiosity.

"No, where did you hear *that* one?" Stuart asked.

"I . . . don't know, I just—"

"The story goes. . . There was a railroad track that used to run along these parts back in the eighteen – hundreds. There was a break-man that worked one of the trains that traveled through here. One night, somehow, his light sent a false signal, and the train took off when it wasn't supposed to. That is how he . . . lost his head," Stuart explained.

Stacy tried to hide the lump in her throat, but her forced swallow revealed that she was not handling the story, or position that she was in very lightly.

"What was the Break-Man's name?" Bobby asked.

"No one knew his name. Some say that the light that is seen out here is nothing but swamp gas. Some have other theories. My family has actually witnessed it, first hand," Stuart boasted as the car came to a stop on the side of the road.

Stacy's breath started to quiver as her heart sped up by leaping bounds. She could feel it wanting to burst out of her chest and take off into the night, leaving her in the dust to fend for herself. Bobby killed the engine and took the keys out of the ignition. Even though Stacy was against the idea and suddenly decided to recant her choice to go along for the ride, they were destined to be staying for a quite a while. In her mind, they would be setting up their metal, mobile tent until the sun came up the next morning. She knew that everyone in her presence wanted to see something happen, anything to give them the fuel and motivation for something to converse over for months to come.

"I'm getting out and taking a look around. Is anyone coming with me?" Bobby stated as he opened the car door.

"I'll go with you, Bob," Diane said as she unbuckled her seatbelt and exited the car.

Stuart looked at Stacy with a hint of concern. He could tell that she was not adapted to her surroundings, only the company that was around her. "Do you want to get out? We can just stand by the car if you'd like. If they decide to walk around, we can wait for them," Stuart said kindly.

"Well, okay," Stacy reluctantly replied. She got out of the car along with Stuart. "How long has your family been coming up here?" she asked.

"Since my grandmother was a kid," he said with a slightly sinister smile, "this legend has been around for ages, ever since this place has been called Bragg Road. They just changed it a few years back though. Some say that if the light passes over your car, or whatever you're driving, it kills the motor."

"Kills the *motor*?" she asked as she waited for an immediate conformational repeat.

"That's right. The light passes above your car and cuts off the engine," he explained.

"Have . . . you . . . ever seen it? I mean the light itself?" she asked before taking a sip of her drink. She could barely swallow it down as her throat tightened. Looking up, she noticed that Bobby and Diane seemed to get smaller in the distance as they kept walking down the mile-long, straight stretch of road. "It's kind of cold out here. I wish that we could build a fire or something," she said as she awkwardly crossed her arms while trying not to spill her drink.

"There's really nowhere to build one," he noted then added, "we would burn the entire Big Thicket to the ground . . . and probably us along with it. Besides, I think it's against the law around these parts."

"So, what do most people think that the light is? I mean, besides swamp gas or some kind of fumes," she inquired.

"If you mean as far as the legend is concerned, some say that it's the lantern that the headless Break-man carries in search of his head. Others think that it's the train he was on at the time of his death. Some have said that the light appears to sway back and forth, hence the lantern theory. Others have seen a huge, single light . . . hence the train speculation. No one really knows for sure," he elaborated.

"I've never heard of this place until you told us about it. I kind of want to go home, Stu," she grumbled. She felt comfortable with Stuart, but at the same time, like she was about to jump out of her own skin. She could feel her stomach beginning to swirl in a nauseating fit of dreadful suspense. It was somewhat of a rush, but mostly a horrifying experience.

"There have been all kinds of paranormal researchers, psychics and people like that from all over the United States that have come here to either check it out, write about it or debunk the theory of a ghost. It has made this little town quite popular," he explained as he began to lightly kick the gravel beneath his shoes.

A coyote howled deep within the forest and made Stacy practically jump into Stuart's arms. "Whoa, everything's okay. I'm not going to let *anything* hurt you," he said then put his hand on her shoulder. Stacy looked at him with a smile as he turned his head. Stuart looked back toward the road and squinted his eyes. Bobby and Diane had already been swallowed and devoured by the darkness of the night.

They were nowhere to be seen, as far as Stuart's eyes could focus. "Yo, *Bobby.* Where are you guys," he shouted with a repeating echo. There was no answer.

"I . . . *really* want to get out of here now . . . like . . . *bad,*" Stacy said as another quiver inducing chill slithered its way down her spine. Something began to move in the trees behind them. A tear tried to squeeze its way out of Stacy's eye, but she looked the other way and wiped it with the palm of her hand. She didn't want Stuart to see her in such a vulnerable state. She was having a hard enough time looking at her own self-perception in the silent mental breakdown that now slowly started taking over her inner core.

The sound in the trees began to stumble closer and closer. Stacy knew that it wasn't the wind rustling through the branches. It had to have been much more than that. Much to their surprise, the swishing of the trees was soon followed by two lights immersing from the patch of forest. Stacy jumped back into the car and locked all of the doors. Stuart, being the only male there to protect her, stayed outside and glared at the beams as they progressed closer toward him as he slowly backed against the car, placing his fingers under the handle. Stacy unlocked the door in which he was blocking for his own safety and hers most importantly.

"Hello? Who's out there!" he called into the forest, waiting for an answer.

Two double-barrels of a shotgun came creeping from between the bushes. "Ay, man. You kids better be careful. We're huntin' out here," said Dennis Sherwood, a Saratoga local. Tagging along by his side stood his younger cousin, Brad Filling.

"I thought they didn't allow guns out here," Stuart said with a strong sense of empowerment, "people come to this road all the time. Entire families come here to see the light. You could get someone killed."

Dennis slowly walked up to Stuart and put the barrel under his chin, pressing his jaw shut. "But you won't tell anyone that we're out here . . . will you," Dennis hissed in a grim tone. Stuart shook his head in agreement.

All that Stacy could see was Stuart's back pressed against the window of the car as it slightly slid in an upward motion. She had no idea what was going on outside and Dennis had no idea that she was hiding in the car.

Because of Dennis' unruly action Stuart feared for Stacy's safety; in his mind, there was no telling what would've happened if Dennis knew she was in the car. Much to his relief, Dennis and Brad backed off and returned into the thick patch of woods. Stuart turned around and looked at Stacy through the glass. He was pale white and slathered in a cold sweat, like he had just seen a ghost. Then, he backed away from the door and Stacy opened it, and got out.

"Oh, my God, what happened? You're . . . so pale . . . and sweating. Are you *okay*?" she asked as she wiped some of the perspiration from Stuart's forehead.

"Uh, yeah, I'm . . . I'm fine. I just wish Bobby and Dianne would hurry up and get back here," he replied in a relieved sigh. He tried his best to calm down from the confrontation that could've easily taken his life with the slip of a trigger happy finger. In the distance, Dennis and Brad could be heard joking about making Stuart almost wet his pants. "You showed him, huh," was the last statement Stuart could make out in an earshot range before their voices faded into the wind. Little did Stuart know Stacy also heard Brad's parting sense of sick mentality.

Stacy began to understand what had unfolded right in front of her eyes, without her even knowing. She just glanced at Stuart and looked down at her high heels, without saying a word. She didn't want to embarrass him any further than she imagined he already was after what he had just experienced. Stuart breathed in long strides and shook all over, but tried to hold back the visuals, due to his feelings for Stacy.

As he calmed, he looked down the mile-long stretch of road for Dianne and Bobby. His watering eyes could barely make out the dark path that lay ahead. Suddenly, his jaw dropped.

"What wrong?" Stacy asked.

Stuart looked dead ahead and slightly squinted his eyes. "Look down the road. Do you see that?" he replied as he extended his arm and index finger in front of him.

"Did I see . . . what?" Stacy inquired as she looked in his hand's general guided direction.

"Look, Stacy . . . right there," he said in almost a whisper.

Stacy leveled her head and eyesight as her heart almost skipped a beat. Something stood staring the two directly in the face. This was not two angry hunters, armed with loaded rifles. It was not a deer. It surely wasn't Bobby or Diane. It was a huge glowing light in the middle of the road . . . and the enigmatic globe of illuminated wonder was headed right for them. It was leveled at what seemed to be about six feet from the ground at the distance they were from it. The light proceeded closer but at a snail's pace.

"Let me in the car! Move out of my freaking way!" Stacy screamed as she pushed Stuart practically onto the ground to reach the door handle. She got in the car, and Stuart followed. They locked all of the doors. When they finally settled down from the scattered-brained fit of fear, they looked through the windshield. The light had vanished into thin air. Stacy and Stuart were panting hard and fast enough to have just completed a marathon. In their minds, that is exactly what they wanted to do, but had nowhere to go; at this point in time and in the dead of the night, they weren't certain if they would win or lose.

"The keys, they took the keys with them!" Stacy screamed in panic.

"Just, just calm down, *please*, Stacy! We are in the car! No one can hurt us now," he reasoned.

He was trying his best to make light of a bad situation, but was not certain what could or would happen next. They both knew one thing for certain . . . they were not about to get out of the car.

Just as the two got semi-relaxed and situated themselves in the back seat, the headlights began to blink as the radio turned on and up at full volume. Stacy started screaming at the top of her lungs. She put her hands over her ears as she kicked the back of the front seat with full force panic.

"Stacy, calm the hell down!" Stuart cried as the radio turned off in an instant. "Please, Jesus!" he blasted as everything was silent around him.

"What is happening, where are Diane and Bobby? I just want to get out of here and go home!" she wailed.

Stuart put his arm around her shoulder. She began to calm down as he requested and put her head in her shaking hands. He turned around and looked out of the back window. The strange light swayed back and forth behind the car as it elevated and descended closer to the long road behind them. He looked down at Stacy without saying a word. He didn't want to push any buttons to startle her.

"It is okay, Stacey, everything is okay, I . . . I promise you," he crooned. He didn't know if she believed him. He wasn't sure if he believed himself. The light backed further away from the parked car and then moved closer, as it crossed back and forth over the street. The gleaming white glow changed to a dim red and back to white as it swayed back and forth. It slowly evaporated into the darkness in a green gust.

Stuart put his head down on top of Stacey's to comfort her and his own cowardly hidden emotions at the same time. Their shared fear brought them closer together, which deep down, is what both of them wanted. They just never thought that it would happen in a situation such as this.

"Stuart, Stacey! Help us, please . . . Heeeeelp uuuuuuus!"

a voice cried in the wind. "What was that? Did you hear it?" Stacy asked lifting her head up too quickly and hitting Stuart in the face with fierce impact.

"Hear it? I certainly freaking *felt* it, that's for sure!" He replied, covering his nose with his hands.

"It was Diane screaming for us to . . . help her. What if something has happened to her and Bobby? What if they are in some kind of danger? What if—"

"Stacy, my nose is bleeding all over my face," Stuart blurted. He lowered his crimson washed hands into the sight of his gaping eyes.

"Did you *hear* me? Did you hear that voice? It was Diane, I'm telling you! Why won't you listen to me? I know I just heard her . . . or someone screaming! They were calling out to us for help!" she wailed.

Her temperature rose and her patience drastically dropped. Stacy's words fell upon deaf ears and a swelling nose as Stuart frantically tried to find something to stop the gushing red. He finally lifted the bottom of his white shirt and pressed it against his face. His eyes watered, causing his vision to progressively blur.

"Oh, I'm sorry, Stu. I didn't mean to do that. I just got scared. I just . . . I know that I heard her voice. I just know I did. I'm not going crazy or just hearing things. This was for real," she explained then reached over attempting to assist Stuart in nursing his nose.

"It's . . . ouch— everything is okay. I know you didn't mean to. Man, it was my idea to bring you guys out here to see this and now I kind of want to go home as well. If anything has happened to Bobby and Diane, it's going to be my fault. I don't know what I would do with myself if something happened to them. Probably commit myself somewhere," he lamented.

"It . . . It is not . . . your fault, Stu. We all wanted to come on this trip. No one can blame the other more than themselves. You know what I mean?" she reasoned then looked around cautiously, biting her lip. Deep down inside she really wanted to say, *'Yes, Stuart, it is your fault that we are in this situation! Why did you coerce us into to coming out here in the middle of nowhere just to see some light?'* But, she couldn't bring herself to do so and sink to such a level of blame. As far as she knew, Stuart was the only one physically suffering from his own decision. She tried to keep telling herself that Bobby and Diane would show up any minute now with the keys to their freedom and peace of mind.

Stacy began to settle down for the most part. However, her inner selfishness took over when she saw the agonizing pain Stuart suffered caused by her accidental head-ram. A slight smirk drew across her face. She leaned back in the seat and closed her eyes as Stuart now had to fend for himself.

Suddenly, the car started and revved up, without moving an inch. The radio turned on once more at full blast. The horn began to repeatedly honk in short beeps and one long one. Stacy could not control herself any longer, and her sliding patience and bottled fear let lose her words as she kicked the back door on the passenger's side screaming,

"Damn it, Stuart! This is your fault! We're going to die in here and it is *all your* freaking *fault!*"

"Just calm down, Stacy, there is no one here to harm us! It's just messing with us!" He screamed over the revving motor and honking horn.

He held on to Stacy tightly as he looked into the front seat. The gas pedal appeared to be held in the downward position as if someone were sitting there inside of the car with them. Stuart balled up his fists and took a swing into the front seat of the car, hitting thin air. The motor died, along with the radio and the horn ceased to honk.

He looked out the windows. The car seemed as if it were moving. "Stacy, hold on. The car is moving forward," he said in the most subtle tone he could use without frightening her more than she already seemed to be. "We're not moving! The car is standing still, and I want out of it! I want out of here and away from *you!*" she cried.

"I'm not doing anything! I am trying to protect you from whatever this is!"

"You know what it is! You know what you were getting yourself and us into when you told us about this place! What really happened to your uncle?! It wasn't a car accident, was it?! I bet he met his maker right here . . . on this freaking road! Answer me! Tell me the truth this time, Stuart! You owe it to me and all of us, including yourself! If it wouldn't have been for you, this . . . would not . . . be . . . *happening!*" She screamed in a showering reign of intolerable animosity.

Stacy knew somewhere deep down inside, past all of

the fright and flying emotions that if they made it off of Ghost Road alive, she would forgive Stuart in the long run. Even though somewhere in her gray matter, this rational logic at this particular moment in time didn't register. Furious, frightened and worried, nothing could control the unleashed retribution which Stacy held against Stuart in this given juncture in time.

Still, she debated whether or not this could be her own mind playing tricks on her, especially when she thought she heard Diane call out to them. But, what If they really were in some kind of serious danger? She knew that if the latter judgment swimming around in her head predicted the correct ruling, there would be no hope for any of them. She teetered there on the verge of nestling her brain into the comforting decision that had to be the only logical cerebral path to be taken in a situation such as this.

'My mind is just playing all kinds of tricks on me because of this freakishly weird environment in which I am trapped . . . I am just . . . hearing things. I am only . . . seeing things because I am telling myself to . . . That is all . . . nothing more . . . None . . . of this . . . is real . . . These are all illusions that are messing with my head . . . . I barely got any sleep last night and I am delusional. ... There is no one here, but Stuart and myself . . . . He knows that . . . and of course, I know that. I . . . am just . . . going . . . insane,' she thought to herself. Quickly, she reached for any tactic of stability to tell herself that everything would be okay.

Just as she scavenged her sanity a little piece at a time, the car alarm began to go beep, along with the car horn. Her cell phone began to ring, but the caller identification did not display a number. She knew that every peaceful shard of tranquil rationalization had just been placed into a solid block of reality. Everything she tried to debunk in her mind was actually true. An unknown force had manifested all around them. This paranormal force found a way into the car, with them.

Stacy began to panic once more and slap Stuart in his chest and arms. "Look what you've done! Diane and Bobby could be already dead and we're next! How could you bring us out here, knowing that this would happen! You knew it all along, didn't you?" she shrieked.

"I didn't know, Stacy! I'm so sorry! I didn't know!" he yelled. But, his words and loving retaliation were lost in the chaotic malfunctions of the car as the horn and car alarm continued to blare. Then, Stacy's phone rang adding to the mix of sounds.

"Hello!" She greeted white noise on the other end of the line, thinking that it was some kind of signaling rescue. She wanted to have faith in her wishful thinking.

"Who is it!?" he asked.

"I don't know!" she snapped. "Hello! Who is this?! Who is . . . ?"

"Sssssstaaaaaaaacy!" a disjointed and raspy voice gargled through the cell phone.

"Noooo!" She wailed as she began to sob uncontrollably and drop the phone onto the floorboard. Stacy began to smash the cell phone with her foot until it broke into two pieces.

"I'm getting the hell out of this car. I can't take any more of this!" he noted. He tried to open the back door and though the door wasn't locked, it wouldn't open. He kicked the door open and stepped outside of the car. Stacy remained in the backseat, screaming with her hands over her ears to block the blasting horn and alarm.

"Stuart, get back in here! Where are you going!? Don't leave me in here!" she cried.

The full moon shown in plain view through the windshield, but as Stuart stepped out of the car, his face lit up by another light. He turned white as the bright light covered his body. As he realized this, he jumped back into the car and slammed the door as hard as he could.

"The light is right over us! It's right above the car!" he screamed.

"We're not going to make it, Stuart! They're already dead! Something must have happened to them!" she hollered.

The ground darkened and the car alarm and horn fizzled into deceased silence. It seemed as if the battery had died in a slow, agonizing act of defeat. Stacy reached down and picked up the two halves of her cell phone and stared at the mutilated communication device.

"Now what am I going to do? I broke my freaking cell phone," she grumbled.

"We still have mine," he noted. He pulled his cell phone out of the pocket of his white t-shirt, now almost completely splattered in drops of red, and held his arm at a ninety degree angle.

"Well, call someone," she implored. "Call Bobby, he should have his phone on him. He never leaves home without it." Stacy realized that for the time being, they had to stick together if they were going to survive the night. She would save every drop of aggression inside of her for when they made it home, if they were going to make it off of the dark and empty mile long Road alive.

Stuart unfolded his cell phone and dialed Bobby's number. Bobby's cell phone started to ring, in his ear and in the front seat of the car. "Aw, man . . . he left his phone here," he groaned. He lowered his phone from his ear and pushed the end button.

"Well, then call someone else," Stacy snapped.

Bobby's phone kept ringing in the front seat. The temperature inside of the car began to drop below sixty degrees. The couple could see their own breath as they began to shiver and tremble uncontrollably. Goose bumps began to rise on Stacy's arm as Bobby's phone ceased to ring in a progressively slow putter.

"I'll try Diane," he noted.

"Is she answering?" Stacy asked impatiently.

"Hold on. It hasn't even rung yet, jeez," he replied with the same degree of impatience.

The phone rang for only half of a second, and then the phone died. Stuart looked down at the energy level which appeared full. "It just rang for a second, and hung up on me," he explained, glaring down at his cell phone.

"What?" Stacy gasped. Her head began to swivel like a garden sprinkler in an uncontrollable spasm, as she tried looking out of every window in the car at once. She didn't have a clue what she was looking for or what she would find, or what would find them. Stacy's head moved one way as her wide-open eyes moved in every direction in a jerking motion. Her scrambled psyche had taken hold of the mirrors of her soul, pulling it along for the twisted trip to the lucid state of phantasmagoria. She knew that what was happening before her eyes was very substantial, but tried to deny the brutally obvious reality, with every ounce of withering sanity that she had to grasp onto.

Stacy tried to awake herself from the swirling nightmare that slowly unfolded all around her, but she wasn't asleep. Not only was she experiencing this vividly gripping moment in graphic detail and emotion, but Stuart endured this terrifying reality as well. They were right beside each other to verify that this could not be a bad dream.

In an unselfish act of shared sympathy, Bobby and Diane may have been physically lost, but they both constantly walked through Stuart and Stacy's blackening gray matter. The four of them had been good friends for many years. Stuart and Stacy were worried about Bobby and Diane's safety, even while in a compromising situation of their own well-being. This painful fact did nothing for them but add to the mounting stress presently bestowed upon the couple's crumbling psyches.

"Look! It's Bobby and Diane!" shouted Stacy in a

relieved breath.

"Where are they?" Stuart asked. "I can't see them!" He strained his eyes to look through the windshield.

"They're right there!" Stacy said. "Open your freaking eyes! They are running toward us!" She pointed straight ahead with a shaking hand.

"I don't see . . . Wait! There they are!" Bobby and Diane were running for them at full speed. They were both screaming but neither Stuart nor Stacy was able to hear or decode a word that spewed from their gaping mouths. Bobby and Diane both seemed to be as pale as freshly applied wet glue onto a pitch black canvas. From out of the dim-sighted background, something appeared behind them in a fading presence that grew brighter by the second until it became a glowing, white light. Stacy and Stuart had already become far too familiar with its unwanted acquaintance.

"Run! It's right behind you! The light is right behind you!" Stuart screamed at the top of his lungs. He hung the front half of his body through the backseat window as he called to them.

"It's gaining on them! It's coming right for them . . . and *us!*" Stacy screamed. As the light got closer it changed to a dark crimson color, but as it passed between Bobby and Diane, the brightness increased back to a blinding white beam. The radiant ball of illuminating terror kept getting closer to the parked car. Stuart squinted to look past the light and could not see anything, but the blackness that devoured the night. The once guiding vision of the tranquil moon had been obscured by thick storm clouds lingering above in the nocturnally painted sky. All that could be seen was the light that barreled at them and progressively became closer and brighter. Bobby and Diane had vanished into the night once more. This time, they disappeared right in front of Stacy and Stuart's own eyes. They could not believe what they had just witnessed. They didn't have much time to think about where Bobby and Diane had gone, as the light became so close that it impaired their collective vision.

"Where did they go, Stuart? I can't see Bobby or Diane! Where in the hell did they go? I could hear them calling out to us!" Stacy yelled. She put her hand over her eyes as a visor as she peered out into the light trying to see beyond.

"I don't know! I can't see them either! They just vanished, something must have happened to them!" Stuart screamed. He retracted himself back into the car.

The light swayed from one side of the street to the other. A loud hum accompanied the glow as it reached the hood of the car. The huge light elevated and hovered over the hood and then began to crawl up the windshield. The car vibrated like an earthquake had a firm grip on it with monstrous hands, as the earth stood still around the violently shaking couple.

"What is it doing to us!?" Stacy cried in a fit of terror laced shock.

"I don't know! Hold onto me!" he yelled.

The humming roar overrode his vibrating voice. It felt as if the lantern had transformed into a train and the railroad tracks in which it traveled were connected to the top of the car.

"Make it stop, Stuart, please make it *stop!*" she screamed and she burst into uncontrollable tears. The back of the car lit up as the shaking died down to a complete stop. The huge light glared through the back windshield. The blinding beam began to slowly circle around the vehicle as it changed from white to dark red and repeated the process as it enclosed them. The two felt as if this were the light at the end of their tunnels of life. The only difference was, instead of them traveling into the tunnel as most would have imagined, the tunnel had come to them and seemed to be sucking the two into the light against their own free will.

Bob and Diane could be heard screaming as the strange and unexplainable light revolved around the car. Their echoing voices faded in and out, as they got louder, lower, closer and distant with every motion around the vehicle.

"I can still hear them! Where *are* they!? Bobby, Diane! Where are you?! We can hear you!" Stacy screamed. A thunderous, eardrum-busting audible torture of a train horn drowned out her cries.

Stacy knew for certain that the legend involved a train, as opposed to a lantern, as some of the legends had noted. There was no way a lantern could be so large in size and produce such a horrendously awful racket. Not only did the chaotic noise almost make her wet herself, it gave her a skull splitting headache. At this point, she started praying for the subtle glow of a lantern. The force that this illuminating spirit possessed was much more powerful than that of a lantern. As the light reached the back of the car, it began to slowly back away into a distant, fading luminance in the rearview mirror. Bobby and Diane's shrilling voices coincided with the light as they began to fade away into the blackness behind them. "What are we going to do, Stuart? I . . . I don't want to die out . . . in the middle of some deserted road," she cried. She put her head on Stuart's shoulder.

"I don't think that we're going to die. I think, if this thing wanted us dead or wanted or heads for that matter, it would've already done something to us. Don't you?" he answered. He rubbed more dripping blood from his face and contemplated his own answer.

"I'm still so worried about Bobby and Diane. I mean, who knows what has happened or is happening to them out there in those woods, or on this street. I'm just so scared for them, and us," Stacy said. She wiped her tears on Stuart's red stained white shirt.

'You're not the one with the freaking broken nose,' he thought to himself. "Everything will be okay. We'll get out of here. I just don't want to go walking down this street looking for Bobby and Diane. They could come back while we are gone . . . and I don't want to leave you here all alone to fend for yourself. Those hunters could still be out there," he explained while looking out each window.

"Do you think that they did something to Diane and Bobby? Those hunters, I mean? What if that light did something to all four of them?" she worried. "I know you're here to protect me, and you have been. I'm very thankful to you for that . . . but—," Stacy's voice faltered as she put her head down and began to breathe heavily.

"But what? You can tell me. I understand if you are mad at me for getting us into all of this. It's very much my fault and I apologize to all of you. I just wanted to have a good time . . . and . . . get to . . . know you a little more than we already do, that was all. I have always heard that the light was harmless from my family. They have come out here to see it several times, like I said before. It's supposed to be about as harmless as the ghost of Sarah Jane road . . . or the kissing statues in that old cemetery," he pleaded. "You know, just something to see that can't cause any harm. I didn't even know that it would do everything that it has so far. No one ever told me that it could—"

From out of nowhere, a gunshot went off, followed by two more. "Get it! Shoot it again! Kill . . . !" A voice that sounded like Dennis' shouted from deep inside of the wooded area.

"It won't stop! It's blinding me! Noooooohohohohhhoo!" Another could be heard screaming that could have been Brad, his voice fading away into the night.

Stacy's cherry red lips started to quiver as she looked around in panic. "Who was that?!" she shouted in a high-pitched yelp.

"I don't know. Maybe it was those hunters. Maybe something happened to one of those hunters. I don't know . . . I'm not going out there to check on him and make sure he's okay though. I know that much," Stuart replied. He wasn't sure which hunter it was, what they took a shot at, what they hit, or their condition, but he did know that one threatened his own life as the other laughed at his distress. That fact alone was enough to make Stuart keep his distance. Deep down inside, he was laughing a little as well. He worried that they could have done something to Bobby and Diane, but would not say the wrong thing that would upset Stacy.

"I don't know what to think or believe right now. I'm so confused," Stacy said. She looked out of the car window and saw a light glowing in the forest. It kept getting closer and closer to the road. "Stuart, look!" Stacy screamed into Stuart's ear at the top of her lungs at a deafening point blank range.

Stuart rubbed his ear vigorously with the bottom stump of his palm to stop the lingering ringing. It took a moment for what she had said to register into his mind, from the volume that she used expressing it into his ear. "What . . . what is it?" he asked feeling slightly irritated.

By the time he had looked out of the window, the unexplained light was already staring them both right in the face. He could see a translucent image of Brad screaming within the glow. Brad evanesced in a subtle fade as the light slowly made its way around the car once again. Seeming to have more energy behind the brightness than before, the entire car became engulfed in a blinding illumination and the temperature inside started to rise at a rapid pace. The couple began to sweat from their instilled fear and the external heat that glazed their skin. The radio turned on at full blast as did the motor and security alarm. Bobby's, Stuart's cell phones, and even Stacy's broken phone, began to hum a constant ring without spaces in between. To add to the shrieking confusion, an all too familiar train horn began to blast at a window rattling volume.

As the light circled in a three–sixty around the car, the colors changed from an incandescent white, to a vision-impairing red. Stuart and Stacy felt as if they were trapped inside of a chaotic prison of blinding sights and deafening sounds that would surely become their shared catacomb. This mutual feeling was far from romantic in any way, shape or form.

"Just go away! Leave us the hell alone! What do you want from us!? Why are you doing this to us!? What in the hell . . . *are yyyyouuuu!?*" Stacy screamed. She began to beat on the front seats in a heated tantrum of fear-drenched confusion.

"Calm down, please!" Stuart suggested. He felt angry at himself and Stacy at his failed attempt to settle her snapped and entangled nerves.

"What do you want me to do? How do you want me to feel? Safe? Like nothing can happen to us out here? Is that it?" she asked. "This thing will not stop messing with us! Bobby and Diane are not coming *back*! We've been out here for hours! I'm hungry! I'm thirsty, and I haven't eaten anything since breakfast yesterday morning! It's three o' clock, Stuart! Three o' clock! Do you know how *long* we have been stuck out here because of your bright idea of seeing this? Our families are probably worried half to death about us! What else am I supposed to do? How else am I supposed to act?" she screamed over the train horn, cell phones, radio and security alarm with the greatest of ease.

The blazing concoction of animosity and terror that boiled inside of Stacy boosted her voice level over all of the other sounds that surrounded them. In the same effect of retaliation, her ranting raised Stuart's held back feelings of annoyance toward her to almost a bursting stage of unleashed verbal assault. He morphed inside from forgiving, to possessing the ability to burst at any given opportunity or moment.

'Why can't you just shut your whining mouth the hell up? You're making me want to throw you out of this car so that light can do whatever it wants with you. I could be spared of all of this whining! Please, just shut, your, mouth! That's all I ask, just for one solitary moment of what little peace I can have with all of this going on around me,' Stuart thought to himself in silence with his eyes tightly clenched to the point of tears. "It's okay. I'm sorry," Stuart mumbled among the blaring noises from the cell phones, car, and circling light.

"What did you just say to me?" she asked.

"I said I was freaking sorry! What do you want me to say or do at this point, Stacy? This thing is not going to leave us alone! Do you hear me? Can you hear me?" he shouted. Stuart's repressed intolerance had finally reached breaking point of negativity that began to raise its ugly head above the calm surface.

The light came to a stop in the back of the car. A bright beam radiated through the interior and down the long road in front of Stacy and Stuart. In the far distance, Bobby and Diane were running as fast as they could. Stuart and Stacy looked at each other, knowing they had witnessed this before. What they were seeing was just in their minds or the apparition that held them captive playing tricks on them.

The beam of white light turned red and moved forward, through the back windshield it and hovered above their heads inside of the car. Stuart and Stacy screamed as if it were the last time they would be able to do so. The light passed through the car and proceeded down the road in front of them.

The combination of the horns, alarms and phones ceased as the light made its way through the front windshield. The beam passed in between Diane and Bobby, and Diane vanished into thin air. Bobby looked beside him and saw that Diane wasn't running beside him anymore. He looked behind him as the light evaporated. He ran faster screaming at the top of his huffing lungs. His legs felt as if they were about to give out, trembling beneath his body, but he sprinted in full speed toward the car.

"It's that freaking light playing tricks on us again! That's not Bobby! It isn't him!" Stuart said.

Bobby kept running toward them now only about a hundred yards away from the vehicle.

"How do you know that it isn't him? And where did

Diane go?" Stacy asked.

"I don't know where she went! She vanished with the light! It must have taken her or something!" Stuart snapped.

"No! That can't be Bobby! It just can't be! It's just playing tricks on us again!" Stuart said.

Bobby got up to the car and slammed his hands on the front door, driver's side window. "Unlock the damn door! Hurry!" Bobby screamed.

"Is that you, Bobby? Is it really you this time?" Stacy asked. Cautiously, she leaned over the front seat of the car to get a better look at him.

"Yes, it's me! Who else would it be! Open the door, Stacy . . . now!" Bobby shouted.

"Where is Diane?" Stacy asked.

"I don't know! She was running right beside me and disappeared! I don't know what happened to her! The light was coming for us and she—" Bobby was saying when Stuart yelled.

"Bobby! The light is coming down the road again! Let him in, Stacy, now! It's really Bobby this time! Open the door!"

Stuart pushed Stacy out of the way and leaned over the seat to unlock the door for Bobby. His nose began to drain more running red than before. A humming noise grew louder and the light came closer. Bobby opened the door and dove into the front seat and closed the door, fumbling over the assortment of keys latched to his keychain. He stuck the key in the ignition and started the car. "Let's get out of here,"

Bobby said.

"We can't just leave Diane out there. Are you mental? What if something bad happens to her?" Stacy asked.

"I'll drive around and look for her, okay?!" Bobby asked as he turned the key.

The car started and Bobby revved the motor, shifted the gear into drive, and released his foot from the brake pedal. Just then, the light hovered over the hood and the motor died instantly. Bobby turned the key and nothing happened. Suddenly, the radio turned on at full volume to the sound of static, causing Bobby to fly back into the driver's seat in a startled jolt. The horn began to repeatedly honk and the headlights simultaneously flashed along in a series of short and longer beeps.

All Break-men were trained to use Morse code, just as cub and boy scouts in the later days. Unfortunately, no one in the car had attended a single pact meeting, Cub, Boy nor Brownie. All three remaining passengers were clueless to the message. The beeps and flashes were nothing more than fuel to their flames of fright that burned inside each of them. The series of honks and light pulses sent the message of warning, "I . . . h-a-v-e . . . h-e-r . . . l-e-a-v-e . . . t-h-i-s . . . p-l-a-c-e."

The light evaporated one last time, into the murkiness of the night. Bobby turned the key and the car started. He slammed his nervously twitching foot on the gas pedal without thinking twice and skidded off down the mile-long dirt path formerly known to the locals as Bragg Road. Stacy, Bobby and Stuart wanted to make its former entity, Ghost

Road, nothing but a bad memory. They didn't care what lie ahead of them on the way out, as long as they could leave this road far behind in the dust.

Bobby notified Diane's family and informed them she had mysteriously disappeared the night before. Diane's mother, father and older brother drove up and down Ghost Road all day until the night fell once again. Diane, nor a single trace of her, was ever seen again. Bobby, Stuart and Stacy were all considered suspects in her disappearance and extensively questioned by local authorities, until all three were ruled out as potential offenders in the eyes of the law.

Cal's Cutoff
by:
Herika R. Raymer

The phenomenon of 'vanishings' has captured the imaginations and embodied the fear of many; not to mention it has been the launching ground for many urban legends and lasting folklore. For those who have come close to or experienced this phenomenon, it has often caused a memory lapse or shadows of doubt as to what they really saw and experienced. This odd thought was what was on her mind as she visited her home town.

Celina Park had been on her way to a family reunion in Arkansas from Georgia, when she decided to take the Collierville-Arlington exit off of Interstate 40 to see how her old neighborhood had changed. She drove west along Winchester Road, marveling at how different Collierville and Germantown looked. She found it remarkable to see how Collierville had expanded out from rural houses with a small town square with a grocery store into a small city area. There were banks on just about every corner, fast food joints, at least two big groceries, churches everywhere, a large water park, and even some strip malls and car dealerships. In the same vein, Germantown was almost like Memphis - only cleaner - with suburban neighborhoods, clinics, stores, parks, and a large library.

She shook her head in amazement; in her imagination, she could still see the wide spaces where she and her friends had met to have bonfires and generally hang out. Still, she had to wonder if one particular change was done. She was circling around back to Germantown Road, if she wanted to check out an old haunt, the decision had better be made soon.

Celina experienced a moment of doubt, her knuckles whitening a bit as her grip on the steering wheel tightened briefly. Then, almost automatically, she turned onto Germantown Road and made her way south towards Bill Morris Parkway. The destination, a dirt road across from the polo field properly known as Callis Cut Off Road; she knew it as Cal's Cutoff.

Turning onto the road, she was not surprised to see the 'road blocked' sign strung across the entrance. She was careful to pull over and turn on her hazard lights lest another driver be blocked by her, even though she was well out of the way. On impulse, she exited her vehicle and made her way to the sign, standing there looking down the dirt path and seeing where it disappeared down a tree-lined pathway.

She felt an unnatural chill, and crossed her arms over her waist to hold herself.

Cal's Cutoff had been a source of many folk legends and tall tales for as long as she could remember. A couple of the stories involved a tragic accident and murder. A high school girl was being driven home by her boyfriend and the car apparently lost control while swerving along the treacherous winding route of Cal's Cutoff and crashed - instantly killing the girl. The boyfriend walked over to her house, the now abandoned house of Cal's Cutoff, and her mother answered the door. Upon realizing that her daughter was dead, she picked up an axe and chased after the injured boyfriend and killed him. A second tale had an enraged father patrolling the grounds of the road, armed with an axe, looking for his son that never returned home one night. Another version of this fable said that the father actually murdered the son with the axe, and wandered the grounds looking for more victims.

Thinking of the house, Celina recalled that it was the main attraction of Cal's Cutoff. Once known as the 'Cult House', it was located in the middle of a field surrounded by a wooded area. Its name derived from the rumor that satanic groups would meet out there and hold their rites by a large bonfire. Those who had managed to find their way to the house would find graffiti or other objects around or in the house. The porch light, however, could be considered the main point of interest concerning this house in the teenage mind. As strange as it may be, day or night, the generally held belief that if the porch light was blazed on then anyone on the road should vacate immediately for their life would be in peril.

Naturally, none of the stories were true, but adults and the authorities felt these stories would keep high school kids from messing around on a back road at night. Of course it actually did the opposite. Dares to see who could brave the road, or better yet brave the night at the bonfire site or in the Cult House, were common.

It had been one such dare that had caused Celina's current trepidation for being anywhere near Cal's Cutoff.

A light breeze rustled through the canopy and brush far ahead of her. Celina started visibly and her eyes scanned the greenery furtively. There was nothing there except the wind. Unable to relax, she released the breath she had not realized she had been holding. Her hands clutched her elbows more firmly, but still unable to control the tremors that now ran through her. Another cool wind fluttered by, causing the hairs on her neck to rise and her instinct to flee to build inside her. Celina was remembering, even if she did not want to.

A sophomore in high school, Celina had already heard about Cal's Cutoff. The common dare would be for anyone to try and drive the dirt road at day or night, but the real show of courage was staying in the house overnight. Celina had no interest in proving that she could stay in a haunted house, but her friends were delighted by the idea.

"This is dumb," she had said for the umpteenth time.

"But, you are here," Monica said from the driver's seat.

Her sister Rena, a senior, grinned at her from the front passenger seat. She merely glared at her older sibling and crossed her arms. They had plenty of homework to finish, projects to do, and she could not see what was so important about spending the night in a haunted house. Why in the world had she agreed to come along anyway? Oh yeah, she hadn't. They were supposed to be going to see a movie then having a sleepover at Monica's house. Celina's friend, Noelle, who looked just as spooked, but also excited, sat in the back with Celina. Noelle's excitement didn't surprise Celina since this kind of stuff fascinated Noelle, just as it fascinated Rena. Monica was basically driving and coming along for the fun, and Celina was... well... she felt kind of hijacked really. She had been looking forward to a movie.

"Oh, stop sulking," Rena chided her as she turned slightly in the seat. "It is only for the night, then we get back to the house and you can do whatever schoolwork you want."

"What is the point of this, though?" she pressed. "Just to say we stayed over in Cult House? C'mon! That is so lame."

Noelle grinned. "No, it's way cool! I can finally have some first-hand experience of this place, and maybe even write a book about it."

Celina rolled her eyes and settled into the seat. Realizing this was a done deal, she might as well make the best of it. It wasn't as though she was unfamiliar with 'roughing it', after all her family went camping often. They had sleeping bags, a cooler full of food and drinks for the brief stay, and even a small skillet for cooking and some cleaning wipes. Normally, she enjoyed doing something a little different, but tonight she wasn't so sure. Something seemed off, she had a nagging feeling that they should not go to Cal's Cutoff tonight; a feeling that she dared not voice aloud, because it would undoubtedly make her the target of some unwanted ribbing. Still, she could not shake the feeling. Every once in a while, she could see her sister shiver and look askance at Monica, but Monica never noticed. These little clues told her that her sister felt the unease too, but just as reluctant to say anything about it.

Back then Bill Morris Parkway did not exist, just a bare Winchester stretching out past Germantown. No shops or strip malls, just a neighborhood and trees. Then the Germantown Road turned off, where Monica turned the car onto. The eerie shade of pink and orange in the sky announced the coming of night, and seemed somehow more ominous as the vehicle shimmied and shook from the condition of the road. Celina looked across the empty polo field, watching the darkening sky, wishing they would turn around. But, their fate now sealed as the car turned right onto Cal's Cutoff.

Monica slowed down as the dirt road fell into rough shape and foreign objects on the road became harder to see due to the shadows of twilight. Celina could see the approaching darkened tree-line, and the sense of foreboding increased. The other riders were remarking on the road and how creepy it seemed, but more in a teasing tone as if trying to get a rise out of each other. She didn't join in, her throat seemed to tighten, and she felt cold. They continued to follow the winding path at a cautious speed. Noelle would point out a worn sign, while Rena said she saw a doll in a spooky voice. Monica just laughed and continued to drive.

All too soon, the car pulled to the side to follow a narrow path after about the third curve. They were able to see the house through the skeletal brush, and Celina was happy to see the porch light not on. However, the decaying fence around it did not help allay her fears.

They pulled up just outside the main gate and waited for a few moments. Four pairs of eyes looking up at the dilapidated house, mustering the courage to exit the vehicle. Finally, Monica turned the ignition off.

"Gonna be dark soon," Monica said matter-of-factly. "The sooner we get in and set up, the better."

In a flurry of motion, the four girls got out of the car and went to the trunk to gather their gear. Celina and Noelle grabbed the backpacks and sleeping bags while Rena and Monica carried the cooler. The small group approached the door, their footsteps slowing as they got closer until finally, they were at the threshold.

"Well, here goes!" Rena announced, and she tried the door.

It was unlocked.

They made their way in and turned to the living room, where they agreed to set up 'camp'. The inside of the house smelled musty with age, sour of old beer from previous visitors, and hosted some uncomplimentary graffiti and signs. This all added to the impression of it being a vacant house, so they did not have to worry about anyone coming home and declaring them trespassers. The four of them quickly selected areas to sleep, not surprisingly close to the door, and set the cooler between them. Celina and Rena had brought some electric lamps to help with the dark, but the gloom of the house soon settled on them. Celina's sense of doom increased, her stomach clenched and the hairs on her neck were standing on end. She really wanted to leave. Looking at her sister, she could see the older girl rubbing her hands along her knees from where she sat crossed-legged, a nervous habit to those who knew her well. If the other two had any fear, Celina could not see it. Maybe they were just better actors at keeping their feelings hidden.

The night dragged on, with the girls talking about nothing in particular. She was grateful that they were avoiding telling ghost stories, she wasn't sure she would be able to sit still. As it was, they talked about school, what bands they liked, the latest concerts and movies they had been to, just anything to keep their minds off of where they were. Before long, the tension in the air finally seemed to be diminishing.

A sudden thump upstairs quieted them.

No one moved, straining their ears to determine where the sound came from, or if it even had come at all. After a few heartbeats, they gave a collective giggle.

Then they heard another thump, this time louder.

The girls looked at one another, as if mutely confirming that they each had heard the sound. Moving closer to one another, they looked upward and around to try and see in the darkness beyond the lit perimeter of the electric lamps. Celina reached back, relieved to feel her sister's firm grip.

An eerie moan whistled through the house.

As the girls huddled together, Celina could feel herself going numb with fright. Her ears were tuned into all the sounds around her. Every creak, each settling, and all the drops from any leaky pipes were the focus of her hearing. Her eyes were drawn to the shadows as they played along the walls, creating illusions of movement. Her nose tickled unpleasantly at the increasingly pungent smell of the house. She swallowed convulsively even though her mouth was dry, and beneath her clothes her skin felt uncomfortably cool as she shivered unpleasantly. Celina felt certain there was something in the house with them. As she felt the huddling bodies of the others, she knew they felt it as well.

Celina was sure she saw something move in the kitchen.

She gripped Rena's hand hard, and tried to see in to the dark. She could swear that there was something in the kitchen. She searched the shadows, certain it was hovering in there, just out of her perception. She leaned forward, squinting her eyes, trying to pierce the gloom with her will. The others apparently noticed her attention focused on the other room; because one by one she could feel them flanking her and trying to see whatever had caught her interest. Celina wanted to know if her friends could see it, or rather feel what she felt; the slightest disturbance in the varying degree of darkness ahead. Her voice had abandoned her, her throat tight with fear. She wasn't surprised that she didn't feel compelled to move away from the security of the group to investigate. All she really wanted to do was grab everyone and run outside, get in the car, and get away from here as quickly as possible.

"Boo!"

A collective scream erupted as several boys burst into the living room from the front door and the window. Their raucous laughter ignited a fury in the others, who, after taking a moment to recover from the shock, realized that the noises they had heard had been their unwanted guests. As the boys continued to point and laugh, the girls began to advise them of their ire at being the target of a practical joke.

"You jerks!" Noelle was bristling.

"What do you think you're doing?" Monica snarled.

"Oh man!" one of the boys howled. "You should have seen your faces!"

"Priceless!" another chorused.

There was a blend of voices as the girls, incensed, proceeded to severely reprimand the boys on their poor judgment and the boys, in turn, enthusiastically teased the girls on their cowardice.

All of this had been lost on Celina as her mind was still focused on the corridor between the living room and the kitchen. The movement there had not stopped. If anything, it had become more pronounced.

At first, she had seen a slight warp, as if a bubble moving through the area. Now, with so many people about, the almost invisible distortion became more active. She could swear the gloom of the other room seemed to be heaving a bit, as if the kitchen was breathing. What was worse, the shadows seemed to be being pulled inward. They curled, stretched, and swirled.

It was about that time that one of the boys stumbled into her line of vision, between her and the thing beyond. Celina could not recall the names of the other boys, but this boy she would remember. His name was Doug Turner, and he had been a junior at their school.

Key words being 'had been'. Unfortunately, she would recall his last moments vividly until her dying day. It played before her now, vividly as it did in her recurrent nightmares.

Doug was laughing at them, enjoying the joke. His hair and clothes rippled for a moment, as if encountering a phantom wind. The temperature in the room plummeted to where she could see the wisps of his breath. A foul stench almost overpowering filled the air. A strange expression crossed his face then. It was as though he knew something was behind him and he did not want to look, but felt compelled to.

Celina opened her mouth to warn him of the now wispy vortex behind him, to not look, to get away, anything – but yet again her voice failed her.

Doug turned, stood still for a few heartbeats as his entire body tensed. Then, he screamed.

She had never heard an actual scream before. It was horrifying. That sort of sound should not be able to be emitted from a human throat.

The next things happened to her in slow motion, but the others said they never saw anything.

Doug turned back to the group, as if to try and get away. However, the vortex swelled to where its outer rim caressed Doug's body. As the swirls cascaded over him in waves, he faded. He literally faded from existence until finally there was nothing left, and he and the vortex vanished. The echoes of his scream still reverberating off of the walls.

Terrified, Celina dared not turn away from the kitchen. Even as the boys starting calling for their comrade and began combing the house for him, she did not move. Finally, when they began asking the girls where their friend had gone, Celina turned to the girls, her face pale, and managed to finally speak.

"We need to go," she said simply. "Now."

A silence fell for a moment, and she actually felt afraid that they would refuse. She could not see her expression, but apparently there had been something in her face that captivated her audience. Rena came forward to take her hand and lead her out of the house, leaving Noelle and Monica to gather the gear and make their way back to the car. They left the boys still searching.

When the police arrived, Celina was still in shock. She didn't want to lie though, so she told them what she saw. In front of her parents, her sister, and her friends she described to the officers taking notes what she saw that fateful night. It was not surprising when they asked if she had been drinking or doing drugs, of which she naturally denied and offered to take a test to prove it. They were lucky to not be cited for trespassing because the disappearance of Doug Turner overshadowed their escapade. Unfortunately, the missing of Doug Turner had never been explained. It was another curious vanishing, like David Lang in 1880, Benjamin Bathurst in 1809, and others.

Now, two decades later, the only witness stood at the edge of the same stretch of road that had haunted her in that time. It didn't surprise her that plans to try and develop the area had fallen through time and again. It was as though this place was just plain haunted. The folk lore she now understood were meant more as warnings than just to tantalize youths to go out drinking and make stupid dares. It was unfortunate she had not been able to share this epiphany with the others. She had tried, but they had just shrugged her off as a bit spooked by that night and making things up, even though anyone who knew her well knew better than to assume she would go around spinning yarns.

Another cool breeze went by, causing her to shiver again. She really wanted to get in the car and go, but somehow she felt rooted to the spot; her eyes still scanning the area, trying to discern any pattern that might indicate the recurrence of that vortex. Celina didn't want to admit it, even to herself, but she often scanned around anywhere she was – looking for that hungry apparition. To her the idea that disappearances could happen anywhere and at any time was terrifying, but at least she had some clue of what to keep an eye out for. She planned to use that to her advantage.

Suddenly, she saw movement near the tree lined section of the road.

Her stomach clenched, and a cold sweat broke out. It was happening again. She was sure of it. She focused all her attention on that area, trying to find where the vortex was forming. The problem being, she could see no beginning distortion in the form of a warp bubble.

This time she saw a faded human figure; a shade made almost completely of light. If she told anyone about this, they would undoubtedly say this had been a trick of the light. She knew better, mainly because she could hear him. It was Doug, and she could hear him faintly, calling out for help. His essence was there, in front of her, caught somewhere beyond her reality. What made it worse were his vague calls that sounded terrified and in pain. His voice faint, but having been burned into her memory she recognized the same voice from her high school years – he had not aged and he was alone, wounded, and wandering helplessly.

That was it.

Celina muttered an apology, turned, and ran to her car. She put it in gear and speedily made her way back onto the Bill Morris Parkway. She drove on into Memphis and then into Arkansas without looking back.

Nothing would ever make her look back.

The Shack
by:
Diane Ward

Clayton pressed his forehead onto the Dodge Ram Charger's window, still nothing. He flopped over onto the seat next to him and stared out the front of the car. They hadn't passed a house for miles. He'd watched the telephone poles that ran along the sides of the road gradually disappear into fields, pastures and piney forests. The yellow lines had faded off the asphalt. *Or maybe they never painted them here*, he thought, *it's not like there would be anyone to appreciate it.*

"Does grandfather own a car?" Clayton asked, still lying sideways.

"He doesn't need one anymore," his dad said without taking his eyes from the road.

His mother glanced back and frowned, deepening the thin lines that had started to show around her mouth. But, she didn't say anything. Hours ago when they had first left Houston, she would have told him to sit up, that it wasn't safe, however after seven hours of driving, she was tired.

Clayton was tired too, tired... and disappointed. This

wasn't how he wanted to spend his fall break. He wanted to stay in Texas and go with the rest of the fifth grade class to boy scouts, or at least stay home and play with his neighbors Nathan and Trevor. He would have even settled for attending church camp.

He did not want to drive to central Mississippi. He did not want to visit grandfather.

His dad had told him stories about how his grandfather would teach him to ride and train horses, hunt and to take care of himself better than any camp. Normally, his parents stayed with him when they went to visit, but this time was different. His parents were going away on one of his father's business trips—of course he imagined it was more of a vacation—and leaving him here. Clayton felt like he was being gotten rid of.

Looking out, he wondered if it would be odd having no neighbors around for miles, just the forests and the occasional pasture or farmland. It was as he watched the brownish blur of the dying trees pass, that he dozed off.

"Honey, we're here." His mom shook his shoulder. Clayton sat up groggily.

Outside he could see the tree line, tall and dark against the sky and stars. Unlike Houston, there was no distant glow of buildings, nor was there the distant rumble of traffic that could always be heard from his house.

His father stood outside of the car next to his grandfather, who was little more than a hunched silhouette in the distance.

Grandfather's house lay in front of the car's headlights,

and Clayton shivered looking at it. The house tilted to one side as if it were sinking into the ground. Cinderblocks elevated it above the soggy, dying grass. It had never been painted, just built with water-sealed wood that very nearly matched the wintry brown of everything else.

"Clayton, are you coming?" his mom asked. Reluctantly, Clayton grabbed his bags and hopped out. His mom led him up to grandfather. His grandfather (whose real name he'd forgotten) grinned at him toothlessly. Grandfather's lips pulled towards his ears in an expression of happiness, but his eyes were cold. Clayton forced a smile of his own before hurrying past him toward the house.

Inside, the house smelled slightly of mildew and slightly of leather. It was such a small house he guessed he wouldn't have any trouble finding the guest room. And he was right. There were only three real rooms to the house excluding the hallway: the kitchen, the master bedroom and the guest room. His room, the guest room, only had a bed and a bathroom which was set off in the corner. No dressers or bedside tables. No other furniture at all. The only decoration was a picture hanging by the door. Clayton squinted, staring at it. They had a similar picture back at their house.

His grandmother stared back at him from the picture. She was dressed for her wedding day in a white point de gaze veil draped languidly over her head. Her kind, dark eyes looked a bit like his dad's, Clayton thought. He was sure that if his grandmother were still alive, he would have liked her. At least if she were here it wouldn't be so bad. At least he wouldn't be alone with his grandfather.

When he walked back outside, his parents were already drifting towards the car. After they'd said their good-byes and everybody hugged everybody, he watched the car drive down that dark road till the night swallowed it.

It was only when they were truly alone that his grandfather returned to the house. Clayton watched with rapt attention as he took a rifle from the cabinet and started to clean it. As his grandfather cleaned the rifle, he laid down a few rules.

It started out normal enough: "always clean up after yourself, you'll be mucking stalls and putting up your own tack, don't ever touch the horses if I'm not there, and don't pet them either…they're not pets" and so on. Clayton could feel his eyelids start to sag, still groggy from the drive.

He jolted awake when his grandfather gripped his shoulders. Even though his grandfather's skin was wrinkled and his head tanned and nearly hairless, his hands were strong.

"Do not go into the woods," his grandfather said, biting off each word. He held Clayton's shoulders until Clayton nodded. That was it. His grandfather had nothing else to say to him, and he knew there would be no dinner.

Later, Clayton saw the way his grandfather would whip and slap the horses, sometimes hobble their feet to get the fight out and humble them. The horses would fight throwing themselves down over and over again. When they finally gave up, his grandfather would sit on them. His grandfather told him that this was how you broke a horse. In the week that Clayton stayed with him, he didn't need to go against his grandfather to know that he would severely regret it.

Now, he just went and crawled into bed, unable to sleep in the creaking house. It was like his grandfather, he supposed, its bones never seemed to settle. The sheets felt damp and smelled musty, scratchy against his skin. It took him hours to start to fall asleep only to be awakened by footsteps in the hall.

Clayton lay very still, pretending to sleep; however, the footsteps passed his room and then seemed to leave the house entirely. After a few moments, he got up and crept beside the window. He peeked carefully over the edge in case his grandfather was outside watching.

It was then that he first saw the glowing.

***

A homeless man had started living deep in the woods. Once, he wandered up near the house, groping about the yard, staggering and falling, and picking himself up. Emaciated, his skin hung off his bones. Dirt and mud clung to him, and he smelled vaguely of urine.

The homeless man stared at the sun with wide eyes as if trying to drink it in. There was something strange on his head like he'd pried off the shell of a sort of typewriter—which Clayton later discovered was a ten key's covering—and used it like a helmet with his matted hair piled under.

Clayton had been pushing out a wheelbarrow of manure to dump when he saw him.

Their eyes met for a terrifying moment. Clayton could see the tendons sticking out on the man's sunburned neck, his sinewy arms held taunt. He was certain the homeless man would attack him like a wild dog.

Like a jolt of electricity, a wave of fear spread through him. Clayton dropped the wheelbarrow and grabbed the shovel he had been using. The homeless man lunged at him and Clayton jumped backwards with a cry. He swung the shovel at the homeless man wildly, not once making contact but the man backed away some.

By then, grandfather had seen him too.

Grandfather flipped the rifle down from his back in a single, practiced motion.

The shot seemed to hang in the air after it was fired. For a moment, Clayton wasn't sure what had happened. Then, the homeless man turned and ran back into the woods. Clayton stared after him still clenching the shovel, his hands shaking, and his heart pounding. His grandfather clapped him on the shoulder and Clayton jumped a little again.

"It's time again for them to be coming about," his grandfather said, so steady he may as well have been talking about winter itself. Then, he slung the rifle back over his shoulder and returned to the horses.

Clayton's hands still shook from the ordeal. He knew his parents wouldn't believe him if he told them a homeless man had run out of the woods and attacked him. He knew they wouldn't believe his grandfather always carried a rifle. He knew they would rationalize the glow deep in the woods that burned like a great pyre. Eventually, he thought it would all become too much and smother him.

He glanced over to the horse his grandfather had been tending to. It hadn't even spooked at the gunshot. Was this so regular the horses didn't even jump at it anymore?

His grandfather patted the horse's shoulder and bent over again to rasp the horse's hoof where the toe had grown long. Sweat gleamed on his nearly bald head, making it look eerily skeletal. Even though it was supposed to be November it still felt like August, the summer still clinging, and the heat made everything seem out of place.

Later, he finally worked up the courage to go down by the woods where the homeless man disappeared. Looking into the dark canopy of trees, he could see the beer bottles left by the homeless man. The bottles were often brown and broken and blended in with the fallen leaves. Clayton always tried to wear boots down there.

He wanted to ask about what his grandfather had said: "It's time again for them to be coming about," but the question always seemed to stick in his throat. He didn't know what they were coming about for, and he wasn't exactly sure what they were. But, he knew the homeless man and his grandfather were waiting for something, just like the feral dogs howling in distance, and Clayton felt maybe he too was waiting.

***

Clayton slept in his clothes. After he heard the footsteps recede down the hall and the door swing shut, he waited a few more minutes just to make sure he wasn't coming back before slipping out of bed.

The floor was cold and slick underneath his feet. He kept his hand on the wall to guide himself as he walked to the mudroom. Even though he knew his grandfather was far into the woods by now, he was still careful to be quiet.

Outside the night air was sickly warm. The Indian summer dragged the heat long past its natural life, and Mississippi's winter wasn't very harsh to begin with. Still, it was cold enough that there were no crickets or cicadas to hum in the air. There was only the distant call of the feral dogs.

Clayton followed the horse pasture to the edge of the woods and then ducked into the dense forest. The branches seemed to squeeze out the rest of the moonlight. He had packed a few matches in his pockets just in case, since he couldn't bring a flashlight if he didn't want to be spotted. Besides, he reasoned it would be harder to follow the glow if he had his own light.

His breath was shaky with excitement, and he felt that unsteady anticipation like riding the carnival rides the time the fair rolled into town. But, unlike the fair, he also had a deep sense of foreboding budding up deep in his guts that told him that things could go very wrong very quickly.

Finally, he saw it. Waxing into existence like a fire blown back from the embers. He crept further, holding his breath and taking care to step slowly to keep the leaves from crackling too much.

The shack glowed as if a raging bonfire had been captured inside its decaying boards. The shack itself was a small thing, only one room with a tin sheet roof, and one door and one window. It was set on uneven jagged stones to keep the floor from flooding.

Clayton saw the homeless man staring at the shack, eyes wide and gaping. Clayton froze realizing he was only a few feet away. His body went limp with fear. He couldn't move without being seen. Saying a silent prayer, he crouched low, trying to slink back into the bushes.

As Clayton backed away looking for an escape route, he saw it wasn't just the homeless man with the helmet anymore. There were dozens of them hidden by the darkness among the trees, as if they had made some sort of pilgrimage here. The homeless men stood clustered together, yet seemingly unaware of each other, like moths and beetles drawn to a lamp.

Clayton didn't see his grandfather.

As he was backing away, Clayton tried to look in the shack door. He could see something moving inside. He stretched to look within.

Inside, his grandfather danced with a flaming figure dressed in her delicate wedding gown of point de gaze just as he had seen in the portrait. The lace showed designs of tiered flowers and ferns that became more intricate towards the edges of the gown where roses and ferns of rococo scrolls nestled. Under the lace she wore nothing, and yet she didn't appear naked. Her body was smoothed over like a porcelain doll. The bouquet seemed to be melting into her hands, her face dripped like wax becoming more and more indistinct.

His grandfather released the specter and stepped out of the shack. Clayton inhaled sharply. *He's seen me*, he thought. He crouched ready to sprint off. He needed to get away. He felt his head pounding, his pulse throbbing under his eyes.

But, his grandfather didn't go towards him.

The homeless man had started walking towards the shack, very nearly touching it, his eyes filled with rapture like a crazed zealot. His grandfather drew his long hunting rifle from his back and shot a hole through the homeless man's head

The ghost light wavered, dying and jolting back to life. Clayton placed both hands over his mouth to make sure he didn't scream and crouched even lower behind the underbrush. The shot buzzed in his ears.

His grandfather dragged the man into the shack. It was like someone blowing on a candle to strengthen the flame and the shack glowed its brightest. His grandfather then clasped hands with the thing wearing his grandmother's dress, their hands oozing together like tree sap.

Blood seeped out from the homeless man's wound, trickling downhill and hiding under the dead leaves. Before it could touch him Clayton panicked, not caring whether or not he was caught, he ran. The forest seemed to try to stop him as its branches and shrubs clawed at his face and arms, thorns sticking his legs through the jeans. He felt his face wet, his breath coming in quick panicked gasps.

He ran all the way back to his room and flung himself in bed. The light from the shack filled the whole window and spread through the entire house. Clayton shut his eyes tight when he heard the rifle shots. Morning seemed it would never come.

When his grandfather returned the next day, he had a certain glow to him, like he was covered in a very fine shimmery substance. *It's the wax,* Clayton thought. He didn't speak to him the following morning, just went and silently mucked the stalls and rolled the hay.

He never saw any of the homeless men again, and there seemed to be fewer and fewer bottles at the edge of the woods.

***

Decades later, Clayton inherited the house after his grandfather passed away. His parents never knew of the shack, he didn't guess anyone knew but him and his grandfather. If they had known, they wouldn't have sent him off there so many years ago, so they didn't balk when he offered to clean up the house and sell it.

He found the portrait of his grandmother still hanging in the guest bedroom with her thick hair tucked away under the point de gaze veil, her dark brown eyes seemingly black in the old photograph. The more he looked at his grandmother, the more he wondered if what he had seen that night had even been her. When they buried his grandfather, there was a headstone inscribed with her name set beside his, but he suspected the earth underneath was empty. His grandmother was buried under a shack deep in the woods in central Mississippi.

He tore the shack down himself and burned the decaying boards in a great bonfire. He felt dirty just looking at it. He didn't want to even *think* of how many bodies rotted under that ground, hundreds of others on top of her. The deaths of those homeless men plagued him, causing him many sleepless nights that he could explain to no one, absolutely no one. The secret had rotted up inside him until now.

He stood far off in the woods with a hose in his hand, his glasses reflecting the glare. He watched it burn, so hot it felt like it peeled the skin off his face. In a way, he found it cleansing.

Even after the shack burned, sometimes late on a November night, he would hear the feral dogs crying. Sometimes he would see a homeless man wandering down the road when he drove to the house. Sometimes he would see a glow deep in the woods.

Haints
by:
Roland Mann

I was thirteen years old the first time I seen the haints. Before then, I just always thought Uncle TB was pullin' my leg when he talked about them. I'd heard the stories so many times, I knew the endings before he was finished telling them.

Uncle TB lived in an old house that the family thinks used to be a preacher's house at some time way back. It only sits a little bit away from the Gravel Hill Baptist Church. The church has been there forever, too. We were General Baptists. Mama thought if the Lord came on Sunday morning before you had a chance to say you're sorry and ask for forgiveness and all that, you'd go straight to hell. Other Baptists I know say that once you're saved, you're always saved. None of this falling from grace stuff. I think that's the part that made for the "General" in the General Baptists.

I've been going to the church since I can remember. I thought it was just like any other church, small chapel and a few rooms to the back and front for Sunday school. There wasn't a paved road for at least 4 miles. The membership was nearly fifty on a rainy day. Not so many on a good day.

But the church sat in the middle of a graveyard, Gravel Hill Cemetery. Some folks around there say the graveyard was started during the Civil War. The Saint Francis River runs nearby and separates Missouri from Arkansas. There was a fight a few miles up the River, now they call it the Battle of Chalk Bluff, where a handful of soldiers died. Well, the Yankees won that fight and were content with the victory of having chased the Confederates out of Missouri. The General made camp on the hill where the church is, and they just buried their dead around the church grounds where they wanted.

Part of that story must be true because I've walked around the graveyard several times and in the oddest of places you can see a Union soldier grave marker, indicating the place of final rest for a couple of Yankees.

But Uncle TB's house was on the upslope of the hill, the northernmost beginnings of what is known as Crowley's Ridge. It was mostly farming land then and still is today. There are big open clearings for crops and for livestock, set apart by large acres of woods or gullies or fence rows. The hill wasn't good for much other than livestock and hunting and there were lots of woods around the church. You could stand on top of Uncle TB's barn and look over a small portion of the farmland toward the Saint Francis River.

He had the same type of house that everybody around there did; a wooden house that looked like it'd blow away in a big wind. We knew it would stand though. In 1916, a tornado came and snatched one of Mama's newborn twins out of her hands. Killed the baby — it's buried at Gravel Hill — but the house stood. The doors and windows all had screens on them, so you could keep them open for the breeze and still keep out the bugs — especially the mosquitoes, which get really bad in the late summer.

It was this house that Uncle TB said the haints always came to. He swore up and down that if he was ever gone from home over night, no matter what he did to the front and back door, they would always be undone and opened when he returned.

I reckon I've asked everybody in the family why Uncle TB called them haints. All other people call them ghosts or spooks. Mama just laughed when I asked her. She might have known...but she didn't tell. Besides, haints sounded so funny that it just kinda stuck with the family.

Uncle TB would swear up and down, and even threatened to swear on his grave that what he was telling was the truth. He wouldn't do it though, said it was too close to home!

Uncle TB said he would sit on his porch in the evening, and about the time the sun went down, the haints came out. Said most of them would just walk along the road up to the church. Uncle TB couldn't see the church from where he sat; it was around a bend in a road. He said the haints came in all shapes and sizes...but you could surely see them. Every now and again, one would wave to him just like they's going to meeting.

Every sane person around thought Uncle TB was just a drunkard. But, he never touched a drop of alcohol in his life. Said he came close one time, though. It was before World War II. His uncle had passed on. The family only had one car then, don't know what kind, but I've seen pictures—it was old.

As was family practice in Clay County, Arkansas back then, the family sat up with the dead uncle. No funeral homes were built yet, at least not way out in the county. The corner bedroom--doesn't matter whose it was, it had two windows, one on either wall—this was the visiting and setting up room. Uncle TB's uncle was laid in the room and one member of the family was to sit with him the whole night, kinda watching over his spirit, I guess.

Well, Uncle TB said he wasn't more than a high school kid himself then, and this was the first dead person he'd ever really seen up close. But, he wanted to feel all adult and all and he'd wanted to take a turn setting with his uncle.

And he did. But about one or two in the morning, he dozed off. He woke up and all the hair on his body stood on its end. There was at least a dozen cats all scratching and clawing and screaming at the windows. Uncle TB thought they was trying to get in and do Lord know what. Well, he pissed his pants right then and there, and he wouldn't go home until the sun came up the next day. The preacher came in the next morning and told him that those cats had the devil in them and that Satan was trying to steal the spirit away from the Lord.

Uncle TB said that if there would have been alcohol in that room, he'd'a been a drunk all the rest of his life.

But anyways, he said he never did figure out where all the haints were going or what they were doing out on the road in front of his house, but they scared him for all of his adult life. But, you couldn't get him to even consider moving out. He'd said his family was there and that was that.

He did a lot of speculating, though. See, he figured they all had to be the ghosts of folks buried in the Gravel Hill cemetery. Why would they be from anyplace else? He figured that, like most buried in the graveyard, they had all been to the Gravel Hill church at some time or another. So, Uncle TB figured they was going to church to say their sorrys and be forgiven. I'd said once before that it could be he was seeing the ones that didn't say their sorrys when they were alive, and now they were stuck here, saying sorry all the time.

It was this conviction that was probably the reason that Uncle TB went to church every Sunday and Wednesday, and never had a mean thought for anybody, least ways not that any of us knew.

One thing that he never could figure out though, was why they would always open his door. As time passed, he gave up and just left it open. He had tried nearly everything to keep it closed.

The screen door just had a hook latch on it, but the main door had a key-lock and a deadbolt. He had people come look at the house and they told him that he was just leaving it unlocked and the wind was blowing it open. But, Uncle

TB and the family knew different. I was there one time when he did all the locks and then proceeded to stack empty soda bottles on a small stool behind the door. If someone came through, they'd wake up everybody in the house when they opened the door.

I woke up about 5:30 the next morning to see my Dad looking at the door. Uncle TB was just getting up. When he saw the door, he yelled for everyone to come see—his yell scared us half to death.

The small stool stood just as Uncle TB had set it out the night before...except that it had been pushed against the wall...as if someone had just slowly scooted it over to move it out of the way. From the front door, we all turned and looked down the hall straight out the back door—it too was wide open.

Uncle TB got sick when I was twelve. I spent some time with him the summer that he died—that's when he told me most of the stories. I never did see the haints when I sat on the porch with him. He would swear up and down and point to the road but I never could see them. Dad told me that it was the sickness that was making him do those things, and for a long time I felt real sorry for him.

But, that all changed.

Uncle TB had only been dead about a month when I turned thirteen. I had gotten permission to go camping with some of my friends, and as kids can sometimes do, we got this crazy idea to camp out in the graveyard. Lord only knows what we were thinking.

Everything was big fun while it was daylight. When it started to get dark, we started to get a little scared. My friends knew my Uncle TB's house was just down the road and wanted to go there. After he died, my Maw-maw came to live with us, so the house was empty. They knew that too, but felt it was better than sleeping on top of somebody's grave.

So, we ran like scared kids all the way to Uncle TB's. But, I stopped just short of the house. And when I stopped, all my friends stopped and actually ran back to where I was, thinking I'd seen something and not wanting to be the first one to whatever it was I'd seen. I hadn't seen a ghost, though. What I did see was the front door, wide open. I knew I was the last one to have left that house. I had helped Maw-maw pack up and move out. She had given me the only key to the house and told me to lock up all the way around. And I did. I checked and double-checked the windows and doors. They were shut and locked. Period.

However, as I stood there with my friends, the door was swinging wide open; we could see a few feet inside. Even now, the hair on my neck still stands on end when I think of the feeling I got that night. We walked slowly up to the porch, but I turned around on the top step and looked back to the road. My friends turned too, and we saw the haints for the first time that night. There were about ten of them walking up the road toward the cemetery. I don't know of any sane way to describe a ghost, but it was there all the same.

As they got closer, one of them turned off as if to walk

over to us, and did. But, we were so scared that we didn't move. Just stood there, and watched as the haint went up to the house and proceeded to close the front door. He slowly moved to rejoin the others. On the way back, I got the weirdest feeling that he was smiling. I didn't tell my friends that though.

My friends and I vowed to never breathe a word of this to anybody because we weren't even sure we believed what we saw. And we didn't want to be called crazy or drunks like my uncle TB had been. I'm not scared of them like he was. Well, no, I won't go out in the graveyard at night or anything like that, but that don't mean I'm scared. There's a difference between my haints and Uncle TB's. Uncle TB always complained they was opening his doors. Mine are always closing doors.

You Will Come to Meet Your Demise
by:
L.S. Nadler

In the northern county of Carolina, the weather is warm, and the people have warm hearts. On the angriest of summer days, sunlight mixes with cool air above the surface of the fiery asphalt, displaying a mirrored image of the sky. Children frolic through sprinklers on grass long dead. Men go to work, sweat perspiring from their foreheads as they shovel through the dirt. Women sit rocking in stiff wooden chairs inside their shotgun homes, waiting long hours for sheets to dry in the humid air. Blazing heat, thunderstorms, manual labor; it is a difficult life, but you would never hear a complaint from the townspeople. The tiny houses are stacked on top of each other, built of old wood and cracking concrete, creaking floorboards that nobody would dare replace for the sake of history. They are diminutive houses, dark inside.

When those blistering days turn into nights you can see candle flames flickering in windows like a thousand tiny dancing spirits, the shadows of people's lives decorating the walls. They sit inside their houses with the curtains drawn and the radio on, silently awaiting the storm that brews in from the coastline, like acid in the stomach of a beast.

Charleston is a religious town, with crippling steeples towering far above the homes of men. Part of the reason they are so welcoming, so willing to withstand the heat; it is what God bids them to do. Nearly every weathered door on every street is painted a violent crimson red, a message to the angel of death who may come sweeping down from his perch any day to carry away their offspring in his black, cold, skeletal arms. Garlic wreathes hang below peepholes, crucifixes dangle inside each home, and statues of the Virgin Mary adorn the mantel to ward off the demons, reminding them that once you pass beyond this point, you're on holy ground.

On Sunday mornings, every home in Charleston is vacant and soulless and the churches overflow with zealousness. They call it The Holy City, but the citizens know that the town belongs to the devil. They may not know much in the ways of the world, but they know that the devil is as real as you or I. There are no reported sightings, no circumstance happenings, no coincidental acts of evil, for they catch sight of the devil in the midst of his evildoings on those smoldering summer evenings. Walking through the streets, his hooves clacking like those of horses, his rough grunts resounding into the dark homes, his silhouetted form lurking in the shadows of the darkest pathways. And when the witching hour strikes, the devil takes unfortunate souls to dine and laugh mirthfully with him in the mortuary as they feast on the remains of the warmhearted.

There is perhaps no street more frequented by the devil and his minions than Franklin Street. Paved with age-old cobblestone, Franklin Street stretches from the vast Oceanside all the way up to 2nd street before coming to a swift dead end. Few are able to afford the Oceanside view, where light is prevalent and the sun shines thoroughly, the crashing waves on the shore offering a cool breeze that you would be hard struck to find elsewhere in Charleston. The remainder of the street is barren, a desolate wasteland. The rustics abandoned their houses, which then fell, vanquished and claimed by the souls who once lived but live no longer. On the hottest days when the sun is at its highest point in the sky, shadows still wander aimlessly about; they are most adrift and darkest around the orphanage, The Jenkins Institute, halfway down Franklin Street, far past the breezy shoreline.

The Jenkins Institute has long since been abandoned, left to wither away and rot at the hands of the relentless sun and countless thunderstorms. Once a spectacular white abode this massively wide rectangular building is lined with archways across the front with two sets of stairs leading up from either side and meeting in the center where large sequoia doors grant entrance. The townspeople would not tear it down in fear of what the devil might do; rather they choose to endure the melancholy voice that emanates from within.

In his ethereal form, he awaits on the second story of the now decrepit orphanage in his tattered garments. His monumental groans resonate through the halls, echoing as they travel through empty chambers filled only with lost memories: *You will come to meet your demise; you will come to meet your demise.* The boy himself is an empty echoing hallway, a simple creature of repetition. The voice is a sweet croon, practiced, to be admired, yet it intones with a sense of helplessness, as if calling out to a once epidermal form, begging to perish in the eternal depths and termite his hollow existence. His voice is both song and sorrow.

He sits upon one of the dozen empty mattresses, soaking wet with water from last night's storm. The phantom child reaches out his boneless hand and drags it through the air, which he is a part of. He tries to curl his delicate fingers around a toy doll with one button eye, only to have it evade his touch, slipping through his opaque grasp. The doll is more alive than he and craving the touch of another, he begins singing the only song he knows. His song is composed of words not known to any language, not even he understands their meaning. Unlucky travelers passing through Charleston are enchanted by his call; it brings them up the white steps beyond those monstrous orphanage doors, into his dwelling place.

The walls of his chamber are lined with floral wallpaper peeling away from the cold, damp stonewalls, now home to rust and mold. The beds that line the boardroom are soiled. A ragged black velvet curtain, pushed to one side, frames the cracked windowpanes, allowing the sunlight to shine through him in all his spectral glory. Tiles on the floor are scattered in and out of place, mismatched like a jigsaw puzzle that will never be finished, revealing a splintering wood underneath. In the far corner of his room is a floor-length mirror reflecting nothing but a dust coated surface and a chamber as empty as he.

There are many other rooms inside the monstrous institute. He meanders through the manor, through the walls and corridors, alone. Portraits of children line the hallways, their demented eyes following wherever he steps. They are his brothers. He is both one, and a legion of many. They find their voice through him, and together they call to travelers on humid nights of summer, when even the sticky heat cannot stop a chill from crawling up your spine.

He has never aged a day, yet his voice is mature beyond his years. Some say the boy is no boy at all but an old man who traded his soul to the devil, now condemned to roam the land forever. Others say the boy never had a physical form to begin with, but rather is the son of the devil himself.

On those horrible stormy nights in Charleston, as the clouds play hide and seek with the moon, a blast of lightning will flicker through the decaying orphanage and offer a brief glimpse of the skeletal remains that lay in piles on the institute floor. Inside the white walls, he holds the remains of affectionate travelers.

His routine is the same each time, monotonous, like his song. When an unwise stranger walks down the cobblestone road, in from the coast and pauses to admire his white abode, he begins to croon. He will enchant them with his song, with his honeyed voice, like the sirens hymn to the seaman, and they will obey; they will follow his words. He will look up with hollow eyes, asking only that they care for him; he is lonely. He knows nothing of love, of nourishment, of affection. He knows only resentments, misery and evil.

All day and night he lingers through the halls, offering a glimpse of his spectral form through the windows, waving to the shadows in the streets. He loathes the very floor he cannot walk on; he detests the toys he cannot play with. He yearns for the company of others, but knows he cannot have it. He will beckon them into his room at night, and they will find him crying on his stained mattress. He will offer his hand, hoping for some semblance of physicality, to those fools and gypsies who dare follow his voice. They will look into his cold, dead eyes and see the stillness of life within. His tattered clothing gives him a certain air of desperation and the wanderer feels the need to comfort him.

He will smile up at them, reaching out his hand, and when they realize his ghostly form, they will go in for a touch to see if the boy is a mirage brought on by a fever. But, when they feel the icy absence of his touch forming around their skin they perish into nothingness, for that is his curse. At daybreak, the sun will shine through the windows and their skeletal remains will add to the despondent scene of a transparent child surrounded by death. He has never felt the touch of another.

You Will Come to Meet Your Demise

On one of those stifling midsummer days while birds chirped and the cicadas furiously rubbed their hind legs, a young girl with blonde hair and large brown eyes journeying through the southern parts of her country, decided to spend the night in The Holy City. Happily, she walks along the coastline and sees a sign for the Franklin Street Inn.

She is a pure soul. She has not yet been in bed with a man, and this gives her a special quality of innocence. The new world has made her grow weary of religion, yet she still holds tight to the ideologies laid out so long before her. She has motherly tendencies; her womb has bled; now it pulsates, yearning to be occupied by a child. Her curiosity is insatiable, she is fearless, she does not believe in the devil, but he sure as hell believes in her, and this is her weakness.

She walks in from the shoreline, and the boy in his disconsolate chamber feels her presence. It is a presence he has never felt before, one filled with warmth and love, an openness he has never encountered in all his long days and sleepless nights. He trembles then walks to a window on the second story of his abode. The portraits of his brothers follow him, and they fight within him to peer out his eyes. Who could she be? For the first time, he feels something outside his malevolence. For the first time he does not want to sing, but he is lonely.

As the sun begins to set behind that vast body of water, beams of light stream through Franklin Street, welcoming the slender shadows. The traveler wanders further into the street, approaching the inn; her bags are heavy, and she grows weary from her travels. The hot sun has taken its toll on her slim figure. Her stomach groans with hunger, and her feet are black with dirt. She does not notice that all the houses on the street have long since been abandoned, the cascading sun is too beautiful and blinding. She feels the warmth of the northern county and at this moment her ignorance is truly bliss. Many of the roofs are old and full of holes, many windows are barred up, black shutters hanging from their hinges, but she pays them no mind. All she seeks is a pillow to lay her head.

Entering the inn, a bell chimes overhead and the concierge lifts his drowsy head in surprise. He is old, with a weathered face like worn leather; he is a man of the land. He sported a pair of black slacks, a white collared shirt, and a black rawhide vest. His long graying hair gathered in a neat ponytail that drooped over his left shoulder. Collecting his thoughts, he greets the woman and offers her a glass of water. She immediately accepts, and pours it down her dry throat.

The Inn had the smell of burning wood, which she only noticed as the innkeeper handed her the keys to her chamber. Candles and torches lined the walls lighting the inn. The haunting glow of the flames cast shadows upon the wooden walls leading all the way to her room on the second story.

Her room filled with an eerie light from the setting sun, almost over the horizon now, a few beams cutting through the half-closed curtains hitting the foot of the bed in the center of the room. The bed frame was a beautiful brazen black oak, the headboard going nearly to the ceiling. The blankets were crimson, almost black when hidden from the light, and three pillows sat atop the covers. The dim-wood flooring creaked melodramatically as she walked across it. A small dresser, made of the same oak as the bed frame, lined the wall closest to the door, and in the corner rested an elegant mirror with century old carvings.

The elegance of the interior of the inn shocked her despite the cobwebs and dust covered surfaces; a room, though dim, more elegant than she had seen in all her travels. She almost regretted stopping at this guesthouse. Perhaps she could find another closer to the center of town, closer to other life, but when she rested her head upon the pillows, she remembered that she was no longer a child and her thoughts passed along away with the setting sun.

She awoke to a humble knock at the door and the intoxicating aroma of prepared beef. With this, she realized how hungry she had grown after a day's worth of travelling. She opened the door to a familiar weathered face, the concierge was holding a large silver tray with meat, potatoes, bread and lentils beside a tall glass of red wine, and a box of matches to light her chamber. She placed the tray on the oak dresser and before she could offer her thanks the man had darted off somewhere into the black hallway. The woman stuffed the meat down her throat, like a pack of ravenous wolves fighting over the corpse of a doe. Only after tearing off the last piece of bread did she realize her haste and unladylike manners.

After lighting the candles and clearing away the cobwebs she soaked her feet in a warm bath. With each quiver of the flame her body became limper and her eyelids grew heavier, the tall glass of red wine took effect on her petite figure. Before she could remove her summer gown, before she could let her hair down, before she could draw the curtains closed, she gave into the solemn night hours and fell into a peaceful sleep. The hot summer rain began to fall.

When the witching hour approached, the maiden awoke with an irrepressible shudder to the sound of thunder crashing; she sat wide-eyed with the feeling of remorse impressed into her chest as if some heavy creature were perched on her lungs. At length she sat unsettled on the edge of her bed glaring into the darkness, for the candles had long since retired. With a sudden instinct she rose to her feet and wandered to the window, the rain hammering down like pebbles on the old glass.

In between the sounds of the brewing storm she thought she heard a low hum, the sweet voice of a child from somewhere beyond the curtains, beyond the dark unlit streets. Pulling open the black curtains to unveil the window, she could barley see past the glass with relentless racing of beads across the pane. She pressed her face gently upon the surface of the window, her warm breath created a layer of fog on the already obscured windowpane, making the way across the road seem like an insurmountable gulf.

With difficulty, the traveler could just make out what lie beyond the pane, beyond the dark cobblestone streets.

You Will Come to Meet Your Demise

The glow of the lurid building across the street she found disconcerting; the foreboding white of the orphanage seemed askew in contrast to the utter darkness of Franklin Street. Suddenly, she heard the voice. The voice of a young child singing a song she had never heard, yet it was beautiful and intoxicating, like the aroma of a blooming rose. The notes were not any she could place on a scale, the words not any language she recalled hearing in her travels.

The voice rings out with the authority of thousands, but the song is only for her, and it is requiem: *You will come to meet your demise; you will come to meet your demise.*

She could not deny the child's call; she must abandon her slumber and venture out into the storm, she must seek out the child that sings with such distress, take him in her arms and caress his shivering body. Many would be frightened, many would remain in the comfort of their home, like the good people of The Holy City who have ignored his chants for so long, but the woman lives to wet her curiosity, to pursue the requests of evil.

On his bed on the second story of his white abode, the devil's orphan sits patiently waiting, singing the only song he knows. *I wish not to hurt you; I wish only to keep you.*

The traveler instinctively picks up the box of matches from the oak dresser, for she knows the importance of the light when entering an abyss. Down the theatrical creaking stairs, her shadow joins the others, for it is the witching hour and they dance freely. As elegant as a prancing rabbit she passes the innkeeper who sits slumbering behind his desk, his hair let out, his lantern shining bright. She does not know the orphanage is the devil's threshold; she wants only to answer the call from beyond, a song that is so wretched with ecstasy.

You will care for me, and you will disappear like all my mothers before you, and all my mothers before them. I will let you go gently.

On Franklin Street there are no lights, no houses filled with flickering flames, only darkness, a stark black that mimics the deepest chambers of the ocean. Were it not for the crashes of lightning she may have fell victim to the cobblestone road, but the brief offerings of blue iridescent light showed her the way to the orphanage where she ran up the slippery steps. The huge sequoia doors groan like a background choir to his melancholy incantations. His song grew louder.

She lit a match and saw the surprisingly dreadful condition of the interior of the orphanage. Despite its animated exterior, the inside was as dead as the day is long. Rubble littered the entrance hall, tiles piled in the corners, puddles gathered on the floor from the leaky ceiling, the walls were full of holes - home to devilish creatures. Dust lined every inch of the room, and the mirrors that once stood were now in shards on the floor. The air stung like a northern winter inside the decaying house; exhaling, the traveler could see her breath. She wondered what a boy was doing in such a cold and lonely place.

The song reverberated through the halls, echoing down

each corridor, giving it the power of giants. No longer lost in betwixt the clatters of rainfall, it became clear that the voice emanated from the second story of the building and called to her, the same incantations repeating over and under her thoughts with sadness. Lighting a match she saw the staircase hiding beyond the front hallway, past the empty rooms, across the shards of glass. Her radiance brings her forward into the darkness; she makes her first step into the hollow dungeon where lost souls are kept hidden, where he awaits.

Up the stairs on the second floor, the boy basks in his evil splendor. He has not had a traveler for three long years. He has been alone with no one but the shadows to keep him company, and he hungers for the brief touch of human flesh, though he knows it will give him no redemption, offer him no salvation, for he is beyond the saving grace, he is beyond evil. He will serenade her with his cloying refrain, as the people of the town dwell within their homes, and as mice squeak in trepidation between cracks in the walls.

The traveler will see him and feel a deep sense of regret, her motherly nature will well up inside her chest, in her womb, and she will follow him when she sees the tears streaming from his phantom eyes. She will obey his ever-tempting voice. She will attempt to kiss his forehead and touch the pale skin of the lost boy. But, lightning will strike and she will see his monstrosity, realize he has no face to kiss. She will try to hold him in her arms only to have him slip through her grip, and she will perish like the rest. The unfortunate traveler will pay the price for venturing into the darkness, and he alone will be left to sing the sorrow.

After a few wrong turns in the murky orphanage hallways, where portraits of youth gazed into her soul, the beguiled traveler discovered her performer's chamber. Sitting on his foul mattress in the ebony lighting, she cannot tell his ethereal form, all she sees is a sweet child with a gaunt face like an unmarked canvas. His song ceases and he beckons her to his side.

Slowly, with a deathly pace she follows his call; she is frightened for the first time since she can remember, of a child, of his loneliness. She wants to hold him in her arms and tell him it will be alright, she will care for him, she will shelter him from the storm, tell him to rest his tired voice, for now it is her turn to sing.

The boy looked no older than eight in the flickering flame of her match, but something wasn't right. His gaunt appearance changed to a dreadful opaqueness, and looking in the mirror behind the soiled mattress she saw only her reflection. He was a damnation, an abomination of adolescence. He trembles in a forlorn ache, her rationality tells her she is wrong and she must care for him. He raises his arms like an infant reaches for his mother, letting out a whimper. The singing voice could not possibly have come from such a weak child, only a boy, malnourished and sickly.

Awaiting her touch, her final demise, he feels something he has never felt, the care of another being. He feels her true sympathy. It saddens him further to have to annihilate a human of such beauty, such purity, but he knows he is the devil's boy and nobody can love him.

Once throwing the matches on the ground, only the sounds of rain resonate through the halls. Meeting the reach of the child she begins her own song, a soft humming lullaby, a song he has never heard before, a nursery rhyme remedy, a song to lay him to rest. Touching the boys frail arms, she picks him up, pressing him against her chest, and he feels the bulge of her bosom. Still humming, she places a kiss on his forehead. Tears fall from his eyes, mixing with the puddles on the rotting floor. She herself is the holy water, the Eucharist, the holy trinity, though she is too naïve to know. She lays her touch of purity on the miserable creature.

She holds him through the night on the putrid mattress and as the day begins to break, the storm clears and sun gleams through the holes in the ceiling. The place is no longer cold; it is warm and humid, as the south should be. The spectral form of the orphan child is gone, she no longer hears his crooning requiem, and there is no sign of him except the small tattered doll with one button eye on the floor. Rising to her revitalized feet, she walks through the halls, down the stairs, and out the sequoia doors. The sky is a pale blue, the sun a blazing fire in the sky, and a cool breeze ushers in from the Oceanside to greet her face.

The boy from the depths of evil, from the abysmal chasm of eternity, he vanished with the dawning of a new day. His song is lost, for no human could ever reproduce such sweet melodies with such gloom.

Finding her bags in her chamber on the second story of

the inn, she gathers her belongings and sets forth down the cobblestone road, marching along the coastal line to her next destination. Her countenance glows in the morning sunlight, and she feels a sense of fulfillment in her chest, the feeling of tenderness on the morning after a long night's rest. She wanders aimless, as curious as ever, letting the road take her where it will, no further thoughts fill her mind. She hums her lullaby as she ventures forth into the distance.

The devil continues to walk freely in The Holy City; he is seen wandering through the county, dancing with the shadows, peering through the windows of the holy, sunbathing in the graveyard. The devil always attends to his offspring, sees them off to a home warmer than Charleston, but he will forever roam the lands of men.

Hell's Gate
by:
M. R. Williamson

The crackling sound of a warm campfire coupled with a clear, crisp October night was everything Larry Cullum needed to fall asleep. As the eighteen-year-old dozed, he could still hear the coon dogs in the distance.

Somewhere in Insley Bottoms, close to the endless parcels of land that Old Doc Hall bought up during the Great Depression, he thought. He then winced and removed a pinecone from under his blanket. As he did so, he opened his eyes to check, Shorty, his father.

"You'll miss it," quipped Shorty, brushing his brown hair back. "Hugger will tree and you won't even hear it."

Shorty's infectious smile always worked its magic with the eighteen-year-old, but as far as coon hunting goes, Larry didn't need much encouragement. Besides, his redbone had never treed a coon. He could find them, and hold the trail like a steam engine, but he always missed the tree somehow.

Then, one of the dogs bayed again. Dauphus Armstrong, a big, blond-haired Swede, quickly raised up as though sparking a new interest. "Is that what a redbone sounds like when he barks tree?" he asked as Shorty's grin widened.

Larry frowned. "If you weren't my neighbor, I'd shoot you," he quipped.

"Shhh," hissed Shorty as he sat up, peered out into the darkness, and then added, "We've got three blue ticks and a redbone out there. I hear Blue and Chigger and even Larry's Hugger, but I haven't heard Get It one time."

"Bet they've got something," pondered Dauphus as he slowly stood.

"It's not a coon," insisted Shorty. "Get It only barks coon."

Larry slowly pulled himself to a sitting position, stared into the campfire, and listened. "They're not moving," he said. Then, as he started rolling up his blanket he added, "Hugger's not barking tree and he's not barking at a man." Larry then looked at his father and added, "He's barking scared and the others are growing strangely silent."

"You're right, and they're close to Richardson Landing Road," agreed Shorty as he scrambled to his feet and then grabbed his blanket. "We'll take the Levee Road around the bottoms. That should put us close to the open field to the north."

"Sounds like they're in the field," noted Dauphus as he emptied the coffee pot on the fire.

"But, there are no trees in the field," said Larry as they all headed for Shorty's old, white Dodge truck. "Why would coon hounds be baying there?"

Dauphus shrugged his shoulders. "Exactly why we should go and see," he answered as he threw his blanket in the bed of the truck.

"Get in quick. This doesn't sound good," said Larry as he held the cab door open for Dauphus and then jumped in behind him.

Loose gravel flew to the shoulders as Shorty slid around the curves of the old levee road.

Larry rolled the window down and then leaned close to it. "I can't hear a thing," he complained. "When are you going to replace this muffler?"

"Wouldn't worry on that if I were you," quipped Shorty. "I'd be more concerned about that storm in Arkansas. That lightning looks like it's getting close to the river."

As Shorty made the turn around the ridge, he slowed to a stop, turned the engine off, and then got out of the cab.

"That's more like it," responded Dauphus as he all but pushed Larry out of the truck.

"Can't hear mine," said Shorty, "but Hugger's still there and he's in the field close to where that old black walnut is-."

"Not good," complained Larry. "He's always been a fighter and if whatever has scared the other dogs to silence presents itself, he'll fight it."

"Come, let's go to him," suggested Shorty as they piled back into the old Dodge again. "We might just have a bear. That tree isn't far from the river and that critter might have just swum it."

"Doesn't sound like a bear, Dad," said Larry as his

father started the truck. "He's not scared of bears and he's barking scared. He just doesn't have the sense to leave."

No sooner had Shorty put the old truck in gear than they spotted his three blue ticks running toward them in the headlights.

"Well, I just will be dammed," said Shorty weakly. "Get out and put 'em in, boys."

Larry quickly bailed out of the Dodge and all but raced the dogs to the back of the pickup. When he opened the doors to the dog box, they all bowled him over getting in.

"What do you make of that?" asked Dauphus.

"Not a clue," replied Larry as he shut the doors and then added, "They're all huddled to the back of the box."

"Maybe the lightning spooked them," guessed Dauphus.

"Not close enough," said Larry as he pushed the big man toward the truck door. "We've got to find Hugger, and quick."

"Get in," said Shorty. "I can still hear Hugger."

As Shorty raced the Dodge down the levee hill toward the delta flats, Larry strained his eyes, hoping for another lightning flash.

"Look close," encouraged Shorty. "The tree is just the other side of that old shack up ahead on the right."

Larry eyed the old house as Shorty slowed the truck and then pulled past it. Its windows were mostly intact, but they were without screens. The old, rusty-looking tin roof looked as if it had been there before the depression. Imitation, red brick siding had once adorned the old place, but it was now hanging loose in more places than not.

"Look," noted Dauphus as he leaned forward to look around Larry. "Looks like someone put in a brand new door."

"Imagine that," said Larry as his father slowed the truck to a stop. Larry then turned to Dauphus and added. "I think I saw a gold cross on it," he added as he opened the truck door.

"Missed that," said Dauphus, "but look at the lamp in the window."

"Don't get spooked," chuckled Shorty. "That's old Elam's place. That old black man must be at least a hundred years old. My father knew him when I was a kid. I think his father was some kind of a preacher—Pentecostal I think."

"Let's get out if we're gonna look," suggested Dauphus as he looked toward the lightning flashes. "Looks like that storm's getting closer."

"Well," said Shorty as he joined the others at the side of the road, "there's the old walnut tree."

Larry looked out across the freshly plowed field. About fifty yards away stood a tree that looked like it was older than time itself. Mother Nature had not touched it—not a limb was missing.

Larry then heard Dauphus chuckling. As he turned toward his neighbor, the Swede said, "If they're any spooks in this area, they're probably living in that old walnut."

"Thanks a lot," mumbled Larry as the lightning lit up the field again.

"I see him," said Shorty as he pointed toward the tree. "I think he's digging for something."

"Digging?" echoed Larry.

"Come on," added Shorty as he stepped across the little drainage ditch. "If that storm gets here before we get Hugger out from under that tree, we'll be covered in mud before we get to the truck."

"He's barking a warning," said Larry as he and Dauphus followed Shorty into the field.

"Warning? What do ya' mean?" asked Dauphus.

"It's like he sees something we don't—like a burglar."

"I can see him now," exclaimed Dauphus, "and he's still digging."

"Leave him be!" shouted an unfamiliar voice from behind them.

They all stopped and looked back toward the road. A dim, yellowish glow seemed to be floating down the road toward the truck. As it got closer, they could make out an old man with a cane, hobbling as fast as he was able.

"Oh Lord," said Shorty with a bit of a smile. "You'd best let me handle this. He's about half a bubble off plumb."

Shorty quickly stepped around the others and picked his way across the dirt clods toward the old fellow.

Dauphus then nudged Larry with his elbow. "Do you know anything about that old man?" he asked.

"I know no one has ever lived with him since his wife died back in the sixties. They say he watches a haunt."

"A haunt?" echoed Dauphus.

"Yes," answered Larry. As they started plodding across the field to join his father, he added, "It's a place where something stays or comes to pretty often."

"Shhh," hissed Shorty as Larry and Dauphus approached. "I think he said something." He then turned toward the old man as he walked up. "Pardon me, Mr. Jones," said Shorty, "but I didn't catch that."

The old fellow walked up within five feet of them, held the oil lantern as high as he was able, and then said, "Dat's my name," He then looked closely at Shorty and then added, "You one dem Cullum boys ain't ya?"

"Yes sir, I am? This young fellow beside me is my son, Larry and the older one is-"

"Armstrong?" said Elam weakly. Then, as he moved the lantern closer to Dauphus, a smile began to form on the old fellows face. "Bless my soul," he said. Then, as tears welled up in his eyes, he added, "Your pappy was preacher, weren't he?"

"Yes sir. He was a Methodist."

"Finally, I get to rest," said Elam as he wiped the tears from his eyes with his shirtsleeve. He then turned and looked toward the old tree and said, "Dis not Doc Hall's land. Wouldn't sell it to 'em, but he works it anyways and gives me a little money to boot. My pappy was a preacher too," he added as he continued looking at the old tree. "His church burnt some time ago. It used to be right across the street from my house, but yawl white boys never came did you?"

Larry leaned close to Dauphus and whispered, "It burned in nineteen and sixty five."

"No sir. Not that I remember," answered Shorty.

"Den ya'll don't know," he replied as the lightning flashed and lit up the old tree, but only for a moment. It seemed to bring a smile to Elam's face. "Dey don't always come in every storm you know. But, when dey do come, it always be stormin'. He jus' waits for 'em you know. Always waits for 'em; been doin' it since Genesis, probably."

"They?" asked Dauphus. "Who waits for what? Who are you talking about, and what do you mean by 'you'll finally get some rest?'"

Elam then turned from them, worked his way across the shallow drainage ditch, and then looked back at them. "I know you come for your hound, but he got more than jus' a little treed. Jus' like you Dauphus Armstrong," he added as he pointed a crooked finger at the young man. "He got a callin' too, and I think it was to bring you."

"What's he talking about?" asked Dauphus.

"I don't know, but all this is starting to spook me," replied Larry as they started to follow the old man toward the tree and the still-digging Hugger."

"We just come for the dog," said Shorty as they neared the tree, "go get him Larry."

"No!" exclaimed Elam, making Larry freeze in his tracks.

The old man's tone was much more than insistent. It sounded like a warning.

"He'll put up with de animal," continued Elam, "but you might not be so lucky."

"He?" whispered Larry as he glanced back at his father.

Shorty shrugged his shoulders and said not a word.

"Here Hugger, here Hugger," called Dauphus as he bent down and clapped his hands together.

Hugger looked toward them, back up in the tree, and then proceeded to dig and growl at the same time.

"Did I mention spooked?" reminded Larry.

"Stop it!" shouted Elam as he slammed the foot of his cane down in the dirt.

The hound immediately jumped to one side as if a stone had hit him.

"Come here Hugger," called Larry as he patted his thigh.

The hound immediately ran to Larry's side, but eyed Elam as if he was afraid to get closer.

"Put de animal up, Sir," said Elam, "and don't hunt dis side of de road any more, especially when it storms."

"Yes sir," answered Larry. "We'll keep that in mind."

"Come," added Shorty as he turned toward the truck. "Let's get out of this field before the storm breaks."

As a reminder of the storm flashed again, Larry put Hugger into the box with the other dogs. When he shut the door, he noticed Dauphus, leaning on the open truck door, staring back toward the old tree.

"Is this place rubbing off on you?" said Larry as he walked up by Dauphus. "What's got your attention?"

"Devidian!" exclaimed Elam as he struggled up the near side of the drainage ditch. "Devidian be his name, at least dat's what my father, Elijah, called him. Not many see him but me and--"

"Thank you," interrupted Larry loudly as he all but shoved the big Swede into the truck. "We'll remember what you said," he added as he climbed in behind Dauphus and shut the door.

"He's dizzier than a wing-shot mallard," said Shorty.

"Not so sure," said Dauphus as he leaned forward for another look at the old tree. "I think I got a glimpse of what had Hugger's attention."

"Was it a ghost?" Shorty quipped as he fumbled with the keys. The smile on his face irritated Dauphus a bit.

"It looked like some kind of bird," explained Dauphus. "The biggest, blackest bird I've ever seen."

"Turkey?" guessed Larry. "Hugger might bark tree at one of them."

"Bigger," replied Dauphus, "and the sharp bend of the wings were held up strangely above its head." He then turned and looked at Shorty, who was still holding the keys and added, "He was sitting on a limb no larger than a child's arm."

"Devidian!" exclaimed old Elam as he hobbled closer to the passenger side door.

"Start this thing," said Larry as he hurriedly rolled up the window.

As the starter turned the engine over and over, Elam

hobbled up and tapped on the window. "You saw him for a reason, Dauphus Armstrong. He has a plan for your life, Sir, jus' like me."

"Finally," sighed Dauphus as the engine started.

"You'll be back Mr. Armstrong, Sir! You'll be back!" shouted Elam as the truck pulled back onto the road.

As the lightning flashed once again, big drops of rain started to splatter upon the windshield. Dauphus turned for another look at the old, black man as the old Dodge rolled away. He was still standing on the side of the road, holding the lantern high.

"Turn around, Dauphus," complained Larry. "Your knee is killing my thigh."

"He's just an old man," said Shorty. "Don't let him spook you."

"Yes . . . but I've never seen him before tonight, Mr. Cullum," said Dauphus as he turned from the rearview window. "How did he know my name?"

"I'm working on that one right now," answered Shorty.

"He only knew of you," guessed Larry. "You do favor your father. He was only guessing."

"But, what was Hugger trying to dig up?" asked Dauphus.

"Don't know," answered Larry as he also looked back toward the old tree.

"One riddle at a time, boys," chuckled Shorty. "We'll think on this tomorrow. Perhaps the storm will be passed by then." Shorty then glanced at Dauphus and added, "You can move your things into the spare room tonight. That'll do until we get a new roof on the guesthouse. If you're determined to rent it, we'll fix it up a bit also."

***

The next morning, Larry was up early and sitting on the back porch with his cup of coffee. As his mother, Dorothy, cooked breakfast in the kitchen, he listened to the hounds playing in their pens. After a minute or two Larry stood up, stepped to the front of the porch, and then scratched his head.

"Something wrong?" asked Dorothy from the window, noting the worried expression on his face.

"Not really sure," answered Larry. "I don't hear Hugger, and he's usually the loudest. As a matter of fact, I don't think he's there at all," he added as he stepped from the porch and walked briskly toward the end of the yard where the pens were located. "Ah nuts!" he complained, noticing that Hugger's pen door was ajar. "Hugger! Hugger!" he shouted as he neared the pen, but there was no movement from anywhere inside.

Larry then turned and trotted toward the house. As he neared the porch, Dauphus stepped out sipping his morning cup of Joe.

"Hugger's gone," said Larry, "and there's only one place that would be on his mind right now — old Elam's black walnut tree."

Dauphus rolled his eyes, looked at Dorothy through

the screen window, and then replied, "We're not going back there are we? That old man told us to stay away from that place."

"Not really," corrected Larry. "He told us not to hunt there. Besides, that's my dog and I'm going to get him with or without old Elam's consent. Now come on. You gave me that hound and he's the last living redbone from your father's line."

"Good grief," grumbled Dauphus as he gulped his coffee and headed for Larry's black, Ford Ranger.

In little time, the powerful V-8 was rolling toward Black Bottom Ridge and the grade that would take them down to Elam's shack.

"He said I'd be back," grumbled Dauphus, "and here I am — led by a dog just like he predicted." He then turned to Larry and added, "Why don't we give Hugger a little time. He's never stayed lost for too long anyway."

"Nothing doing," said Larry as the Ford raced around the ridge and headed for the grade and Dock Hall's land.

"Well, at least it didn't rain much," noted Dauphus, "and it's clear as a bell."

"And cold too," said Larry as they rolled down the grade toward the old house and walnut tree.

Larry slowed the Ranger as it flew past the house and then slid up right across from the old tree. He then leaned forward and looked around Dauphus toward the haggard-looking walnut.

"There he is," noted Dauphus, "and he's not digging."

"Yes," agreed Larry, "and judging by that pile of dirt, I believe he's finished. Let's go and see what he's found."

Dauphus reluctantly got out of the truck, rolled his pants legs up, and then followed his best friend toward the tree in question.

The hound never tried to move as they walked toward him, nor did he even acknowledge their presence when they drew near. Something way up in the middle of the old tree had his undivided attention.

"What are you looking for?" asked Larry, noting that Dauphus was looking at the tree's limbs also.

"Wait a minute," said Dauphus. "Something just isn't fitting the puzzle here." Dauphus then looked toward old Elam's house. "He had to hear you come up, and he's not even on the porch. And look at this," added Dauphus as he walked just under the tree and kicked at the dirt. "My boots are muddy from the field just behind me and this spot under the tree is bone try." He then knelt, felt of the ground, and then added, "The ground is strangely warm here."

"Just another part of the puzzle I guess," said Larry as he walked closer to his hound. "Hey, boy," he said as the two approached. "What have you found?"

"I don't see a thing in that tree," said Larry. He then knelt down and examined the hound's bloody forepaws. "Lord Almighty," he responded just above a whisper. "What in the world has snagged your attention so badly that it would lead you to do something like this?" Larry then looked at the five foot wide and two-foot deep hole Hugger had dug and then quickly stood up. "Get your mind off that old man, Dauphus, and come look at this," he said with a hint of disbelief.

"Good grief," said Dauphus as he stepped up by Larry. "It's some kind of heavily engraved piece of copper-colored metal."

"It's not a piece," noted Larry as he stepped down into the hole. Then, as he moved the dirt about at the edges of Hugger's hole, he said, "I don't see an edge. This thing is one, big piece of metal. I think it's bronze, and heavily engraved," added Larry as he knelt down and brushed at a strange winged being that looked as if he were blowing a long trumpet. "Go get the army shovel, Dauphus, this thing's got writing on it in English."

"What does it say?"

Larry brushed the dirt as best he could from the first three words and read--Through these gates... "That's it. Go and get the shovel. It's behind the seat and . . ."

Larry's voice trailed off as everything suddenly went strangely dark, as if midnight had suddenly fallen upon them.

"What the Devil is happening?" asked Dauphus weakly as he stepped closer to the hole.

"Not a clue," answered Larry as he then looked at Hugger, who had just uttered a low, guttural bark and then sat up.

"Ohhh God," said Dauphus. "Hugger has seen something in that tree and now we can hardly see the limbs.

Just then, the old tree limbs began to move and rake against one another as the sound of a huge set of wings left the tree.

"Hear that?" asked Dauphus as he jumped into the hole, ending up next to Larry. "It's circling right above us. Look at your dog."

"It is, isn't it?" agreed Larry as he watched Hugger follow the curious sound above them.

Then, the sound stopped suddenly as Hugger's gaze froze on something between them and the trunk of the old tree.

"Can you see it?" asked Dauphus weakly.

"Shhh," hissed Larry. "My gun is in the truck. I don't even have a pocketknife."

"Worry is but a human trait," said someone who sounded as if he was right at the top of the hole they were standing in.

"Who are you?" asked Larry just above a whisper.

The voice then came again, "Through countless years I have been mute through this seemingly endless dilemma; yet, here before me stands yet another."

The voice was that of man--tired, but sounding somewhat relieved nonetheless.

Larry grabbed Dauphus by the arm and whispered, "Who is he talking to?"

"How do I know," replied Dauphus as he gripped the back of Larry's arm. "I can hardly see you."

"May we ask who you are?" asked Larry.

The strength in his question was barely enough to be heard only a few feet away.

"I am one in a line of many. One who tells you that the end of darkness draws near."

"Show yourself," said Dauphus, "and bring back the light."

"I dare not," responded the voice strongly. "I am not comely. My countenance will cause you to quake. In your world, I am depicted as fair and beautiful . . . . Hear my words," he continued softly. "When my Master comes, Night and those who find comfort in him will soon lose their protector. The light that proceeds from the Master will rip that dark veil asunder and end evil along with its father."

"You are the one Old Elam spoke of," said Dauphus.

"I am Devidian. I watch the West Gate," exclaimed the voice loudly.

As he stepped a little closer to them, the area around him brightened, but just enough to define his features a bit more than just a silhouette in the darkness. Cole-black hair he had, not unkempt, but with many curly tufts that pointed all about. Eyes of ice—ones that reflected light as it would be reflected off of chrome. His ears were pointed and curved upward into his hair. His nose, although not pointed or hooked, was still thin and long.

Larry sat down hard on the edge of the hole and noted the sharp bend in the being's wings, which was now three feet above Devidian's head. He then noticed the pearly-white teeth in the 'I told you so' grin on the being's face. He was looking straight at Dauphus. Strangely enough, Hugger had moved and was now sitting at Devidian's right side.

"Have you already forgotten your father's ways?" asked the angel.

"No . . . No Sir," answered Dauphus as he knelt a bit closer to where Larry was now sitting and then added, "We still attend church."

"Your father, Johansson as he was called, was a good man. He believed in the place whereupon you are now standing."

With that, the ground began to shake, roll like a lake, and shift. It was so violent that Larry and Dauphus fell beside one another and pleaded for it to end. When the quake finally ceased, the floor beneath them began to glow and turn strangely warm.

Larry and Dauphus scrambled to their feet, climbed quickly out of the now much larger hole, and then looked back at Devidian.

"He's an angel," whispered Dauphus weakly as Larry helped him to his feet.

"Dauphus Armstrong," spoke Devidian softly, "look upon this gate, and read what you see."

Noting that Dauphus could hardly take his eyes from the angel, let alone say anything, Larry looked down at the glowing floor of Hugger's hole. Two huge doors fashioned as an arc as they met. Each of the glowing, brass doors was twelve feet wide and ten feet tall where they touched. Figures depicting angels and cherubs were carved upon its edges-

-the larger holding swords, and the smaller ones, trumpets and scrolls. All faces were turned toward the writing across the middle of the doors.

Larry stepped closer to the edge of the hole and read, "Through these gates, all hope is lost." Before he could say another word, or look up, he noticed the angel's feet. He wore a dark, burgundy robe that reached almost to the ground, but his feet were plainly visible nonetheless. His feet were as dark as his arms, with almost an olive tone. His toenails were hard-looking, brown and curved like the talons of a predator.

"Dauphus Armstrong!" exclaimed the angel loudly, sending Larry right back to his friend's side. "The time of my Master approaches. Your seed and the seed of all mankind will soon be cut off. Elam Jones is at the end of his days and has kept the curious from this place, as did all the guardians before him. I do much the same for Satan's remnant from time to time. Behind those doors are the rest of his legions put there after the first Great War."

Dauphus wiped the sweat from his brow and said weakly, "What have I to do with you?"

"Stay with old Elam for his time is near. When his health fails, comfort him. He has been my servant for almost thirty years. He will teach you what to do and how to do it. Fear not, neither for your safety, nor for your wellbeing, for Elam will also make known to you the one who has taken care of him. In less than two years, another much like me will come. His name is Adrian. He will have the keys to this gate. Care for him as you would any other Christian."

Devidian then backed slowly away from the two. His ice-colored eyes reflected the glowing gates giving him an eerie and unsettling look as he faded into the darkness.

"Come out, Dauphus Armstrong, and bring your friend with you," called Elam from somewhere behind them.

Then, as quick as a cat's sneeze, the morning's light returned like a silent explosion. Both, Larry and Dauphus stood there shielding their eyes from the light of day as they looked for the old black man.

"It's gone," said Dauphus as he looked all about the area where they stood. "There's not a sign of even Hugger's hole. It's like it was all a dream."

"Hugger's still here," noted Larry. "He looks as if nothing has ever happened."

"No dream," said old Elam. "Things dat happen here are never imagined, and never left to your own interpretation." Elam then looked at Hugger and said, "Go and wait at de truck."

The hound stood, sniffed where he had located the doors, and then raised his head and looked at the old man.

"Go on, I said," repeated Elam loudly.

Hugger then bounded off across the field toward the truck.

"He won't do that for me," mumbled Larry as he followed the hound a bit and then looked back at Elam.

The old fellow just stood there and grinned at the young men for a moment or two. Then he finally said, "Not many souls blessed to see an angel afore they die." He then looked straight at Larry and added, "He make a believer out o' you?"

"You bet," was all that Larry could muster up.

Elam then pointed his walking stick right at Dauphus and said, "How 'bout you?"

"You were right," agreed Dauphus weakly. "I was lead back here by a dog. Now, I'm looking to you for answers. What now?"

Elam then looked at Larry and said, "You can go with your animal."

"Please, sir," asked Larry, "let me hear what you have to say."

Elam then looked at Dauphus.

"He's honest. I'll swear to that," assured Dauphus.

"Very well den," said Elam as he again glanced at Larry, "but what is said here, stays here."

"Yes sir," responded Larry quickly.

"No sense in me explainin' Devidian. I know he did that himself. There's a young, blue-eyed girl, 'bout eighteen I'd say, who brings me food and things I need," said Elam as he stepped a bit closer. "Mind you, she's no white girl. Her hair's de color of corn silk and she talks a bit funny. It's a dialect I haven't been able to place. When my time comes, she'll fetch you."

"Devidian said to stay with you, Elam," explained Dauphus.

Elam stopped, looked back at the old walnut tree, and then to Dauphus. As his eyes welled up with tears, he tried to speak again. "It's true den," he barely managed. "When last she came, she said my reward was near. Guess I misjudged her meaning."

Elam then turned and started slowly picking his way back across the plowed ground toward the road.

"Sir," said Dauphus as he caught up with the old man," I feel awful funny about crowding in on anyone, especially a perfect stranger."

Elam then stopped dead still and turned to look at Dauphus. "You do as Devidian said. I'll show you de ropes, and I'll introduce you to Dana. She's de one takes care of me . . . and now you." As he turned and continued toward the road he added, "Got a radio, but no television. Don't need one. Things never dull around here especially when de storm clouds gather above dat old tree. De ground shakes 'neath de old shack's blocks somethin' fearful, but de old house, she don't move at all."

Larry put his hand on Elam's back and said, "I'll help you fix up the old place a bit."

"No need," responded Elam. "If you did dat, it would look out of place. Besides, my old house looks lots better on de inside," he added as he started laughing. "It be dry when it rains, cool in de Summer, warm in de Winter, and interesting as Hell itself," he added, laughing out loud as he did so. "Jus' like dat angel you jus' seen — un-measurably awful on the outside and solid gold where it counts."

Maddness
by:
William R. Eakin

An ambulance was outside the Gray House, just in the gravel driveway. They'd parked it as if to showcase it to the world right there in front of the gaping double door of the turn-of-the-century gray-planked barn the Grays used as a garage. Just above where they'd parked the white, metallic ambulance with its own rear doors open, the Gray's first and only son Bobby Star had scrawled in black spray paint across the lintel of the barn the misspelled MADDNESS. He'd been thirteen, and was sent away for treatment. He came back home when he was twenty-one, and lived upstairs in what was supposedly the old nursery.

I was on my daily walk and the County Sherriff Orvil Kellner was standing big and round as Humpty-Dumpty lording over the whole procedure with a thick stogie in his hand. He was a friend of mine. He motioned another cigar at me and I took it as I asked: "What's happened?"

"He finally killed 'em," said Orville looking with disgust as the EMTs hauled the gurneys over the porch steps and to the back of the ambulance: I saw only white lumpy landscapes on each of them, and streaks and clots of blood, as if the lumps were volcanoes pressing out gunk from some deep center.

"Oh my God," I said.

"I knew he would all along."

"Guess we all did." And it looked like we were all right about that.

"Used then hid somewhere that antique Bowie Knife, the one they'd mounted above the fireplace. You seen it."

"I seen it," I said. The fireplace was rock, old: built in 1830 with the house, broken up in cannon fire as the union army came up the street, crumbling through the rest of the war with men dying on stretchers to every side, broken more through years of disuse and never really fully repaired. They'd tried to restore the house back in the 1920's: they walled up the narrow staircase next to it for reasons never really talked about, but never touched the fireplace. When the current Gray family moved into the abandoned home in the 1960's, they'd hammered a big hole back through the barrier into the stairway so that the then-young hippy husband would have it as a study — or a place to smoke his dope. It was 1968. There were two unused ratty cobwebbed dusty children's rooms up there: the husband's study and then the old nursery itself eventually cleaned up a bit for the son they called Bobby Star. The hole in the ragged old brick and mortar barrier to the stairway stayed exactly that, ragged and old like the fireplace. Old hippies. Part of the dilapidated nature of the place was just because of that, projects half-started and then too much dope for a now old couple to mess with. As if no one in that house could finish a project.

I guess I mumbled that aloud, because Orville said, "Well Bobby Star finally did."

"Did what?" I asked.

"Finish a project."

"Hmm," I shook my head. I could see the old couple lying there in their bedroom downstairs as if they were there now, though they were being loaded into the ambulance. The bedroom was between the ragged opening into the stairwell and the wood frame door into their little yellow kitchen. I could see them quite well, too, as if still alive and going to bed: they lay there, in their late 60s, early 70s, old lumps. I could envision them reading their damned books as they always did, invading the house as they obviously had with weird ass thoughts and dreams and hopes. He read: mystical trash, freedom-through-TM, and aliens and Egyptology: the stuff of metaphysical bookstores. She read: *Bury My Heart at Wounded Knee* and *An Anthropological Investigation into the Spirituality of the Native American*.

She once said mornin' to me at the shared post that held our mailboxes. And she got this weird dazed look in her eyes like you can see in old women who were once raised on coke and acid and free love and now had plenty of natural high in pseudo-mystical psychic stuff: "I can almost feel them, walking down this road, walking toward

Indian Territory, giving up their beautiful rich mountainous forested homelands to the greedy sucking land-owning, land-sucking bastards who slaughtered and beat them and made them walk the death march to some god-forsaken unknown, arid and miserable land like—Oklahoma!" And while those words might have sounded angry coming from anyone else's mouth, she had this dazed romanticized calm about her, as if all that horrible stuff was simply meant to be in the course of nature, like because of the Wyrd of the old Anglo-Saxons or Druids or some such nonsense.

"Uh, yeah," I said. "Me, too." I hadn't been over into Oklahoma. I just knew Orville went there to gamble and came back with cigars to share. He and I both detested the Grays, me especially, since I considered them whackos and we shared the tail end of my driveway. From their barn you could see my little brick house at the bend in Cabin Creek.

Orville was talking about finding them dead, and, again, I could envision them, little lumps under their sheets with creaky old heads sticking up illuminated only by their reading lamps. I could see the knife rising. I could see their eyes jolt up startled. I could see the knife blade coming down and watched it strike the sheets, slash through the sheets down into skin, rise and do it again. I could feel the harsh and unforgiving jolt of their bodies and hear the skin ripping like fleshy fabric. I could peer into the sudden shock on their old faces and watch the light in them go out as one, then the other, was taken off into the nothingness that really awaited them. Or to what they would have called Sunyata.

"Some folks said they got what they deserved," said Orville.

"Huh?"

"With that boy."

Oh, yeah. I'd been one of them. You do enough crap in the style of the 1960's and no telling what you've done to your gene pool. They'd had family here all along; they themselves had abandoned the place as if it were nothing anyone cared about when they flit off to the West Coast; their family had owned it—theoretically--since they'd taken it over as a make-shift hospital for confederates coming back from Pea Ridge carrying in the dead and dying and bloodied to lie about in agony on the floor in front of the fireplace. But even when the current Grays were gallivanting around in California they wouldn't let the place go back to the original owners, oh no, they wouldn't. Under that new age facade was the same greedy genetic makeup that had been in their grandparents, and their great-grandparents, the ones that stole the place from my great grandmother. And her daughter.

"And Bobby Star?" I said.

"What's that?" asked Orville through his smoke.

"What about Bobby Star?"

"Oh, he ain't never coming back. My boys took him right away; you know he was nuts. But did you ever think— he'd do such a thing?"

"Thought I heard sirens—you know I walk down the creek and back every day." Usually when I walk, I leave my own driveway, walk past the Gray House and go down to the old foot trail that follows Cabin Creek into the deep woods. There's an old railroad bridge there that I take across the creek to come back the other side. I follow the creek where it snakes around the back of the Gray house and then mine — the small section we kept of the three hundred acres my ancestors once owned. From there Cabin Creek rushes down to the river and on to the sea. I cross it at my place where the stones are big enough to make a little footbridge.

I'd heard the sirens from down in the black woods, standing on that old railroad bridge.

"Poor bastard had to be restrained to get him off the premises. No sir, he ain't never coming back."

"Good," I said.

***

It was late. Moonlight came in through the front door they'd left hanging open. They had crime scene tape all over the porch and all around the house. But inside the crumbling place seemed peaceful suddenly. I looked out the window at the old barn and could still see in the moonlight MADDNESS where that boy had scrawled it. MADDNESS.

And then I heard the voice, the little girl's voice; sounded like a little girl playing, talking to her dolls, up in one of those rooms at the top of the once walled-in stairs, the nursery. They should never have opened that stairway, much less put that invalid Bobby Star in her room. The air in the house grew cold.

I looked into the bedroom. The stripped mattress glowed white in the moonlight, white, except where blood had gushed onto the mattresses. I imagined I saw them there again, reading their hippy books. And now I felt I had to say something and I spoke as if they were there: "You shoulda took that boy outta here when he first started hearin' them voices."

I waited as if they would respond and they did not, but I could hear her, the girl, her voice sing-songy, up the stairs.

"You shoulda took that boy out soon as he showed signs of being crazy; brain like that will fester until it starts to feel the injustice all over, feel what's been done to a family when smart greedy bankers take over in the midst of— tragedy, horror."

When suddenly a brilliant, bright, eerie, strange light burst through the windows and illuminated the bedroom and the whole house: and I saw it in my mind's eye, cause I'd seen it before, a lot of times before—and the Gray ancestors had relocated my own family (in an act of what they called charity) into that little cabin right at the edge of Cabin Creek. And right now in that empty big house I saw the light only as I always saw it, as if from the little log cabin that the Gray family had long ago put those two in, the mother and the girl, after the Grays took over the house and most of the property, after the War Between the States killed my ancestor's husband and left that little girl fatherless, and both of them destitute. The Grays took it over and they relocated her into the cabin of Cabin Creek. And when the meteor split the sky and thundered like God in the heavens, of course, of course! They all saw it, the Grays from what had been my family's house, from what had been that little girl's room; and that ancestor of mine, that woman and her child standing at the back of that old even back then dilapidated cabin, the one that shared the little dirt road up into that gray barn where one day that boy Bobby Star would paint MADDNESS. And mother and daughter saw the brilliant Christmas star insane thing fizzling out of the sky and sparkling and suddenly shattering into the water of the creek right behind their cabin. And they say the hissing could be heard from seventy-five miles away; and the hissing was a roar that shook all the walls on my family's old property and the roar was a great release of steam, volcanic, and it hit them like a hammer, hit that old cabin like a hammer, wrapped around them like a fist of white and gray and terror and suddenly they were gone, the woman and her girl. All gone except the ruins of that cabin where they'd had to go live after the Grays took over, and except for the Gray House, where that family stood in the window of her bedroom--her bedroom, damn it!—and watched the mists recede.

Only they weren't gone. There in the creek right at the spot where I myself would someday build a tiny brick house, there in the water right at the bend, in the night that still crackled with the explosion of the meteor, stood countless spirits called up from the cosmos: the ghosts of confederate soldiers tattered and ripped by war come to die in this place and to be buried out back of the big house; and with them the stone-faced feathered women and men and children, who'd walked their moccasins into nothing but blood tamping down our road with it, dying and bleeding on the trail of their tears. And amongst them, with the Civil War dead and the dead of injustice stood my forebears, that woman and that little girl. And then with the steam they were all gone. And then it was just that little girl left alone, to be taken off to some orphanage and no longer even allowed to stay at Cabin Creek.

Orphanage and asylum. And in those times a young girl in an asylum was ripe for all sorts of terrible things, a beating that broke her jaw; much worse; lone rooms with cold attendants helping her birth my bastard ancestors, in blood and frozen steam and hate. And I know there are stories that she came back, somehow escaped and came back, tattered, broken, bleeding—I know these stories directly from the horse's mouth—and that she slept her last nights in that ole barn between the shattered cabin and the Gray House, the one that would eventually cry MADDNESS. And I know from more than just stories that she watched the big house with the family never knowing she was there, watched with jaw slack from some horrible beating along the way, the saliva running down from her mouth, watched that building until she died and those people rose again from the creek to take her away, watched that bedroom that belonged to her, to her and no one else, not any of those Grays, not even the little boy who those hippies named Bobby Star and who thinking he saw her one night in the barn painted above it the inscription that described what the place had indeed become.

***

So I stood looking in at the bed. I could feel the knife in my hand though that was just a memory. I could feel my arm raising it up and the downward slash, and the downward rush, and another downward slash, and the great mists moving my arm with a ferocity I myself could not possess. And I had felt the knife in my palm for real one last time before I tossed it from the old Union Pacific bridge and stood and watched the deep green water there until I heard the sirens and knew they'd finally taken mad Bobby Star away and her room was hers again.

"No sir, he ain't never coming back," Orville had said. And now thinking of that, looking at that mattress, I realized the little girl had stopped singing upstairs.

For a moment that startled me, but then I turned and saw her. She stood at the broken barrier wall, one foot on the stairs. The same little girl who'd talked to me over and over when I myself snuck into the barn those countless times to look up at her window in the big house.

"Thank you," she said.

And the MADDNESS was over.

Wellspring
by:
Roman Merry

"What is it?"

"It's a well, dummy." The other boys laughed.

"Shut up Johnny Ray, I can see that." Darl's voice cracked like a rusty fiddle and echoed across the parched, sun-drenched pines.

"Then why'd you ask what it was?" They laughed again, but just for a moment, as they turned attention to the weathered structure that must have endured the blistering heat and humidity of many a Mississippi summer.

Cautiously, as if creeping around a sleeping tiger, four sunburnt boys from Neshoba County circled the broken, brick cylinder that hid a hundred yards inside the tree line near their fishing hole. They gravely kept their distance from the pit as it yawned open a blackness of unknown depths. Each boy quietly hoped one of the others would be the first to move closer, but they all just stood like statues.

"I dare you to look over the edge," Johnny Ray finally smarted to the others.

"No way, man. I ain't going any closer."

Johnny Ray looked at the smaller boys and smirked. "Wussies."

"You are."

"Hey, shut up. I thought I heard something." Cash held his hand close to his ear. Then Darl imitated his twin brother, straining to hear whatever it was before Willie started laughing.

"You guys didn't hear nothin' at all. You're just chicken to get near that thing and look over the edge."

"No, maybe he did. This well is haunted, you know." The words curled up a smile on the oldest boy's bologna lips.

"Shut up, Johnny Ray. It's not haunted."

"Oh yes it is. I heard one of the Sartoris clan got mad at his wife and threw her in the well. She died down there and they never got the body out. It's why they stopped using it."

Willie spat some imaginary chaw toward the crumbling structure, just missing the abyssal hole. "Nawp, it was his sister he threw down there. And it was a Compson. Quentin, I think was his name." He spied the twins looking at each other nervously as he spoke, so close to a possible murder scene complete with skeletal remains.

"Is that true? Someone died in there?"

"I swear it. It was in all the papers back before we were born. Everyone in town knew about it."

Darl inched toward the circle of brown brick and broken mortar, trying to sneak a glimpse of a bone sticking up. "How far down you reckon it goes?"

Johnny Ray shrugged. "Fifty feet. A hundred. Who

knows?"

"Yeah, you sure don't," Willie taunted.

"Hey, I know I can kick your ass, *Willie Nillie*."

"Shhh! Did you hear it that time?"

"Hear what?"

Cash took a couple of steps back from the well. "Sounded like a voice. A woman's voice. Coming from there." He pointed a shaky finger toward the well and Darl also moved back.

"Man, you didn't hear anything, especially coming from inside that stupid waterin' hole."

Cash shook his head as he stared wide eyed and pointed again. "I heard it. Darl, let's get out of here."

As he turned to leave, Johnny Ray stepped in his path. "No one is leaving until somebody looks over the edge and proves they got hair on their chest." To show he wasn't kidding, Johnny Ray pushed Cash toward the maw. "Are you all chicken or something?"

"Why don't you look, Johnny Ray?"

"I already did when I found it out here in the woods. Wasn't scared a bit and I was all by myself."

Laughing like a drunkard, Willie dismissed the bold claim with a wave. "You are so full of it. I'll go look and then you can all cook me dinner and do my laundry like you're my maids, you sissies."

"Don't do it! Let's just get out of here. I heard a voice coming from the well. Twice. I ain't kidding."

"No Willie, let Cash look over the edge. Maybe he

can make out with his girlfriend at the bottom of the well." Johnny Ray laughed and made kissy faces at the younger boy. Willie followed suit, cackling as the twins looked more frightened by the minute.

"No way, let him go." Darl stepped to Johnny Ray but he pushed back hard and Darl landed flat on his butt.

The biggest of the boys had a slack grin on his face now. "Willie, make sure Darl doesn't try to save his brother again." Johnny Ray pushed Cash harder, nearly causing the boy to lose balance but he turned and stopped just short of a trip-ready brick hidden by leaves. His legs trembled and sweat covered his brow as he stood barely a foot away.

"Johnny Ray, please, I heard it. There's someone down there. Some *thing*, I swear. Don't make me look."

The pleading, however, fell on deaf ears. "I already told you, nobody leaves until you look over the edge. And it's starting to get dark. Better look already so you and Darl don't get grounded again for coming home late." Johnny Ray reached out slowly, putting his hand on the scared boy's shoulder, feeling the pushback. "Do it, wuss."

Cash started to kneel and Darl cried out, "What are you doing?" Willie occupied the space between them and threatened a kick, keeping Darl in the dirt several feet away from his brother.

"That's it. Just lean over and look down into the well for five seconds. You won't see nothing but a black hole and you'll feel foolish for being a scared little baby all this time."

Hesitantly, Cash reached a shaky hand for the rim of

the well. It felt loose, like the last hundred years had worn out the mud holding everything together. Cash bit his lip nervously and leaned down toward the mouth. The acrid air wafting up from the well assaulted his nostrils and reminded him of his uncle's waxen face just before the casket closed on it forever. From above, Johnny Ray cast a long shadow over him as the sun dipped below the skinny pines anxiously peering down around them.

"Go on, Cash. It's almost dark. Do it already while we can still see."

Darl tried to stand and Willie pushed him back down. "Cash?"

"I'm okay, Darl. It's just a crummy well. Ain't no such things as ghosts."

The closer Cash got to the well, the wider it seemed. Probably so wide, he couldn't reach across and touch the other side. His stomach turned like a washing machine inside him as he imagined himself falling in and down; forever falling, flailing into the grinning mouth of Hell. The more he waited, however, the scarier it got as light continued to fade away in the distance. *Just do it,* he thought. *It's not like someone's gonna reach up out of the well and pull me down in it. Right?* He inhaled deeply, counted to three, and forced his head right over the opening in front of him. The loose brick gave under his weight and fell forward into the well, making Cash lose his balance momentarily. He screamed, which caused the other boys to scream. Then he stopped, watching the brick trail off into the blackness beyond. No one breathed as they waited for what seemed like a full minute with no sound of the brick landing.

Finally, the boys heard the brick plop distantly into the dank water at the bottom of the well, immediately followed by a high pitched shrill like a thousand tomcats screeching at once. The pernicious scream echoed up from the depths, riding a geyser of foul and decrepit water gushing toward Cash's frozen face. He swore he saw two red eyes cresting atop the black jet just as Darl grabbed the back of his collar and pulled him away from the well as sludgy, brown water shot up over the bricks and cascaded down where the boys had just been standing. "Cash, let's go!"

Willie and Johnny Ray were already running as fast as they could out of the woods. The twin brothers followed suit, never once looking back as the banshee howl still rang in their ears. Cash knew if he looked back, a waterlogged corpse with red eyes would snatch him up and carry him down into the bottom of the well and he would never be heard from again. They all somehow knew it.

Not until the twins got home did they stop running, collapsing as soon as they closed the door and felt soft, incandescent light fall on their blowhard faces. Mother had just set the table and was walking toward the door to call them to dinner. One last shriek howled through the oncoming night, then died off like a dog bark as Mother shivered with a knowing fright as she looked out the window and locked the door.

The Bequest
by:
Kalila Smith

In spring of 1897, Clayton Montgomery ventured to New Orleans from Mobile, Alabama to take care of some unusual family business. A New Orleans attorney, Herbert Girard, had telegraphed Clayton several weeks prior, informing him that his uncle had left him a substantial estate in New Orleans. It was in fact, one of the most prestigious homes in the French Quarter; a large mansion on Rue Royale. Clayton thought it odd that he had been bequeathed property from an uncle he never knew, but nonetheless intrigued.

A handsome, successful man at thirty- three years old, Clayton had recently decided to settle down and marry twenty year old, Mattie Lawson. Mattie's father had been a business associate of Clayton's for many years. The house would make the ultimate wedding gift for his new bride. The couple planned for a large family and hoped to begin having children immediately. The lavish mansion would serve as the perfect place to raise a family. He anxiously waited in Mr. Girard's office to discuss the property.

"I never met him," Clayton said quietly, "I recall my mother mentioning that she had a much younger half-brother who lived in New Orleans, but she spoke very little of him. He wasn't much older than I."

"Your uncle had no living children of his own. He was the only child of your grandfather from his second marriage. It was your uncle's wish that in his absence, you, his only nephew, receive his property," Mr. Girard coldly stated.

"How did he die?" inquired Clayton.

"I beg your pardon?" responded Mr. Girard.

"I'm curious how a man of his age died, and with no other heirs," said Clayton, leaning forward in his chair.

"He didn't," responded Mr. Girard.

"I don't understand," Clayton muttered, "If he willed the property to me in the event of his death…"

"No one said that he died, Mr. Montgomery," Mr. Girard explained, "What I said was that he wished the property be granted to you in the event of his absence; but he is not dead. Your uncle has been committed to the state sanitarium. To put it bluntly, he went mad. I'm not at liberty to discuss the full nature of his condition with you. You would have to speak to his doctors at the state hospital."

Mr. Girard handed him a large envelope containing the paperwork and keys to the property. "I assume that, as you are not from the area, you are unaware of the history of the property. The house has had, let's just say, a fair share of misfortune associated with it," affirmed Mr. Girard, "Simply put, it's said to be haunted; cursed to be exact."

"I don't believe in ghosts or curses, Mr. Girard," laughed Clayton as he rose from his chair.

"Good luck, Mr. Montgomery," Mr. Girard replied morosely.

Clayton chuckled to himself as he left the office, "Ghosts and curses are the delusions of old men," he mumbled.

Clayton stepped onto the St. Charles Avenue streetcar, which took him to the French Quarter. He strolled leisurely down Rue Royale allowing his senses to take in all of what was the Vieux Carre'. The sound of music and aromas of exotic cuisine filled the air. He crossed Dumaine Street and noticed that it had become quieter. *This isn't so bad*, he thought, *it's just another neighborhood, just a bit more colorful.*

He arrived on the corner of Rue Royale and Governor Nicholls Streets and stared in awe at the gray stone mansion. "1140. This is it," he whispered to himself, "Well, you don't look so haunted to me."

Haunted or not, Clayton knew immediately that this house would fit perfectly into his future plans. As he wandered through the home, he found himself pleased at its exceptional condition, right down to the furniture left by his uncle. He gazed out of the back window to find that the courtyard area left a bit more to be desired. The courtyard garden had become overgrown with weeds. The second floor balcony seemed to be missing a few posts and the railing unstable. What formerly served as slave quarters, now boarded up, stood precariously, a dilapidated reminder of the past. "Ok, so you do need a bit of work," he mused.

He gazed out onto Governor Nicholls Street from the balcony. A woman stood across the street staring up at him. She appeared frightened. He smiled and waved to her. The woman gasped and quickly turned away hurrying down the street.

"Maybe you are haunted," he joked looking down at the shabby balcony.

Clayton secured the house and left through the courtyard doors. He saw a neighbor watching him through a window. As he stared back at her, she quickly drew the curtains shut. Apparently, Mr. Girard had not exaggerated. The beauty of the manor was tainted with rumors of ghosts and shadows that lurked in its majestic halls. The property acquired its reputation for ghosts after a grisly discovery in 1834. Earlier owners were believed to have tortured their slaves; committing unspeakable atrocities. Even though much time had passed since the incident took place, many locals still refused to walk on the same side of the street as the house. Whispers in the night spoke of screams and cries coming from within its dark corridors.

The property had been acquired in 1831 by a wealthy socialite and her surgeon husband. The good doctor and his wife maintained celebrity status amongst their peers throwing frequent lavish soirees. The most prominent and influential members of society were the usual guests at these events. The Madame gained more notoriety in the early months of 1834, when she was blamed for the death of young slave girl. She attended to the Madame as she prepared for one of her parties but displeased her while combing her hair, pulling a tangle.

The angry woman screamed at the child, chasing her about the mansion. In an attempt to escape the Madame's wrath, the girl ran out onto a small balcony that extended over the courtyard. The hysterical girl foolishly climbed onto the balcony railing and lost her footing. She fell to the courtyard below, dying instantly. Neighbors reported seeing the Madame standing on the balcony, bullwhip in her fist. The girl had been buried on the property. An investigation took place finding the couple guilty of mistreating their slaves. But, the incident was forgotten until April 10, 1834 when a fire broke out in the home revealing a darker secret.

During a party, the kitchen, located in the back of the property, caught fire. Black smoke billowed out of the building attracting the attention of neighbors and party guests alike. A curious mob gathered on the banquette across the street. Onlookers witnessed the fire brigade entering the property through the courtyard gates. After extinguishing the fire, they returned to the street with the frail body of an elderly slave woman found unconscious and chained to the stove in the kitchen. Upon being revived, the old woman directed authorities to an attic above the slave quarters. They found the attic door bolted and locked from the outside, but muffled screams could be heard within.

It took several tries with a battering ram to knock down the heavy oak door. When the door finally released, the putrid stench of death forced police and firemen to their knees vomiting. The attic room was filled with operating tables, medical implements and body parts in jars on shelves. Numerous slaves were chained to the walls, obvious victims of crude medical experiments. Their faces and bodies were maimed and mutilated. Those that were still alive were malnourished, scarred from beatings, and wore spiked collars allowing only minimal movement. The bodies of the dead as well as the survivors were removed from the property and medical attention given to the injured. The couple fled New Orleans to escape investigation as angry neighbors ransacked the house leaving nothing but bare walls within.

From that night on, residents of the French Quarter began calling the home "The Haunted House." Some swore they could hear screams echoing throughout its barren halls. The house remained vacant for over forty years. It then became a tenement, offering housing to poor Italian immigrants. One by one the families vacated the property, telling tales of shadowy figures walking the galleries. Some claimed to hear a young girl's scream in the courtyard late at night. Mutilated animals were often found in the courtyard.

In 1885, the house was purchased by an elderly man who died in the house five years later, adding to the myriad of ghostly inhabitants. He bequeathed the property to a trusted friend who had been the most recent owner, Clayton Montgomery's uncle. Locals believed that the house was not only haunted but cursed by the slaves who endured torture at the hands of the maniacal couple.

On June 16, Clayton and Mattie were wed in Mobile.

The Bequest

Young Mattie made a beautiful bride in a silk and lace wedding gown and a long veil that fell perfectly over her golden curls. Her blue eyes shone brightly that day in anticipation of her new life with her husband. Shortly after a honeymoon in Niagara Falls, the couple set off to their new home in New Orleans.

"I can hardly wait for you to see it, Mattie, it's quite a spectacular manor," boasted Clayton.

"I'm sure it is," giggled Mattie, "since you are moving me all the way to New Orleans and away from my family."

"It'll be worth it, I promise," he vowed, "Now some of it does need a bit of work, but we can handle it."

Mattie smiled, "I'm sure I'll love it."

For the first several months, the couple enjoyed their new home. They walked about the square and shopped at the market on Saturdays. They attended the opera and the theatre in the evenings. Once the newlyweds had settled in things changed. Clayton began to spend more time away on business leaving Mattie home alone. She sometimes heard footsteps on the stairs and the sounds of doors slamming. Often believing it Clayton returning, she'd race out into the hallway to find no one there. Late at night, she'd awaken to voices whispering and what sounded like a young girl crying outside. She would walk out onto the balcony and see nothing. *It's only the wind,* she thought.

One night during a thunderstorm, she noticed something moving outside of a window. Mattie stopped and stared at the window. Nothing happened. As she walked away, she again saw something move. She tiptoed to the window and pressed her face against the glass peering out into the darkness. Suddenly, a large shadowy figure of a man appeared, glaring back at her. His dark face covered with blood and chains across his massive chest. She screamed and turned away. When she finally gained the courage to look again, the figure had vanished. From that point on, she kept the heavy drapes drawn tight in the evenings and ignored sounds of the night. Clayton convinced her that she had a vivid imagination spawned by superstition and rumors in the neighborhood.

He consoled her, "The only phantoms here are the ones in your mind, Darling. You must ignore it and you'll see that it will go away."

Mattie spent a lot of time in the garden area, removing dead weeds and replacing them with beautiful flowering plants. Across the back row, she planted four white crepe myrtle saplings. She closed her eyes and envisioned the trees in full bloom. A smile ran across her face. Her moment of bliss was short lived, as a loud thump coming from the slave quarters startled her. Alone in the courtyard she heard something inside, a dragging sound, as if someone moving furniture. Then, again, a loud thump reverberated from the boarded rooms. She felt that something was staring at her through the boards, waiting and watching. Too afraid that she might see something awful, she didn't dare look inside.

In October, Mattie announced that the couple would be expecting their first child. Mattie's fears were set aside as she focused her thoughts on her baby. Clayton hired a woman to help Mattie with the house and garden and keep her company. Ophelia Jackson was a widow in need of a job. She moved into one of the guest rooms. Ophelia had heard the rumors of ghosts in the house, but didn't believe them.

Life became calm and happy for Mattie and Clayton as they awaited the birth of their child. It was then that Clayton received word that his uncle had taken his own life in the mental asylum. He felt guilty that he had never attempted to visit him, and ask questions about the house. "What did it matter, anyway?" he rationalized, "He obviously had been very sick."

As Mattie decorated the nursery one afternoon, she was startled by a woman dressed in a long black dress. The woman appeared in the doorway of the nursery, then darted down the hallway when Mattie noticed her. Mattie ran out behind her only to find nothing. As her pregnancy advanced, Mattie grew more and more anxious. She would pace the floors alone at night clutching her belly. "I won't let anyone hurt you," she would tell her unborn child.

Ophelia woke one night to find Mattie wandering aimlessly in the hallway mumbling about a woman in black. She tried to walk Mattie back to her room but she became hysterical. Mattie pushed her away, screaming at her. "I won't let you hurt my baby!" she cried.

"You're having a dream, Miss Mattie," Ophelia assured her.

But, Mattie would not be consoled. She fell to the floor

crying and screaming. Ophelia left her there, only to find her asleep on the floor the next morning. "You poor child, it was just a terrible nightmare," Ophelia told her as she helped her up in the morning.

"That woman," Mattie explained, "She's trying to hurt my baby."

"No, no," Ophelia said, "I tried to wake you but you were walking in your sleep, there's no one here that wants to hurt you or the baby."

Exhausted, Mattie staggered to bed still mumbling about the woman she feared.

On April 10, Mattie began to feel the pangs of childbirth and told Clayton to bring the doctor. Clayton stood outside the door of the bedroom feeling helpless as his young wife screamed in pain. He waited impatiently to hear the cry of his newborn child but instead a dead silence befell the house. Ophelia raced from the room, her hands covering her face. The doctor emerged from the room shaking his head quietly, a small, blanketed bundle in his arms, "I'm sorry, it was stillborn. I did all that I could do, Clayton, sometimes it's just God's will."

Clayton trembled as he stared blankly at the doctor. He heard the muffled sounds of Mattie's sobs. Several days later, the couple buried their son. From that day on, Mattie grew more and more hysterical. She ran through the house in the middle of night crying and screaming. "It's this place," she'd cry, "It's her place, that evil woman."

One night, while Clayton was away, Mattie awakened

to the sounds of a baby crying. She ran out of her room and watched in horror as the woman in black wandered down the hallway with a baby in her arms. "My baby! Give me my back my baby!" she screamed. The woman laughed and ran down the darkened hallway. The baby cried helplessly.

Ophelia rushed out of her room and saw Mattie standing there screaming hysterically. "Who are you talking to?" she asked as she attempted to calm Mattie.

"That woman, that evil woman, she's here, and she has my baby," Mattie exclaimed as she pulled away from Ophelia then ran down the hallway.

She ran out onto the rounded balcony that extended over the courtyard. "Where did you go?" she cried as she reached out over the railing. Suddenly, something grabbed her arm from out of thin air. It pulled her further and further over the railing. Her other hand grabbed the railing as she fought against the force that was pulling her forward. Unable to maintain a grip on the rickety railing, Mattie's frail body flipped over the top and down to the courtyard. Ophelia ran out onto the balcony just to see Mattie hurling over the edge. "Mattie! No!" she screamed.

Mattie's bloodcurdling scream as she plummeted to her death could be heard blocks away. Ophelia sent for Clayton and explained to him what happened. "She kept babbling about this house; a woman. Losing the baby was too much for her. I tried to stop her but it was too late," she cried.

After Mattie's death, Clayton lost all interest in life. Ophelia went to stay with her family and Clayton was left alone with nothing but his memories. The garden Mattie loved so much had fallen into ruin as Clayton spent most of his time and money in gambling houses, saloons, and brothels. Convinced that he would never recover from the loss of his beautiful Mattie and their child, he lived a reckless, risk-taking life. Late in the night, he would hear the howls and screams of the ghosts in the house. He heard the baby's cries. He drank whiskey to drown out the sounds until he passed out, no longer paying attention to the woeful moans. He no longer believed Mattie had been mad.

One evening as Clayton staggered home from a saloon, he saw a woman standing in the shadows on the side of his home. He darted around the corner and grabbed her by the arm, "Who are you?" he demanded, "Why are you spying on me?"

The woman gently pulled her arm from his grip. She smiled and introduced herself as Delima. "I saw you several times, at the saloon. You seem so lonely, so I followed you."

Clayton looked at her suspiciously but couldn't help notice how attractive she was. Her lustrous long black hair, her pale, flawless, porcelain skin, and her perfume intoxicated him. She stared back with large, ebony eyes into his. He had been very lonely since he'd lost Mattie. Perhaps it would be nice to have some company for a change. He invited her in for a brandy. The two spent the next couple of hours talking. They drank brandy until Clayton could barely stand. The last thing he remembered was the dark haired beauty helping him up the stairs, and into the master bedroom.

Clayton awoke the next morning with a horrible headache. He reached out toward the other side of the bed, only to find that there no one there. Realizing he was alone, he walked about the house calling out to the woman he remembered from the night before but she had gone leaving only the faint smell of her perfume. He wondered if he had merely dreamt of her. *But then how could your perfume still linger?* He wondered.

He spent the next several evenings looking for the mysterious woman. He went from one saloon to the next, retracing his steps from the night that he had met her. She was nowhere to be found. As he walked down to his office on Canal Street one day, he caught a glimpse of her on the corner across the street. She turned and whisked down the side street. He raced across the intersection in an attempt to catch her but had vanished. Perhaps she had been nothing more than a dream, a longing brought about by his loneliness. He spent hours thinking of her, the way she smiled, the smell of her perfume that permeated the house the next day. He longed to see her again.

His mind became consumed with thoughts of her. She appeared to him only in his dreams, yet when he awoke to the smell of her perfume again, he began to wonder if he too was now going mad. He decided that it might be best if he sold the house and moved away from New Orleans. Perhaps this would save what little sanity he had left. He began to make arrangements to sell the house.

Clayton spent the next several weeks cleaning the house

and the garden. He decided it was time that something must be done to the slave quarters. They had been boarded up for so many years. He pulled the boards off the windows and the doors on each floor. The rooms were musty and full of dust but empty.

Clayton set out on the tedious task of renovating each floor into lavish apartments. While working on the third floor room, he noticed a few loose floor boards beneath him. The boards were rotted and falling apart so he decided to replace them. He got a crow bar and began pulling up the loose boards. He yanked the first board loose.

The rotted wood broke into small pieces. There was something under the boards, something white. A peculiar odor emitted from beneath the floor. He gagged and coughed raising the crow bar above his head. Sweat poured from his brow as he struck the floor boards again and again. Dust and splintered wood blew up into his face. He feverishly ripped up the boards exposing the remnants from an earlier time when the deranged socialites tortured their slaves. He dropped the crow bar and fell to his knees, retching at the sight of what remained of those poor souls buried beneath the floor. "Monsters!" he gasped.

He composed himself, staggering out to the street. By the time he reached the police station on Royal Street, he could barely stand from the shock.

Later that day, Clayton watched nervously as authorities removed the skeletal remains from the subfloor. He could have sworn he saw streams of white mist rising and fading off into the sky. *Maybe now,* he thought, *the ghosts of Rue Royale will be put to rest.* He decided to go out for a drink to calm his nerves.

When Clayton arrived home that night, as he stepped up to the front door, he became aware of a familiar scent. Suddenly, something touched him on the shoulder. He jumped and turned to see Delima standing at the front entrance. She smiled coyly and walked toward him. "Aren't you going to invite me in," she asked.

"Where have you been?" He asked, "You left without a word, I looked all over for you…"

"Shhh… " she said putting her finger to his lips. "I'm here now, isn't that all that matters?"

She followed him into the parlor. Clayton poured them both a brandy.

"You have no idea what I've been through today. While I was pulling up a floor, I made a horrible discovery," he told her.

"It's all right now," she said coldly.

"No, I don't think you understand," he attempted to explain, "In fact, perhaps it would be better if you come back another time. I have had quite a frightful experience today," he resolved. Delima smiled, "If you insist," she said.

He stood to walk her to the door. She playfully pulled away from him running up the stairs. "Catch me if you can," she giggled.

"No, this is not the time," he demanded as he followed her.

Clayton stood in the dark, calling out to her. He

wondered how she could be so callous. Could she not see his distress? Perhaps he had not been clear enough. He saw her shadow on the balcony. She laughed out loud.

"Come inside and I will walk you to the door," he offered.

But, she ignored his plea. "Come and get me," Delima dared as she loosened her bodice. She slowly moved towards him seductively. Clayton gazed into her eyes becoming more and more intoxicated from her perfume. She leaned into him, pressing her lips against his. He kissed her passionately, pulling her closer.

Suddenly, something didn't feel right. The sensuous scent of her perfume turned into the putrid stench of rotted flesh. He pushed away from her quickly. He gazed down not at a beautiful face but a decayed corpse. The ghastly specter moved towards him as maggots spewed from its mouth. He gagged as he backed into the balcony railing, feeling it rock from the weight.

The horrid creature howled and cackled as he leaned further back. The last sounds he heard were the cracking of wood and his own scream before hurling downward to the courtyard. His lifeless body lay in the very spot where his beloved Mattie had fallen.

Two weeks later Michelle Montgomery Taylor and her husband John Taylor sat in the office of Herbert Girard. "I'm very sorry for your loss, Mrs. Taylor," he announced as he handed her a large envelope with the address 1140 Rue Royale written onto it, "It was quite a tragedy. It was Mr.

Montgomery's wish to bequeath his property to you, his only living relative."

The bereaved woman took the envelope and quietly exited the office.

A short while later, Michelle and her husband solemnly unlocked the front door. They slowly strolled around the parlor sadly gazing at the furnishings. Michele paused. Her eyes darted about the room. A strange expression ran across her face.

John took her gently by the arm. "I know how hard this has been on you," he acknowledged, "Maybe it would be best if we waited a bit to deal with this."

"Yes," she asserted, "you're probably right."

The couple exited the parlor. As they crossed the threshold of the large white door, Michelle paused again looking back into the parlor.

"Is something wrong, dear," asked John Taylor.

"For a moment I smelled something. Perfume, I think, then it was gone," she responded, "I'm sure it's nothing."

The Cleansing
by:
Miguel L. Viscarra

It is no secret that fury, vehemence and cruelty are well-acquainted bedfellows. They are frequently restricted to an endless spiral of contention that reproduces itself repeatedly and indiscriminately. Acts of explicit disregard and harm do nothing more than breed increased disdain. Nowhere is this more evident than in the contemporary system of corrections, which serves as a revolving door of social deviance. "Cleansing" society of its most repressive criminals and quarantining them, essentially births a great deal of hatred and resentment for the establishment. In this way, it's no wonder things got so severely out of hand. For all intents and purposes, those dilapidated brick walls housed a breeding ground for discord and rage.

Saúl had been lying lifeless in that same old bed every single morning since before even he could remember. He probably wouldn't even have had changed the satin sheets if he could have still smelled her on them. Interestingly, he still only slept on that one side of the bed, which is exactly where you'd expect to find him on a morning such as this. Saúl had recently been contracted by the New Mexico Department of Corrections to be a member of a group of familiar "experts" assigned to the examination of the famed Penitentiary of New Mexico. Unsure of the reasoning behind such a request, he assumed that the state was looking into reopening the hollowed facility, as local prisons were becoming exceedingly overcrowded.

Although, Saúl was definitely a social skeptic, and he wasn't blindly going to accept the guise that this controversial decision wasn't just another chess move for legislative and political gain. An envelope lay on the nightstand near a pack of cigarettes and a half-empty glass of whisky. Saúl was thrilled to receive the urgent envelope, which enclosed the state's letterhead on a quite private note that inflated his ego rather nicely.

Relatively familiar with the prison, Saúl had previously worked as the institution's preacher for about twelve years. Having an extensive and multidenominational religious education, he served to a wide variety of diverse prisoners in the facility's Catholic and Protestant chapels respectively. It wasn't until he met his match that it all came to a crashing, yet romantic end.

After finishing Seminary School in another state, apparently still his claim to fame, Saúl moved back to New Mexico, which is where he'd called home for a great deal of his life. He moved around a lot; staying extendedly across the state in Albuquerque, Alamogordo, Carlsbad and Las

Cruces. However, that nomadic existence didn't last for long, as he eventually met a girl that changed his entire life.

There it is; that sappy tale of emotional self-actualization. Not to sound cliché, but in retrospect, he should have listened to his jaded preconceived notions of adoration. Perhaps he should have been a bit wearier, but they were "in love."

***

December

Thinking about that now, it turned his stomach to think he played into that timeless fairytale. Emily wasn't like any other girl. There was something in the way she talked that kept his thoughtless eyes firmly entranced with the feminine lips from which poetry poured. They could lie around for hours enjoying one another's company and the most unnoticed of daily beauties, but still, none compared to her. Those days, nothing ever quite did. He soon gave up all hope of a religious career after he met his inspiration.

Realistically, Clerical Celibacy wasn't something he saw in his future, especially considering he'd just met the women he wanted to spend the rest of his life with. However, it seemed as though all his motivation had left with the wicked.

He couldn't even bring himself to get out of bed at times, but a visit to where they'd first met held great promise; promise that was nothing like those intangible ties that once decayed with age. Moreover, as the telephone wasn't exactly ringing off the hook with job offers and opportunities for the forgotten, Saúl jumped at the unique chance to explore what many reference as one of the most notorious prisons in the United States of America.

The envelope, from which the letter came, also enclosed a few thorough dossiers regarding the other diverse individuals that Saúl would be working alongside. After previously taking the pages from the manila envelope and examining the credentials of his coworkers, he found that their backgrounds and qualifications were actually quite impressive.

Claire Miller was a world-renowned photographer and journalist with an affinity for the supernatural. He recognized her name but was shocked to find out that he'd be working with an actual celebrity. She'd covered so many well-documented hauntings in countless supernatural publications. Many of her photographs could be seen exploiting some of the latest and greatest of classic and contemporary supernatural hoaxes and haunts, and Saúl couldn't wait to see what she had planned for the penitentiary. Admittedly, he was quite the fan of her extraordinary wealth of work.

Saúl also recalled the name Lee Adams from local political slogans and signs posted across the Southwestern landscape. He wasn't much for politics, but hearing political controversy is relatively unavoidable when morality and humanity are trumped by selfish ideology. In this state, Lee Adams, was a household name. He was a well-known politician with a degree in criminal justice and a history of judicial prosecutions for the state. If anyone knew why New

Mexico wanted the infamous prison reopened, it was surely a big city politician like Lee Adams who demanded such.

Restless, Saúl was cursed with another sleepless night. He desired so badly to be rested enough for his return to the Penitentiary of New Mexico, but the nightmares consumed him once again. As the hands of the clock moved progressively about its face, Saúl's thoughts were an amalgamation of unconscious longing and an insatiable wanting that would remain forever unfulfilled. Lying in an unpredictable slumber, Saúl envisioned a dark hallway lined with bars. The only source of light emanated from a distant room at the end of the hall.

Confused and frightened, Saúl could see flaming silhouettes accompanied by the haunting crackle of scorching embers. As his vision stabilized, he realized that he was outstretched and crawling on the floor. Saúl was completely unaware of his enshrouded pursuer, but he certainly knew the beautiful woman at the end of the hallway.

Often times, he knew her better than she even knew herself. Their eyes met as the woman entered the hall from the room directly in front of the inferno. The flames danced on her red dress like a fateful premonition of things to come. Although he was unaware of his destination's origin, Saúl knew he wanted to save her; to rescue the poor girl from herself. Horrified, he looked on as the fire inched from the room toward the woman.

As the lacy ribbons of her shoes caught fire, the woman outstretched her arm toward the fallen Saúl. He stared in utter shock as the familiar face called out his name with her final breath. Saúl could do nothing but watch intently as the woman's crimson gown went up in flames. As he closed his eyes to hide the fiery massacre before him, Saúl awoke sweating profusely in his own bed.

Wiping the perspiration onto his damp pillow cases, Saúl gazed angrily at the blaring alarm clock. This wasn't the first time the beautiful phantom had woke him at this hour. For him, these sorts of night terrors were a frequent occurrence. Having just seen an effigy of his undying love burn before his eyes, Saúl was reluctant to reach for the pack of smokes he knew Emily had hid in the drawer of the nightstand. As he lit the end of the final cigarette in the forsaken pack, he tasted regret and the carcinogens that would surely cause a toxic headache in the minutes that followed.

With the room filled with smoke, Saúl arose from his bed as the cigarette burnt out completely and not a second sooner. The bed sheets fell gently to the floor as the smoke began to dissipate from the room. Naked, Saúl took the envelope from the nightstand and read the details of the letter once more. In addition to calling for an early departure, the letter instructed Saúl to meet with the remainder of the exploration group promptly at noon on February 2nd. Knowing full well that today was the day; the 31st anniversary of the prison riots, he would have to leave soon if he wanted to arrive on time, especially considering that the facility was nearly four hours away from his hometown of Alamogordo, New Mexico.

He'd wasted far too much time as it was, therefore Saúl

started to gather the various items he required for the trip. Collecting a large notebook and ball-point pen from the nightstand, he compiled the necessities near the front door, which is where he'd also found his jacket, digital camera and car keys. As he stepped into the shower to cleanse for the journey ahead, Saúl could only hope to set aside his nightmarish trauma and past in the facility for the sake of the exploration at hand. He was already under enough pressure without having to deal with the memories that plagued.

With his foot heavy on the gas pedal, Saúl sped past the scenery that he'd become so familiar with over the many years he lived in the state. The environment around Interstate 25 was a blur of cacti, yucca, mountains and sand that seemed endless. It was as if civilization was strategically plotted in 30-minute intervals with nothingness in-between. In the previous three hours, Saúl had already traveled past Carrizozo, San Antonio, and Socorro. Albuquerque was the only populated landmark left to be conquered.

Closer to Santa Fe, the anticipated destination was located about an hour after Albuquerque, and Saúl wanted to knock-out that portion of the drive as fast as possible. The anticipation was killing him, as he'd been preparing for this day since originally receiving the envelope weeks ago. Saúl hadn't found fulfilling work since the prison closed. He spent the majority of his time working in local churches across the state, though he was surprised the diocese even allowed him to do that. A great deal of Saúl's life after presiding at the penitentiary was spent away from the religious identity he once held so dear.

While working at the prison Saúl met a woman that would completely change his life, including the celibate lifestyle he led. Prior to meeting the prison's counselor, he hadn't really taken much interest in any of the females he'd come into contact with. Saúl certainly never thought he'd find Emily; the one he wanted to build a life with. Having survived the riots, there was absolutely nothing holding Saúl back from straying from his position in the church and starting a life with Emily. Thus, he left the religious institution for hopes of a loving longevity.

As Saúl sped out of Albuquerque, he realized that he was mere moments from stepping foot into a nostalgic past. Was he even ready for this? He arrived at the gates of the devastated prison around 11:45. Thankfully, he wasn't a moment later, as a large row of cars was already lined up outside of the prison's first tower.

After Saúl parked his car in an empty spot along the fence, he saw a cluster of people starting to gather near the most ridiculously flashy limousines that now blocked many of the vehicles Saúl had passed. A tall man in a black pea coat stood outside the limo door surveying the crowd as if counting heads. Saúl joined the crowd before the man as the clock struck twelve.

"Thank you all for coming today, and welcome to the Penitentiary of New Mexico," the man said. "I'm sure many of you are wondering why you've been asked to participate in this important overnight expedition, but I hope you'll understand the degree of privacy and anonymity involved. All I can tell you is that we are looking into reopening the facility, but we are unable to do so without a thorough investigation into the functionality of the premises. Many of you have been employed here over the years, yet some of you are new faces to this area. We collected a great group of investigators with diverse backgrounds specific to this task," continued the gentleman.

"Five teams of three will be strategically placed throughout the prison. Considering the establishment's size, I'd expect none of you to run into any other teams inside. So, you will have complete privacy to search throughout your designated area at will. It's your overall goal to report your findings back to me, which will be taken into consideration when reopening or demolishing the prison. Now, who would like to hear about the prison riots?"

***

The NM Riots

"On February 2nd, 1980, the Penitentiary of New Mexico had been overtaken by a percentage of the 1,157 male inmates that were held within," the man began. "These various criminals ranged from child molesters and rapists to thieves and murderers. Knowing that there were theoretical holes in the institution, such as the negligence in not using a standard riot grill, many prisoners saw an opportunity to leave a lasting impression on the society that discarded them to the confines of this place. Guards were overpowered by prisoners during a typical and routine inspection, which resulted in them acquiring the many keys to the prison. Twelve of these guards were held captive and tortured to an inhuman degree."

"In addition to being sodomized violently by numerous prisoners, the majority of captive officers were stabbed and beaten within inches of their lives. However, it's important to recall that not all of these captors behaved so monstrously, as many of them came to the aide of the officers and even protected them from the more vile criminals," the man reassured.

After quickly drinking from a water bottle, the man continued, "The deaths in this place included, but were not limited to, burning, asphyxiation, carbon monoxide poisoning, drug overdoses, hanging, decapitation and more. It wasn't until the inmates reached the sex offenders in Cell Block 4 that the real inferno started. After stealing acetylene torches left by construction workers from the bowels of the prison, the inmates flooded Cell Block 4 with intentions of destruction. They used the flaming torches to burn through the many cell bars to get to the prisoners inside. Once inside, those criminals were burned alive and tortured by the same men they saw day in and day out. Thirteen inmates were murdered violently in Cell Block 4, and to this day, the charred stains of burnt flesh and bone cannot be removed from the prison floor."

"Death and violence were rampant throughout the

prison. The violence was not merely confined to Cell Block 4, as the gym, southwest wing, administration wing, towers, and control center also saw great carnage. Technically, it was the gymnasium and the piled bodies that endured the greatest of fires. Though all twelve imprisoned guards survived, the riots here left ninety inmates injured and thirty-three dead. The riots continued throughout the night, though many prisoners had escaped to the prison's outer walls by this time. The facility was not retaken by authorities until 1:30 p.m. on February 3rd, 1980," the gentleman concluded.

After leaving such an ominous impression, the mystery man left the group to get acquainted with one another and start heading into the hollowed and war-torn prison. A slender, blonde woman with a professional-grade photography camera approached Saúl and said, "Are you Saúl?"

"Yes," he quickly answered. "You must be Claire. I'm a big fan of your work, and it's going to be a pleasure working with you today," he said.

Smiling, Claire thanked him for his kind words and looked around for the third member of their party. The familiar politician approached from behind Claire and Saúl with three sleeping bags, blankets, and a briefcase in hand that looked similar to those being carried by certain members of the other various expedition groups. As Saúl looked around, he noticed that many of the teams found flashlights and other equipment within.

"I brought these for you two," Lee said as he shook their hands. He continued, "With all the holes in that prison's walls, we're going to need to keep as warm as possible tonight."

Admittedly, this sort of caring expression was not what Saúl or Claire expected from such a local celebrity, but they decided to just go along with the many pleasantries being thrown their way. Taking cues from the other four entering groups, Saúl, Claire and Lee thought it appropriate to get their investigation underway. They were all very eager to get inside the prison, as their group had been entrusted with looking over the famed, Cell Block 4.

Staring up toward the prison's Tower 1, the group passed through the fence by removing one of the graffiti-laden boards entwined in front of a large, gaping hole. Saúl could recall passing that same watchtower every morning that he drove to work at the prison. He'd always wave at the armed guards as they kept watch over the yard and outer walls of the penitentiary, though he couldn't really remember any of their respective names.

A threadbare rope, which was thrown neatly over the handrails of the tower, swung in the breeze as Saúl and his companions walked slowly toward the entrance of the facility. Had the group been at a different vantage point, they would have been able to see exactly why the old rope was hung in the first place. During the riots at the prison, a man was dragged from the burning institution and strung up by other prisoners. Left for dead, his body remained there until the authorities were able to safely take him down in the early hours of February 3rd. What Saúl, Lee, and Claire failed to see was the entombed spirit that hung watching their every move, for it wasn't merely the wind that was keeping the rope in motion.

For one reason or another, the ripped orange jumpsuit that clothed the bloody prisoner was not as apparent as one might think. The inmate, whose neck had clearly been broken from the fall, watched eerily with his head slightly cocked to the side to account for the bone that protruded from his collar. With shoulder-length hair blowing in the wind, his blood-stained face let out an uncomfortable smile as the three investigators left his sight.

Saúl's envelope contained a master key to the penitentiary. The letter mentioned that it would be adequate for opening all of the doors within the gouged facility, and Claire was quick to use it in order to get into the building's main corridor and administration wing. Upon entering the prison, Claire began snapping pictures of all the worn scenery.

The walls were encrusted with black soot that was reminiscent of the fires that burned steadily during the riots, and every countertop, desk, and table was covered in a thick layer of dust. "This is better than I ever could have hoped for," Claire proclaimed. "I assumed this all would have been cleaned up by now," she continued.

Claire had made a life of taking risks and photographing some of the most interesting and dangerous situations and places. Her prestigious background had taken her across state lines to controversial areas where few dared to tread, but she had a special affinity for the aged ruin she saw in the remains of mayhem. As Claire photographed from almost every angle, Lee and Saúl looked through the various open office drawers overturning what few papers hadn't been burnt up in the fires.

Amongst the many forms and operation manuals, the two also found an array of handcuffs, shackles, and other tools of the trade. Saúl picked up a page that was scattered on the administration counter, as he wanted to commemorate being thrust back into his old life. He longed for the memories forged then, and not a day passed without wishing for their triumphant return. The page was a roster of the facility's employees back in the 80s, and there was one particular picture that brought him great solace, especially considering that he hadn't seen her in what seemed like a lifetime.

Claire's camera eventually came to focus on Lee, who at the time, was also collecting assorted papers and placing them into his Halliburton briefcase. She snapped a few shots of his intrigued face as he collected the pages, but she couldn't think of any logical reason for him to take such keepsakes.

Collectively, the group decided to move on to the control room that was located next to the administration wing. This is where the normal, day-to-day operation of the facility was overseen, but it was also the initial site of the inmate takeover. At the start of the riots, two officers were held up in the control center, which was enclosed by what was thought to be impenetrable glass. The two refused to comply with inmate demands to open gates and bars that held their allies, which prompted swift and violent action from the assaulting prisoners.

Hitting the glass repeatedly from the outside with various tools and fire extinguishers, the inmates broke through and acquired the institution's various keys. The two guards managed to escape just in time, as the control room's locks were under construction, which was also the case with much of the ill-prepared facility. Claire photographed the broken television monitors and glass that lined the prison's control center, while Saúl and Lee milled about the toppled chairs and broken computers. "I think this is a great place to set up camp for the evening," said Lee. "We can see all around us in this room, and with the multiple levels, we'll each have a lot of privacy and space to ourselves," he continued.

Saúl and Claire agreed with the state politician and decided to figure out the specifics of their sleeping arrangements.

The group's primary exploration and entry into the Penitentiary of New Mexico had taken up some time, as the three were very careful to put great effort into their photographs. In addition to the bright flashes of Claire's professional photography, the gentlemen had also brought their own cameras that were capturing their dark and frightening environment. Between the administration wing and the control center, the three had been unearthing the prison's past for hours, and they could see that night was upon them through the windows in the front offices.

They wanted to continue exploring the grounds, but as

they were the first to enter in a while, special daylight safety precautions were to be taken. Thus, the group decided not to venture further and just chronicle their exploration of Cell Block 4 the next day.

Saúl and Claire hadn't really planned for the evening, so they were especially thankful that Lee had brought them sleeping bags to sleep in for the night. Had he not done so, they literally would have been left out in the cold.

While Claire and Lee slept soundly on the upper tiers of the control room, Saúl chose the bottom portion of the room. For the most part, he just laid around and stared at the smoke-darkened ceiling while the other two slept. However, the night's many unsettling sounds and noises ultimately soothed Saúl into a chaotic sleep.

Two old office chairs sat near the door where Saúl found his rest. Originally, they were faced outward toward the window that overlooked a large portion of the penitentiary. Unbeknownst to the sleeping Saúl, one of the chairs slowly creaked and turned to face his direction. As the chair turned over and fell loudly to the ground, he awoke to recognize a familiar feminine laugh.

As Saúl looked lazily toward the door, he saw the faint exit of a red dress. He looked around to see if Claire and Lee had heard the chair fall, but both of them were still sleeping soundly. As he widened his eyes, Saúl quietly got up from the floor in pursuit of the familiar female. "Emily," he whispered as he entered the hallway leading toward the penitentiary's cell blocks.

The Cleansing

In the distance, Saúl could see a woman running through the open gates that once separated the many cell blocks from the joining hallway. He called out Emily's name louder as he continued down the hallway toward the escaping phantom, but she did not hear his attempts and turned left at the end of the hallway. Saúl knew this would lead the woman directly into the famed Cell Block 4, but he was not reluctant to follow her even to the ends of the earth. As the pursuing Saúl reached the end of the hallway, he turned to discover that the fleeing woman was nowhere to be found.

***

Cell Block 4

Cell Block 4, like many of the other cell blocks, had a long corridor that began with a few shower areas and continued to include 15 cells on each side. Upon first glance, the entire room was completely shrouded in darkness, but it didn't take long for a sole light bulb to illuminate at the far end of the room. As the light flickered on and off, Saúl entered the room calling out to the woman that led him there.

The shower areas on either side of the room were dark and damp. As Saúl walked by these showers, the terrible odor of mildew and rot permeated his nostrils, but nothing would stop him from finding out if Emily was one of the former employees also chosen to take part in this opportunity. He continued down the corridor to the soundtrack of the breeze outside and water droplets from the various pipes that protruded from the shower walls.

He took careful notice to look inside each and every one of the cells in the block as he passed in front of them. All of them were wide open, and the bars had even been completely ripped off of a few. Fearful, Saúl continued onward, since he really couldn't see anything in the individual cells. The small light at the end of the hallway provided only so much assistance.

Constantly turning his head to take in his surroundings, Saúl slowly lurched toward the final two lit cells. Looking left and right, he felt heartbroken to have found empty cages. The woman had vanished, but his attention was now drawn to the grotesque stain in the middle of the floor. The cement appeared dark and disturbingly discolored.

This is the place, Saúl thought to himself, *this has got to be where they burned those guys.*

Suddenly, the surrounding silence was broken by a woman's voice, which uttered something that had repeated over and over in Saul's nightmares. As if within inches of Saúl's ear, she calmly said, "I don't want to be here anymore."

***

Claire had woken up Lee after noticing that their comrade was missing from the penitentiary's control room. She quickly took a flashlight from the briefcase provided, handed a second flashlight to Lee, and they both started for the control room entrance. Together, the two searched the administration wing before getting lost in one of the cell blocks Saúl had passed on his way to Cell Block 4. Neither of them had taken the time to notice the number on the entrance, which would have saved them both a lot of grief.

"Do you smell smoke," asked Claire.

"Yeah, something in here is on fire," Lee answered. The two crept slowly into their chosen cell block.

The stench of burning filled the air, and it totally overpowered the smell of filth that emanated from the cell block's showers. Claire shined her flashlight into the cells on the right side of the room. For the most part, Lee kept to the other side of the room, so the two were able to effectively examine their surroundings.

Claire called out for Saúl, but her shouting remained unanswered. Lee mimicked her inquiries from the opposite side of the room, and his attempts also yielded futile results.

There came a ruckus from one of the cells on Claire's side of the corridor. As she lifted her flashlight to illuminate the cell number on the wall, the number 23 quickly came into full view. There was a brown boot in the center of the holding cell, and Claire could see that the laces had been removed. Lee noticed Claire inquiring closer and asked, "What do you see?"

"There's something hanging in here," she whispered softly.

As Claire lifted her arm to raise the flashlight, she was horrified to take notice of the holding pen's wretched history. There was a hanging in Cell 23 during the 1980 riots. A few of the raging inmates didn't take kindly to the imprisoned, and they took great pleasure in the ridicule, torture, and eventual death they gave in the only sanctuary the prisoner had known in decades. His only safe haven had been transformed into a violent tomb that would keep his soul trapped forever in a repetitive loop of unwanted sorrow and self-inflicted torment.

Claire came to find that the boot had fallen from the still corpse that hung from the pen's ceiling. Upon closer examination, she noticed that the unresponsive body was actually hanging from the laces that had been stripped from its attire. There was a fire burning within Claire. She couldn't believe what she was seeing, and she wanted Lee to reaffirm her visions so badly. The only response she could muster was to blink her eyes repetitively with her mouth agape.

The small circle of light that emanated from the flashlight flickered and moved frantically about the specter, but Claire and Lee could see clearly that the figure had opened its bloodshot eyes and was staring directly at them. "Are you seeing this," screamed Claire.

Horrified, Lee didn't even bother to answer her confused question. He couldn't grasp what was going on in front of him, and all he wanted to do was run away as fast as he possibly could. With Claire left unanswered, the decrepit prisoner turned his attention to the quiet and shaking politician. The carcass opened its sealed lips for the first time in ages, which the two onlookers could see from the slow and stuttered attempt to speak. "You put me here," he quietly uttered with anger and malicious intent.

Suddenly, Lee's extremities felt completely limp. He tried fleetingly to move away from the horror, but something had immobilized him. "I can't move," he screamed, pleading to Claire for any help she could give. Claire watched frightened as Lee's facial expression turned to emptiness. Her screams echoed through the desolate institution, as the two men before her were now fixated in her direction. "What the hell are you doing?" Claire shouted as she felt Lee grab her arm.

The struggle continued as Lee inched Claire closer and closer to the smiling casualty that was now reaching for her with outstretched arms. She tried without success to release Lee's hold, but it was far too late. As Claire was only inches from the hanging corpse, it didn't take long for her to be within its clutches. With one final shove from Lee, Claire was pushed directly into the awaiting arms of the lamented menace. Her flashlight fell to the floor to brighten Lee's footsteps as he walked back down the cell block.

A cold darkness fell over the hanging inmate as he clung to Claire with great ferocity. She screamed loudly for help, but there wasn't anyone around to save her, especially since what little control Lee had was now consumed by the misery that festered in the hollowed prison.

Claire could feel the ghoul's supernatural grip tightening around her throat as she watched Lee fade from her sight. Claire shook violently with fear, which only fueled the maniacal laughter that poured from her rotting assailant.

The overwhelming sadness overtook Claire, and as her eyes filled with tears that eventually trickled down her cheek, she watched the flashlight flicker out beneath her.

***

The Reconciled Chapels

After hearing Emily's poignant and nonchalant murmur, Saúl left the darkened Cell Block 4 to further his search. Walking slowly in the dark, he heard Claire's screams from the distant cell block and feared for what had become of the woman that lead him away from the group. He found himself in an acquainted hallway that he'd traversed time and time again during his stint as the holy man at the prison. Saúl presided religiously over all the devout inmates in the institution, and he even had the opportunity to work in multiple chapels within the facility. For one reason or another, the Penitentiary of New Mexico provided not only a Catholic chapel for its inmates but also one for Protestants.

Interestingly, the two small churches were separated by a thick wall that mirrored the denominational blockade that existed to a greater extent socially. At one time, Saúl took great pride in the solace he and his teachings brought to those faithful prisoners.

He knew full-well that those imprisoned in the penitentiary often had a special connection with the divine. Saúl slowly opened the door to the Catholic chapel, but it immediately fell from its ragged hinges. As it fell to the floor and cracked into a multitude of pieces, he looked inside at his changed workplace. The walls of the chapel were covered in the same black soot that layered much of the prison.

The benches that Saúl recalled being filled at one time were toppled over and burnt. What few religious idols remained were cast aside and worn beyond recognition. Upon walking onto the altar, Saúl noticed that the wall between the chapels had been knocked down. The chaos that he could see in the other room mimicked that of the room he'd just stepped into.

Spinning in observant circles, Saúl was careful to take in his dark surroundings. The only light inside was from a breathtaking moon that shined brightly through the windows in the night sky.

Falling tearfully to his knees, Saúl remembered what he'd given all of that up for. He would forever remain confined in his own emotional prison by the female guard that taunted him day in and day out. He'd loved Emily but she never cared to love him back.

One day, the two lovers ventured into some cliché Texas town like they did whenever they became bored with the Southwestern countryside. He loved spending time with her. What time wasn't spent conversing over random happenings and local news was laced in silence - a silence that Saúl took as a common happiness. That day, he learned that every inkling of their love was nothing more than a convenient arrangement; an escape that would eventually leave Saúl begging for mercy and liberation from his own decaying heart.

Saúl pulled up to a rest stop so the two lovers could indulge in a cigarette. It was no secret that he didn't want to smoke anywhere near his new car, so the two walked off into the scorching desert. As Emily lit the cigarette in her mouth, Saúl coyly lowered his eyes and kicked a few small rocks into nearby cacti.

"We have got to talk," Emily started.

"What's on your mind," Saúl inquired intently.

The next few moments would change his life forever, as he never expected his inspiration to rip down all of the foundation they'd worked to build. Without missing a beat, Emily confessed that she wasn't happy with their arrangement anymore. She went on to list a variety of nonsensical reasons, none of which were anywhere near the reality or severity of causing such a departure.

Saúl tried so hard to hold back the tears, as he didn't want her to actually see how much he was being ripped apart from the inside. All he could do was turn to the car and walk back, hoping he'd wake up from whatever desert nightmare he'd just stepped into.

She watched him get into the car and dry his eyes with a tissue from the container in the backseat. Pain may not have been what she intended to inflict, but she hadn't really considered that the feelings building inside Saúl were the purest and sincerest of desire. As Emily got back into the car, she uttered the seven words that would open Saúl's emotional flood gates for years to follow. She grabbed his hand and said, "I don't want to be here anymore." He never wanted her to leave, and he surely never wanted to do anything to make her consider such a thing. However, shortly after this, the two never spoke again.

Saúl had spent far too much time rehashing that old memory in the burnt chapels, and he picked himself up off the floor to make a safe and speedy exit.

As he walked toward the fallen door from which he entered, Saúl stopped to smell the burning aroma that lingered in the air. Suddenly, he caught a glimpse of the woman he previously followed. She ran past the fallen door and back into the area housing the institution's many cell blocks. "Wait," he called out as he tripped over the door to chase her once more. "Please stop," he shouted as she got farther and farther away.

Again, the beautiful woman turned left and ran directly into Cell Block 4. Saúl quickly sped-up and watched as the woman ran right into an open cell on the right side of the corridor. The light at the end of the room flickered faintly, but it still did not offer enough light to irradiate the contents of the holding cell.

Scared but persistent, Saúl walked into the darkness only to hear the prison bars slam behind him. "Help," he screamed as a steady light turned on above him. "Someone let me out," he continued.

Looking around his surroundings, Saúl grabbed a sheet of dirty paper from the floor. In desperation, he took the pen he'd brought from his pocket and started etching a message for the woman that led him back into Cell Block 4. He considered that he was losing his mind, but he was willing to try anything just in case she returned.

He lifted his head to take in the sights and sounds around him, and saw a dark figure standing under the flickering light at the end of the corridor. Saúl noticed that the figure was substantially small in stature, but the decapitated head in his hand surely compensated for lost height. "Let me out of here," Saúl screamed at the man. "You've got to let me out of here," he pleaded.

The head squirmed in the inmate's hand but chose not to heed Saúl's mournful cries. As the figure turned and started to walk out of the cell block, the imprisoned Saúl called out one final time. "Please don't leave," he begged the inmate. Without a second thought, the prisoner turned and exited the room as Saúl climbed to his feet and clenched the cell bars tightly. He knew that something had to be done if he ever wanted to gaze upon the light of day again. In addition to the ominous scent of smoke that filled the air, Saúl could make out the hint of seared human flesh.

The smell of burning bodies emanated throughout his prison confines, and he could feel his stomach turn with every breath he inhaled. Unable to clearly decipher what was happening around him, Saúl was aware that only a few more hours remained before all the examining teams would leave this place and seal the doors shut behind them. He wondered if they too were experiencing these hellish visions and apparitions. Moreover, he found it exceedingly curious that he hadn't heard their voices or found evidence of their whereabouts during his panicked pursuit of the beautiful woman.

Feeling as though there was not a living soul to come to his aid, for the first time in a long time, Saúl remembered what it was like to be truly alone again. He hadn't felt such helplessness since the day Emily had left his side.

With dying hope, he whispered, "I don't want to be here anymore."

Bath 10
by:
J L Mulvihill

Hot Springs, Arkansas got a lot of history, especially in the old part of town where the government declared it a national park. Everybody knows it's the healing waters of natural hot springs that draw people to this town. When the bathhouses went up, plenty of people come through here over the years, more than half of them with ailments lookin' to be cured by those magical waters. You can just imagine all sorts of things that went on in this town that had nothin' to do with healing waters though. Gangsters, gunfights, politics and money ran those bathhouses. The sick, the dying, the rich, the poor and the greedy, they all partook of the cleansin' waters praying for miracles. Things happen in places like this; human nature tends to write its own horror stories without the help of imagination.

What most folks don't know is that before those bathhouses were built, those hills already had secrets. Dark things lie hidden down deep in those bubblin' wells of crystal waters, things that had been sleepin' for centuries and awakened by the relentless scratchin' of humans as they built their town scarrin' the land and suckin' the essence from the ground; dark things that feed on human greed and fears.

I don't know all the secrets of this place. I don't want to. I'm very sorry I even know this secret I'm about to tell you. But I can't just straight out tell you, I've got to give you a little background so you will understand better why I'm tellin' you this. Why I made this decision and why I got to do this.

I guess I should begin by tellin' you that my family has been workin' in the bathhouses for three generations and now I'm the fourth. After tonight I hope I will be the last. No one in my family ever told me there was anythin' wrong at the bathhouse. My great granny, my granny, and my momma managed to keep it a secret. That part I understand, what I don't understand is how they could live with themselves everyday knowin' what they did. Never tellin' anyone, even in the family, until the day they get a job there. That's what happened to me.

This is my first real job, other than babysittin'. Had I known the true sacrifice I'd be makin', I would've found a job somewheres else. But this was easy and my mamma got the job for me just as her mamma before her and her mamma before her. I hadn't really planned on keepin' the job for very long anyway, just through the summer and then I planned to go to college. Though my mamma backed me on the whole college thing, she really didn't seem like she'd been given it her all; I felt that maybe her priority for me was to take this job and that would be all that mattered. But when Momma decided to retire from the bathhouse, a sudden urgency set in her mind that I had to be the one to replace her.

Whatever understandin' Momma had with the bosses, it must've been a long standin' position open to only those in my family. I suppose this should've made me even more suspicious about the job. I needed money and I knew Momma wouldn't give it to me so I took the job, but secretly keepin' from my momma that this would only be temporary. It's kinda' funny to think that I knew I wouldn't be here long, I just didn't know the real reason why.

Momma waited till I was about to leave for work my first day when she and Granny did their best to explain to me what to expect, what truly to expect. Her and my Granny both came to my room while I readied myself for the grand career of bath attendant. I remember lookin' at myself in the mirror wearin' that white uniform that almost made me look like a nurse, minus the hat. It made me think about the possibility of going to nursin' school. I was thinkin about that when Momma and Granny came to my room and told me this crazy story about somethin' that lived in the bathhouse and that we gotta feed it every now and then or it will take us.

Momma said great granny made some kinda deal with this thing a long time ago that if we kept it fed it would leave our kin alone. Momma said we had to find someone else to give to it. I started laughin, I thought Momma, and granny was funnin' me. But Momma got all serious, and Granny got mad and left the room mummblin' to herself sayin' stuff like I was gonna get them killed. I couldn't believe all this. I just told Momma I had to go and we'd talk about it later. Momma told me there'd be no talkin' about it later and I had to listen good now. So, I listened to what she had to say about the signs to look for and all things I gotta do to cover my tracks so no one would know. When she finished talkin', I left. I had no intention of feeding people to some monster, even if it did exist.

I must admit I came into the job feelin' a bit uneasy, this bein' the first I'd have a boss and all, and then that crazy story Momma and Granny told me, even though I didn't believe, it still stuck in the back of my mind. Those old bathhouses are spooky too; all the bathhouses here in Hot springs have been updated with the modern conveniences society has grown accustom to, but they're still in those old buildins'. They keep it lookin' like its old time like even inside with antique furniture and stuff. Steppin' into any of the bathhouses on Bathhouse Row is like takin' a step back in time.

Those old marble floors still shine like they're new but you can see the places where people walked the most cause it's wore down a bit, and you can hear the echo of those footsteps from long ago when you're all alone and it's real quiet. Sometimes, I swear I could hear the shuffle of slipper-covered-feet walkin' through the hallway.

Those kinda things, they don't bother me, I know there's ghost and spirits. Like I said, they're all over this town. It's those other things, the thing Momma and Granny tried to warn me about, those monsters you gotta be careful of. I didn't know they were real.

Now I can't tell you which bathhouse this is, that wouldn't be fair you know. I mean times is hard and lot of businesses is strugglin' to keep up. I don't want to be the one to cause anyone grief but I can tell you what it looks like inside. After the entrance and checkin' counter, behind a big fancy decorated room, or I think they call it a foyer, there's a swingin' door that opens to a large half circle room. There's a row of chaise lounges right in the center of the room. To the right, there's a line of shower stalls and dressin' rooms. To the left, they put a modern sauna next to the stairs that lead to the massage rooms. Under the stairs is a line of old lockers, which I think they put in as an afterthought because they just don't look right, but that's where people keep their personal belongin's and they can lock them up and put the key around their wrist while they are bathin'.

On the back wall is a row of 12 doors, the kind with the slats in them, I think there called louvers or shutters, or somethin' like that. Each door has a number painted in black over the old crusty white wall. Those doors are the rooms where the baths are at. Momma told me there could've been enough room for 13 baths but 13 is an unlucky number, everybody knows that, so they turned the room into a closet for the towels. I'm thinkin' it's kinda funny now that 13 is considered an unlucky number cause maybe it's not really.

Anyway, each bath has its own little room where those magical waters are piped up through old rusty pipes and into big deep bathtubs that have been set in some kind of frame. You know what kind of tubs they got in those frames? They got those antique bathtubs with the feet on them, the kind rich people pay a mint for. Those bathtubs are old and stained from age, and all around the room from the floor to the ceiling is white tile they put in before my great-granny worked there. Sometimes a little tile is missin', so they just paint the wall to make it match. Every now and again you can see a crack or water stain or maybe a patch of rust from all the years these baths have been used. All the baths look like that except one, bath 10. Bath 10 looks like it's all shiny and new, like it had been remodeled, or at least that's what I figured and I guess so does everyone else.

Workin' in the bathhouse turned out to be not so bad at first. Of course I learned to deal with the humidity; it's always hot and wet in there, and the air smells old. It's not just the smell of mildew festerin' under the tubs and tile, or the rot of the wood in the walls, it's just a smell that gets into everythin' includin' the air of a buildin' no matter where it is after its been there a while.

I didn't have much to complain about though cause the money was good; these rich people come into town even to this day, wantin' to be bathed and pampered, and like the old days, lookin' for those healin' magical waters to fix their aches and pains and make them feel better. I got into a routine actin' real nice and treatin' the old rich ladies like they were royalty bein' healed by the fountain of youth and they would tip me some good money. I started to believe this job wouldn't be so bad and I'd have enough money put away that college wouldn't be so much a dream anymore.

I never told Momma or Granny my plans, I just kept on going and no one at home said nothin' more about a monster needin' to be fed. I got comfortable and I forgot all about it. The months went by and then one day, I walked into bath 10 and started drawin' the water and I felt somethin' wasn't right. Kept thinkin' I heard whisperin' but when I looked around no one was near me. I went back about my business getting' towels ready and I hear whisperin' again. I turned the water off strainin' to hear but except for the normal noises outside the room everythin' was quiet. So I turned the water back on and watched as the hot bubblin' water poured out the faucet, comin' from somewhere deep in the ground.

Then I heard whisperin' again, but a little louder. At the same time I saw a blackness oozin' out in the water. The water itself wasn't black but somethin', like a dark mist, swirled and clung to the water as it poured out and filled the tub. I couldn't move for a moment, I felt frozen like someone had stopped me. Then I heard the whisperin' again, only louder, but I still couldn't make out the words. The room, though naturally hot and humid, suddenly felt cold and I got a chill that hit me right to my core. I don't know how but I managed to move myself outa that room and closed the door tight.

I didn't know what to do. I remembered what Momma and Granny had said, that no one must ever know about this. I wondered if maybe I could run and leave it there and never come back. *Why not?* I thought, *why did I have to feed it?* My heart kept beatin' harder and harder, and I felt so confused and scared that I just ran right out the backdoor. We only lived five blocks from Bathhouse row, so I had walked to and from work instead of drivin' to save on gas money. But that day I ran the whole all the way and didn't stop until I got to my front door.

As soon as I walked in the door my momma came at me yellin', it surprised me. "What've you done?" Momma asked me. I couldn't figure out how she knew. I didn't understand until she grabbed my arm and pulled me into Granny's room. Granny sat huddled on her bed shakin' with my little sister in her arms, all around the bed a cold dark mist was hoverin' like a wild hungry creature.

"No! " I screamed at the thing. I remember telling that thing, that black misty monster thing, that I would take care of it. That I would go back and feed it but to leave my granny and sister alone. The mist disappeared after I said that. I wasn't about to let that thing get my sister or my granny, so I had to go back you see? I never wanted to hurt anyone or let anyone get hurt but I had to protect my kin.

When I got back to the bathhouse, no one had even noticed I had been gone except for one of the other attendants who got mad at me for leavin' the water runnin' in bath 10. It surprised me that she didn't see the dark mist, or hear the whispers. After I apologized I ran into bath 10 and found nothin' out the ordinary, but I wasn't takin' any chances though.

Bath 10

In the loungin' area I watched the women waitin' for their baths. I spied a woman who I'd never seen before and she didn't have anybody with her. She wasn't assigned to me which made her an even better choice. I went up and told her I was gonna help her get into her bath and told her it was ready, and I lead her in to bath 10. When we got in the room, still nothin' appeared strange or out of the ordinary, but as I helped her in the tub I saw out of the corner of my eye a slow oozin' of dark mist drainin' from the faucet. I quickly placed the cool face towel over her eyes after she got comfortable and left the room. I said a silent prayer for that woman as I closed the door behind me. I never saw the woman again.

I went about my business as usual for the next twenty minutes, tryin' to keep my heart outa my throat. Tryin' to keep my mind on my job, strainin' to listen for any strange sounds or screamin', I was scared, I was so scared. I kept moving though, ignorin' bath 10 altogether until at last, I knew I finally had to go in there; I had to know and I had to make sure no suspicions were raised either.

My stomach felt sick as I turned the doorknob, afraid of what I might find inside. I closed my eyes when I walked in and closed the door behind me. When at last I found the courage to open my eyes, the horrible scene that confronted me made me want to close them again at once. I didn't though. I took one look and covered my mouth and nose gaggin'. It was all I could do to keep from losin' my lunch.

When I felt I had managed some control, I turned and faced the carnage that for some reason my family had become part of. I didn't see a body or body parts but blood colored the room from floor to ceilin'. The water in the bath whizzed and churned from the Jacuzzi machine that each tub had installed. I stood there and stared in awe as the blood on the floor and walls began to soak into the room itself leavin' no trace of a stain. All that blood just disappeared as if it never happened, it even seemed to leave the room cleaner and brighter, and I remember how the room had looked dingy and yellowed before. Then it occurred to me that when I had first started workin' here the room hadn't looked so dingy but that it seemed to progressively look kinda yellowish over a short period of time, but the rest of the bathhouse never changed.

Then, I watched in horror as the blood in the water continued to swirl around until I finally brought myself to turn off the Jacuzzi and reach in the bloodied water and pull the plug. Blood and water swirled down the drain leavin' a clean bright and polished bathtub. The whole room looked as if nothin' had ever happened. I wondered where her body went; only the plastic wrist band with the woman's locker key remained lyin' on the floor. I thought it strange how no one had heard anythin'; no screams or sounds of strugglin' had escaped from the room. I couldn't let myself think about how the woman had died or how the monster had consumed her.

Then, an unnatural calmness came over me as I realized what I must do next. I took the key from the floor and left bath 10. Discretely I went to the lockers and removed the woman's belongin's, which fortunately were not much; only a pair of shoes, joggin' shorts, t-shirt, and under garments. A twenty-dollar bill lay neatly on top of her folded clothes. I never even thought about keepin' the money, that just seemed wrong, so I put the money in one of the tip envelopes and dropped in the slot of the attendant she had been assigned to, after all the woman had probably intended to do that anyway. I shoved the woman's shoes and clothes in a bag and hid them away until my shift was over.

After my shift, I snuck into one of the hotels in the old district and went down in the basement where the furnace is. Some of the hotels here still have the antique furnaces from the old days, and they still use them. I threw that woman's clothes in the furnace and watched them burn to be sure nothin' remained. I had been afraid her shoes wouldn't burn so well but it seems that the more money you pay for shoes the more flammable they are.

On my way home I thought about everythin', feelin' that I had gotten rid of all evidence of that woman pretty well. I felt sick to my stomach thinkin' on this. I hadn't committed murder but I might just as well have. When I got home, I saw relief in my momma's eyes. Granny and my sister were fine and though my sister remembered nothin' about it, Granny still fumed at me. I couldn't believe how angry both she and Momma still were at me. They told me that I should've listened and done what I was told to do in the first place. Maybe so, but then why did it need to be done in the first place.

Both Momma and Granny don't have an answer for that. Neither one of them knows what had transpired in the past. No one knows what kind of deal my great granny made with this thing. I wondered why it came awake in the first place. There's no rhyme or reason to it, except it just is. Now I gotta deal with it. I know this has got somethin' to do with my family but I'll never know how it got started; all I can do is hope that I can end it.

I can't let this keep goin' on generation after generation. I can't live with the guilt of knowin' I'd been the cause of that woman's death. I don't know how my momma and granny could live with that guilt themselves. They won't tell me how many lives they had to offer up to this thing just to keep our family safe. I can't live with that my whole life.

I wanted to college so bad one day, that ain't never gonna happen now. All this money I saved up I'm givin' to my little sister. I want my little sister to go to college and she ain't never gonna work in that Bathhouse. As for me, I can't go on sacrificin' people to this dark thing, I won't. If this thing wants my family blood then I'm gonna give it to the monster. Maybe that will stop it. I hope it stops it. When I saw that dark mist comin' out the water again and I heard the whispers I knew it had to be time again. Bath 10 has been lookin' dingy and yellow again.

When you find this letter in the locker you're gonna know what happed to me. At least you're gonna know somethin' of what happened. Even I don't know what to expect when I go into bath 10 for the last time. I know the

Bath 10

water is ready and waiting for me. I just hope it doesn't hurt. I don't even know if this will work, I hope so, oh I hope so. Just in case this doesn't work though, don't go into bath 10, don't ever go into bath 10.

Nightmares at Moccasin Bend
by:
Angela Lucius

Driving down the quaint streets of Moccasin Bend, Mississippi was like driving through the pages of an historical novel for young Ashlyn Taylor. The streets were lined with 19th century Gothic Revival homes, giant magnolia trees, and fragrant rose gardens. She loved mysterious places and haunting stories from history and she was already inspired to begin her writing.

Moccasin Bend was a historic town that had been little affected by industry or technology and she couldn't wait to dig into its untold stories. She had big plans to maybe do a coffee table book filled with photographs of rural churches and cemeteries, or maybe even write a ghostly novel with a haunting Southern twist. She had never had a personal experience with the unexplained before, but she loved a good ghost story. She had spent many nights by the bonfire during her days at UT, telling ghost stories with her friends.

Ashlyn had graduated from the University of Tennessee, just that spring, with a degree in English Literature and Photo

Journalism. She had spent the summer in Gatlinburg with friends from school before making the move to Moccasin Bend. Her parents had been killed in a terrible car accident the previous winter, on an icy mountain road near Knoxville. It had been extremely devastating; she had still not recovered from it. Maybe she never would. But, she had decided to engross herself in her project plans. She had some money put away from her inheritance and she had planned to leave her old home in Tennessee for a fresh start. Now was as good a time as any.

She had made arrangements to rent a small furnished guest house that sat very close to the town square and the public library. Two places that Ashlyn knew she would be spending a lot of time doing her research.

After acquiring the keys from the elderly landlady, Mrs. Crane, and signing the lease, she paid the first month's rent and went outside to unload her belongings.

She was glad that she didn't have to unload furniture. Everything, including dishes had been made available, but she had brought a few things that she could fit into her car to make it feel like her home.

After unpacking her things, she decided to take a drive and look around town and maybe stop off at the market to get a few things. She took her time driving around the small town. There wasn't much to it really, a town square with a small courthouse and police station attached, a small library, a grocery market, post office, a cafe or two, and a gas station that looked like it was still living in nineteen fifty, only now a self-service station. If she wanted to go shopping or find some fast food, she would have to make a bit of a drive. The nearest town was 15 miles away. It wasn't much bigger, but at least it had a Wal-Mart, McDonalds, and a Sonic. For now she could be content with what she had at her disposal.

Ashlyn passed several country churches and a small school which consisted of two red brick buildings, one for grades 1-8 and one for the high school kids. She turned left onto Waterford St. and headed towards the bridge. It was a small bridge and looked a bit old fashioned. Although it was two lanes, it looked like it hadn't been tended to in 30 years. The metal beams were tarnished and rusty in spots. Ashlyn decided against crossing.

She pulled her car into a gravel drive next to the creek and put the car in park. She wanted to take in the setting sun and enjoy the fresh air. As she got out and sat on the hood, she snapped a few photos of the creek and admired the surrounding scenery. Looking down toward the south end of the creek, Ashlyn noticed that the other side of the creek was a higher elevation than the side the town sat on. The creek took a sharp bend and disappeared behind the trees.

On top of the hill, at the bend, she noticed a menacing Gothic Style building that towered over the creek. It was three stories tall and had a sinister look about it. Ashlyn shuddered the moment she saw it. Focusing her camera toward the building, she peered through her zoom lens and locked in on the building, snapping a few photos. Another day she would find out what the building was. But for now, it was getting dark and the cool winds that swept across the creek were giving her the chills.

Her first night in her new apartment passed rather quietly. She had nuked a TV dinner and guzzled down a Coca Cola, unpacked a few things and hung up her clothing. She set up her writing desk and her computer, showered and then headed off to bed. Tomorrow, she would explore the town in more detail. It was 11:30 PM when her head hit the feather pillows and she was tired from her drive, so it didn't take long to drift off to dreamland.

Ashlyn sat up straight in her bed covered in sweat. She glanced at the clock, 3 AM. Her mouth felt dry and she was shaking all over. She fumbled for the light switch and after turning it on, went to the bathroom sink to wash her face. Looking in the mirror, she thought to herself, *relax, it was just a dream, it wasn't real.*

Still shaking, she went to the kitchen and poured herself a glass of orange juice and then returned to her bed. But, sleep was slow in coming. She couldn't get the images out of her head. Flashes and fragments of a girl with dead, black eyes in a white, tattered, and dirty gown, beckoned to her. Images that didn't make sense flashed through her mind every time she closed her eyes; images of scary faces grimacing in pain and screaming.

When she awoke, it was 8 AM and she rose, feeling like she had just closed her eyes.

For the next few weeks, Ashlyn's dreams continued, always the same tattered girl with the scary dead eyes, beckoning her to come. Scenes of abuse, neglect and torture; lifeless cold faces wandering around like drooling zombies; waking to the sounds of screams, that echoed in her head. She tried to blow them off at first as stress from the move, hidden grief about her parent's death and being in a new place, but it was beginning to take its toll.

Several weeks had past and Ashlyn had met some of the town's folk, but most of them were not as friendly as she had expected them to be. Especially when she started asking questions about the building on the hill. Most of them would change the subject if she brought it up.

Betty Sue Baker, the waitress at the local cafe was the only person who would talk to her about anything.

Betty Sue knew everyone and everything about them. She made it her business to know the goings on in the town. She didn't have anything better to do. When Ashlyn asked her about the building on the hill, Betty Sue was more than eager to share.

"Oh Honey, that there is the Moccasin Bend Insane Asylum. It's been here longer than this here town. That's where they keep the lunatics ya know, the real nuts...scary folks if ya ask me. Honey, I'm scared to death of that there place. They say that if ya get sent there, ya never come out til yur in a pine box, I believe it too Honey, cuz I ain't never seen nobody leave that place, lessin they was dead."

She smiled a big smile and popped her juicy fruit gum, poured Ashlyn a cup of coffee and scurried off to the sound of the pickup bell. Ashlyn smiled at Betty Sue's exaggerated

Mississippi accent. Even though she was from Tennessee and had an accent herself, she had noticed that the accents in Mississippi were just a tad more dramatic and different from what she was used to. She paid her tab and headed up the town square to her doctor's appointment.

She entered the front door of the old house, which had been turned into a doctor's office and signed the register on the desk. The nurse told her to take a seat and the doctor would call her in shortly. She took a seat, flipped casually through the stack of Ladies Home Journals and then sat back on the old leather sofa to wait. She didn't have to wait long, as she was the only patient in the office. Dr. Alfred Cameron greeted her from the door and asked her to come into the exam room. He was a tall, stocky man, with grey hair the color of snow; he had a rather crooked nose and small beady eyes, which looked three times bigger than they actually were through his bifocals.

"What seems to be the problem Ms. Taylor?" he asked while flipping over her chart.

"Well, I'm rather embarrassed," she said while fidgeting with a lock of her chocolate brown hair, "but I have been having trouble sleeping lately, and was wondering if you could prescribe me something to help me sleep or relax?"

Dr. Cameron pushed his glasses up on his nose and said, "Well, what is keeping you awake?"

"Nightmares, bad ones." Ashlyn said, "I'm having dreams about a dead girl screaming, and people being tortured. I wake up every night at 3 AM in a pool of my own sweat and it's really starting to get to me. I feel nervous all the time, like someone is watching me, even when no one is there, and I just need to relax so that I can focus on my writing."

Dr. Cameron opened his desk drawer and pulled out an Rx pad and scribbled a prescription for Xanax. He handed it to her and said, "Well, if this doesn't calm you down, nothing will."

When Ashlyn awoke, she was expecting to be in her own bed. She thought she was having a nightmare again, until Dr. Cameron entered the room.

"Where am I?" Ashlyn said in a half stupor.

"You're at Moccasin Bend Ms. Taylor, don't you remember anything?" Dr. Cameron said with no expression on his face.

"No I don't know what happened?" She said.

"Your land lady found you walking around in the yard, drooling all over the place and babbling about a dead girl. You became violent with her and she called me to come see if you needed a doctor. I had my orderlies bring you here for observation. I would like to keep you here until I know what's going on with you and that you are not a danger to yourself."

Ashlyn felt like Dr. Cameron was feeding her a load of crap, but she couldn't remember a thing, so she made little protest at first, that is, until Dr. Cameron ordered the nurse to give her another shot of medication.

Ashlyn began to argue with the doctor. "You cannot

keep me here against my will!" she shouted. "There is nothing wrong with me, I've just been tired, and having these stupid dreams, maybe the medicine you gave me was too strong."

Dr. Cameron wasn't listening and ordered the nurse to proceed with her sedation; the last thing she remembered was struggling to get away.

***

Shivers ran down Ashlyn's spine as she tiptoed quietly down the hallway. She was in her bare feet and soft white cotton sleeping gown. The freshly waxed tiles were icy cold and slick as a frozen pond. She could almost see her own reflection glide along with her every step as if mimicking her from the other side.

The nurse had left her door unlocked by mistake and she had waited patiently until the skeleton crew had exited the floor for their midnight coffee and smoke break.

As she crept past each door of the long, dreary hallway, she could feel the stares of hungry eyes blazing into her back. She dare not look at them. She could hear the moans and cries and rants of the insane behind each door. The same sounds that kept her awake most every night. That and the visions of the dead girl. The nightly screaming had only increased the nightmares and the dark circles under her eyes were proof that she had had little, if any sleep in weeks.

She didn't belong here and she had made her protest known, only to be tackled, drugged, and dragged into her bed, where she had remained tied down to the bed frame for nearly three days. She had cried, begged, pleaded, and screamed to no avail. She had finally consented to the nurses by cooperating. If she were good, they would let her out and then she would find a way to escape. She had been skipping her medication for nearly two weeks and faking her lethargy. She needed a clear head if she were ever going to get out of this place alive. She knew it was the only way out. She had no family to miss her and Dr. Cameron had taken it upon himself to have her committed. He had even taken a statement from her landlady Mrs. Crane, stating that she had lost her mind in the front yard and was behaving erratically. Who in this town was going to believe her over the claims of a sweet elderly lady?

Ashlyn was caught off guard by a piercing scream that shook her whole body. She thought about returning to her room, but this might be her only chance. She had heard the screams every night and wondered if someone were really being tortured. She had tossed and turned in bed for several nights during the past week, wondering and worrying if they would come in the night for her. She could only imagine what gruesome tortures the screamers must be enduring. Several of the patients had disappeared from the dining room lately. Ashlyn believed that they were the ones being made to scream. She had caught a glimpse of the suspected punishment rooms. They were usually locked up tight, but with the lack of proper nursing staff, it had been rather easy for her to wander about unnoticed.

She had witnessed the tub room, where patients were punished for bad behaviors; they were drugged into a stupor and made to sit in deep tubs of ice water for hours. She had seen the lights flicker and heard the wires in the walls hum, when this happened she believed someone was being shocked. She had seen patients walking around in a daze with drool hanging from their mouths, unaware of who they were or where they were. She had to get out of here.

She reached the deserted nurses' station and peered around the corner. There was no one there. Quickly, she scurried down the long, dreary hallway towards the flickering exit sign. Maybe if she was lucky, she would find a way to escape this hell hole they had placed her in.

Giving the handle a firm push, she was surprised to see that it was open. Apparently, the door latch hadn't caught all the way when the nurses left the floor. She stepped through the doorway into the deserted staircase and decided that her best choice would be to go down. Carefully, she crept down each step like a thief in the night.

She wished that she had brought her sweater, as shivers ran over her exposed arms. Her skin was tight and covered in chill bumps. Her blood was pumping hard and her breathing was heavy from the anticipation of being spotted. *What would they do to her if she were to be caught?* She shook the thought quickly from her mind.

Making her way down the dark stairs to the first floor, she pushed on the metal bar, but it was locked tight, a key card was required to open it. So, she started down the stairs to the basement level. Surely, there was a way out of this place. Reaching the door to the basement, she held her breath and pushed. The door opened with a click and creaked loudly as she pushed it open to peek in. It was very dark and damp but appeared to be deserted for the moment. Rusty pipes ran across the low ceiling and she could hear water droplets splashing loudly onto the cold concrete floors.

Which way to go? She must decide before someone caught her or noticed she was missing. With quick paced steps she chose to go right. Going left was darker and more threatening and she was already trembling, almost out of control.

I should have just kept my mouth shut about the nightmares and the visions, she thought. She couldn't understand why Dr. Cameron had not believed her or was keeping her a hostage here, but she had her suspicions that he was up to no good. She knew what she had seen in her dreams, what she had experienced and thought that surely, it had just been stress and that Dr. Cameron would give her something for anxiety, or something to help her sleep, and send her on her way. She had never expected to end up here, locked away in a looney bin.

She had read about the history of this place at the library. Moccasin Bend Insane Asylum had been established in 1850 by a local physician named Dr. Griswold Cameron. How ironic that the past four generations of Camerons had been involved in running the Moccasin Bend Asylum. There was little to go on though, hardly any information about the goings on of the hospital.

Moccasin Bend Asylum was older than the town itself. Situated menacingly in all its Gothic spookiness, high on the hill above the Moccasin Bend Creek, which twisted through the North Mississippi hills like the deadly, black water snake it was named for.

It had been there since before the Civil War. There was one road up the hill to the hospital and it led to the old rickety bridge she had parked near and was guarded by a security checkpoint. There were no fences, other than the main gate wall, as the property was surrounded on one side by a marshy, snake infested slew and on the other side by the high bluffs of the icy black water of the Moccasin Bend Creek. To her knowledge, no one had ever escaped.

It had been documented in the local history book to have once been a hospital for wounded Confederate soldiers in the 1860s and later became a prison for the criminally insane and the unwanted. Not many people ever left this place alive or so she had heard. She did not intend to spend the rest of her life in this Gothic monstrosity of the damned.

Suddenly, she heard the sound of footsteps echo behind her. She stopped in her tracks, held her breath, and listened. She heard them again, coming closer. She ducked into the shadows and waited, afraid to breathe or move. She heard the squeaking wheels of a gurney rolling towards her, along with the eerie, masculine whistle of Dixie.

She waited in the darkness, as the tall black shadow of a crooked man came nearer; his lanky shadow, dancing on the wet stone walls. She could see that the gurney was occupied, but she could not tell by whom or by what. As the squeaking wheels rolled past her, she saw movement on the gurney, a twitch and then a pale, boney white hand flopped out from under the stained white sheet right in front of her face.

She muffled a scream, which she could hear in her mind, but that she did not allow to escape her dry, chapped lips. Reaching over with his dirty, calloused hands, the gurney bearer placed the bony arm back under the sheet and continued on his way.

She could smell the strong odor of whiskey, cigars and putrid body odor, that made her stomach churn and caused the bile to rise into her throat with a terrible burn. It seemed like an eternity before the footsteps and the nerve racking squeal of the gurney wheels faded into the darkness.

For a brief moment, her curiosity got the better of her. She had to know where the gurney man was going. *What if there was a way out?* She rationalized. She slowly rose from her crouched position in the shadows and crept cautiously into the darkened tunnel in pursuit.

The tunnel grew darker and she was forced to feel her way down the slimy, wet walls of the tunnel. A rat scurried between her bare feet. She jumped and sucked in her breath, trying hard not to be heard.

As she rounded the bend of the slimy hallway, she saw a glowing light beneath the large steel door at the end of the tunnel. She knew that she should turn back, that there was probably no way out, but she had to know what was there.

The cold steel door beckoned her to come closer. She crept slowly toward the door, which was slightly ajar.

Nervously, she peered around the steel door and was horrified at what she saw. The gurney man was shoving a body into the flames of the large furnace. Ashlyn realized that the body was twitching as the flames licked their way around the sheet, she realized that the person beneath it was still alive. At that very moment, she heard a piercing scream which took her breath away.

The gurney man suddenly stood erect and paused, then slowly turned in her direction as if he could sense her presence. She quickly ducked behind the door and then turned to run down the long, dark tunnel of slime.

She ran past the staircase door that she had entered, not seeing it in her hurry to escape the clutches of the gurney man. As she ran in the opposite direction, she reached a fork in the tunnel. She stopped briefly, trying to catch her breath; her sides ached with a stabbing pain.

Not knowing which way to go, big crocodile tears began to cloud her eyes.

"No you can't cry now, you have to keep your head if you're ever going to get out of this place", she scolded herself in a whisper.

Sucking in her tears she looked to the left and then to the right. She had no idea which way to go. Her feet were numb from the cold, wet floor; she was shivering and felt sick to her stomach.

Then from the darkness she heard a whisper. "Ashlyn....

Ashlyn." She was frozen with fear. She couldn't move. It was as if she had been paralyzed and frozen to the spot on which her cold feet were planted. Then, she saw her.

It was the girl from her nightmares. The girl with the long, stringy, blond hair, the dark and lifeless eyes, and the tattered and dirty dress; the girl that had visited her bedside so many times. The girl she had tried to tell her doctor about, the girl who had been the cause of her being here to begin with.

"Come Ashlyn, come with me, I can show you the way," The girl said in a raspy, fragile voice.

Ashlyn shook her head in disagreement, but her feet followed the girl without her consent. Disappearing into the shadows, the girl led Ashlyn down the dark hallway; she could feel the green slime on the floor squish between her bare toes. The stench of death and mildew burned at her nostrils.

The girl turned the corner and Ashlyn followed as if in a trance. All the while trying to convince herself not to go, and being unable to resist the urge to follow. Tears streamed down her cheeks now against her will, as she rushed to keep up with the morbid looking girl, who had been her worst nightmare.

As she rounded the next bend in the tunnel, she saw the girl standing there. The girl pointed towards the doorway with her boney white finger.

"Take this doorway, it leads to the graveyard, if you can make it across, there is a stairway near the tool shed that leads down the bluff to the boat ramp where they bring in casket supplies. If you are careful, you can make it out of here when the supply boat comes at sunrise. But you must hurry; they will be looking for you soon."

"Who are you?" Ashlyn muttered in a dry whisper.

"I am Adelia Addison," the girl said. "I brought you here, so that you can tell those on the outside what they are doing here in this place."

"No one will believe me, that's why I'm here to begin with," Ashlyn blurted through her hot tears.

"They will believe you if you show them this." Adelia reached into the darkness and pulled out a stack of worn, leather bound diaries. "These are Dr. Cameron's journals; they contain names and details of the tortures and experiments that have occurred here for the past 30 years. It should be enough for you to expose him and maybe someone will come in and find out for themselves what he is doing to these people."

As Ashlyn took the journals from Adelia's boney hand she said, "But I am a patient here now. How will I convince them I'm not crazy?"

"Dr. Cameron talked about what he had planned for you in his last journal entry," Adelia whispered. "They will believe you."

Ashlyn looked toward the doorway with nervous anticipation. But, when she looked back to thank Adelia for helping her, the girl had vanished into the darkness.

Ashlyn pushed the door open and ran up the crumbling

staircase into the brisk autumn wind. She clutched the journals tightly in her arms like a newborn child and ran towards the Moccasin Bend Cemetery.

The rusted cast iron gate banged recklessly with each breeze, against the chipped, brick wall that marked off the cemetery edges. Ashlyn was scared, but determined to get away and expose this doctor of terror and suffering. She must do it to free these poor patients from having to live with more hell than they already had to endure.

Ashlyn ran hard and stumbled several times on the hallow ground where she had to be careful not to fall into a dusty grave. This cemetery had been here for over 150 years and many of the graves were now beginning to sink. There were broken shards of headstones scattered about the cemetery; an easy place to break an ankle. But she continued to run toward the back gate which led to the landing steps. There was no one at the landing, so she decided to hide in the bushes near the dock. No one would see her there, as the fog was thick and covered her like a white blanket. She shivered from the cold and realized that her gown was now covered in dirty stains and her hair was wet from sweat and stuck to her face like a wet slug.

She waited nervously as the supply boat made its way toward the dock in the thick fog, which swirled like monstrous tendons rising from the black waters of the creek. When the dock loaders had made their way up the staircase with their boxes of goods, Ashlyn slipped into the boat and hid under a tarp. She was almost home free.

***

The Moccasin Bend Tribune Headlines- Monday October 21st read:

Murder and Torture at the Moccasin Bend Insane Asylum, Exposed By Unnamed Source!

An anonymous source delivered the journals of Dr. Alfred Cameron this past week to Mississippi State Authorities. Upon further investigation it was discovered that for the past 30 years or more that hundreds of patients at the Moccasin Bend Insane Asylum were being used for torturous and inhumane experimentation by Dr. Cameron and 21 of his staff members. The State Medical Board has revoked Dr. Cameron's medical license. He and his accomplices have been taken into custody and held without bond. Patients of the Moccasin Bend Asylum have been relocated to a new facility. Charges have been filed for the murders and torture of numerous patients at the facility as well as abuse and neglect charges. Trail dates will be announced at a hearing at the Moccasin Bend Courthouse on Monday Oct 28, The Honorable Judge Archibald Henderson presiding......

A cold breeze brushed past Ashlyn's face as she knelt by the faded stone of Adelia Grace Addison. The date on the stone read 1844-1866. Ashlyn had done some digging into the history of Adelia Grace Addison and discovered that she had once been a volunteer nurse at the Moccasin Bend Asylum during the Civil War, and because she had no family living, Dr. Griswold Cameron had taken her in, in exchange for her nursing service at the age of nineteen. But because she had become hysterical over the news of the death of her husband to be, Brighton Hall, who was killed at the Battle of Shiloh in April of 1863. Dr. Cameron's great grandfather, Dr. Griswold Cameron, had committed her as a patient because she refused to believe that Brighton was dead and had insisted that he would come back for her. Adelia had died mysteriously three years later, from an apparent suicide by hanging herself in the stairwell on the second floor with a bed sheet. There was no evidence of foul play in the historical documents, but Ashlyn suspected based on the history of the facility that something more sinister had happened and the suicide had been a cover up.

Ashlyn placed a red rose on the grave of the dead girl who had saved her life and who had spoken for those who could not speak for themselves.

As Ashlyn rose from the grave side and walked away from the cemetery, a tear ran down her cheek and she felt a peace come over her like she hadn't felt in a long time. She would be forever changed by the experience. She was now a firm believer in ghosts, this was certain.

Adelia stood beside her weathered stone, holding the red rose above her heart and watched as Ashlyn walked away. She smiled with grateful satisfaction and sniffed the fragrant red rose as she gracefully strolled across the cemetery. Now, she could finally walk the deserted halls of the Moccasin Bend Asylum in quiet peace and wait for her beloved Brighton to return for her.

The Top Floor
by:
Alexander S. Brown

It was early October in the city where the springs run hot that Tilbwa Quirk waited on Main Street with her intern friends. Although, Tilbwa, a thirty year old that appeared strong willed, independent, and fearless with the image of, "I am woman, hear me roar," sat prominently, this projection of an empowered female was exaggerated. Behind aquamarine colored contacts and under bleached blond hair rumbled the nervous thoughts, *Why am I doing this?*

She breathed deep, receiving a high from the fresh mountain air. Even though she had lived in this southern Ozark town for a quarter year, she had yet to become accustomed to its purity. Instead, she was used to air that reeked of sewer and fried chicken, like in the old Mississippi town where she had been raised.

Tonight, outside of a bar named Capote's she and her two friends, Janet Thomas and Lillian Fisher, Fish for short, loitered. Fish, who was in her mid-thirties was blessed enough to still look twenty-five years old. Her image, although prim and slinky, would also fit the appearance of a biker chick or as she dressed one year for Halloween, Joan Jett.

With her brown eyes, black hair and thick lips she would likely be the fantasy for a many of recovering patients. Although most times she appeared pissed at the world, she was normally just in deep thought. Such as tonight, she debated if this ghost tour would be full of crap or actually accurate.

Fish smoked a Camel #9 while composing posture as if she had years of ballet training, although her skills belonged to a cheerleader. Suddenly, her prim structure vanished as she popped her hip out, likely hoping that the guy in the leather jacket and spiked hair walking by would notice, to her disappointment he didn't.

As Tilbwa steadied herself from the shots of Jaggermeister earlier thrown back, she noticed Janet texting furiously on her slider phone, her face increasingly grew heated with every typed word. Momentarily, Tilbwa wondered if Janet's anger intensified any further if a line of steam would sway from her head, no differently than the lines that swayed like dancing haunts off the hot springs in the cold Ozark air.

Gradually, a crowd of truth seekers began gathering near Capote's, most were assumed to be tourists as few were eagerly snapping photographs of the city that mobsters once flocked to. Tilbwa and her friends stayed distant, not because they were snobs, they simply enjoyed their privacy.

It wasn't until their tour guide, or what they suspected was their tour guide, arrived that Fish extinguished her cigarette.

"Richard can't make it," Janet sneered.

This was normal for Janet, although she was physically unfitting to her friends erotic or empowered looks, she contributed greatly to women who appeared classy. The man, who had stood her up once again had come in and out of her life many times, each time she would return to him. If she wanted, she could stand alone but for some reason she needed to be adored. Somewhere under her natural beauty and modesty was a girl waiting to break free from her shell, one who literally wanted to scream out, "I am woman, hear me roar!" Until then, she continued hiding behind a mousey smile.

"What's his excuse this time?" Tilbwa sneered.

"Just another lame cop out. They get more pathetic each time," Janet grumbled, not caring to elaborate.

"You need to branch out," suggested Fish as Tilbwa stood, indicating they needed to join the group. Without instruction required, the interns walked to their tour guide.

The man in charge of educating the common folk of paranormal phenomena was an intimidating figure. He stood eight feet tall, dressed in a shade of black so dark that its hopeless depth overpowered the alleys and shadows.

Stepping into the same streetlight that the crowd gathered under, the interns saw that this hulk of a man had a healthy skin tone, which looked as if he had absorbed a daily helping of natural Vitamin D. Up close to their leader; the interns equally agreed that he wasn't as intimidating as they had first simultaneously thought. The reason for this reconsideration regarded his smile that appeared caring and indicated his skills at being a heartthrob.

Being in this man's presence caused Fish to pop her hip out and gain the posture of a poster girl for Calvin Klein or Gap. Although none of the woman made a move directly on this man, Fish and Janet hoped desperately he would pursue something more than taking their money and welcoming them to the group.

Once their money was collected by the guide, who called himself William, the group made small talk until the clock struck midnight and the tour guide announced in his baritone voice, "The witchin' hour is here! Last call for ghost tours! Ten dollas each! Last call!"

When no one else joined the group, the tour guide promised his guests that they were in for a series of extraordinary tales that would cause them all to suffer restless nights. The three interns felt that he exaggerated the reality of the situation. His elaboration had only been said to hype up the crowd and season their imagination with overactive horrors.

For the interns, Tilbwa was the most skeptical as she had greatly sided with science and psychology verses religion or the paranormal throughout life. Fish deemed herself to be more rational. Earlier, she stated during drinks, that hauntings existed; however, she also noted that most peculiar sounds in the typical haunting could be nothing more than an old building settling or bad plumbing. For a house to be considered haunted, she would need more proof before it could be classified as an actual paranormal phenomena. Janet, on the other hand, believed in ghosts one hundred percent. Furthermore, she had mentioned numerous times that she enjoyed watching the ghost shows and documentaries and had read books regarding the paranormal, all of which she was completely gullible to. As a matter of fact, tonight's rendezvous had been suggested by the firmest believer.

Shortly after midnight the ghost tour began near a historic hotel then progressed on the lonely back streets of the city's main stretch. Although the ghastly stories shared were amusing and passed time, Janet was the only one who believed the tour guide's every word. On this hour exploration, a haunted coffee shop and theater were showcased. Later, they were introduced to a full street that wasn't just haunted but possessed. Legend went; the street was damned due to some of the locals in the olden day performing satanic human sacrifice.

At the tour's conclusion the guide had finally seized not only Fish's attention, but he had now gained Tilbwa's interest. As tourists continued snapping photos and filming, the three inters stood in utter surprise. On the same street, not far from where human sacrifice once commenced, loomed a monstrous rehabilitation center, which employed the three interns.

Throughout the walk the three had mumbled and whispered amongst themselves and as of this moment they all grew willingly silent. "This hospital was tha ideal nursing' facility for wounded soldiers durin' tha civil war," William boasted.

The dreadful institution towered fiercely in the night sky and for a moment appeared as if it could come to life and stamp out the audience with possessed architecture. To the heavens, or better yet the dead of space, it reached hopelessly to the spirits that had escaped the structure.

The tower, centered in the damned fortress was crafted from concrete but in this moonlight it appeared that bone had been used for this molding instead of stone. As their eyes followed down the crown of the monster, concrete was replaced by beige brick and windows, some of which gleamed ambiance and the others blackened such as the cold sky.

Wind howled around this goliath kingdom, sounding as whispers of the cries from those tortured souls that had escaped its grasp.

The five bulb light post at the foot of the hill projected an eerie shine upon the base of the hospital. The subtle gleam appeared no differently than that of a flashlight used by a child to demonstrate a scary face while reciting a ghost story.

This same glow highlighted the main entrance that appeared as a separate building but was attached to the monster. Despite its titanic structure that would best fit a cathedral, nothing holy could be described in its existence. Projecting from its main doors, along with the side stained glass windows, was the form of a screaming mouth and two brightly lit eyes of insanity.

Gradually, Tilbwa interpreted its full effect. The main entrance appeared as the head of some demonic hybrid and its brick structure and tower acted as its body. Finally, she was reminded of the giant turtle from *Never Ending Story* but with a *Hellraiser* twist.

"The bottom level," the guide continued, "was once the city morgue and for those who ain't Southern, I have to clarify that our summers have always been smolderin'. With that said, I have to point out that tha hospital didn't receive a coolin' system 'till the 1900's."

An audience member must have assumed where this was going because he grimaced. "Durin' tha civil war it was procedure, such as in any war, which tha government hadda document tha deceased soldiers before they were buried. This took alotta paperwork. 'Cause of this lengthy report, actual burial coulda been as soon as a day or as long a month from tha time of arrival. Now, we all know alotta people died in tha civil war and we know that tha morgue wasn't air conditioned."

The same audience member who had grimaced, sighed, indicating his weak stomach, however, this hint hadn't been taken by the storyteller. "Well, ya can only fit so many bodies in the drawers at the morgue before they run outta space. So, what do ya supposed had to be done?'

A woman at the rear of the crowd coyly suggested, "They hadda leave the bodies in tha open?"

"Correct," the guide stated, "now imagine this… for a whole summer tha bottom level was used to store dead bodies, no coolin' system, and there was a ninety degree heat.... And now ladies and gentlemen, we have decomposition. And what do ya suppose that kinda heat does to a dead body?"

The man with the weak stomach groaned, "It makes it rot."

"Yes, but not just rot; the heat caused tha bodies to actually liquefy."

"Oh God," a teenage girl muttered.

"Oh God nothin'," said William, "in the summer of tha civil war that hospital stored so many bodies on tha bottom level that when they liquefied the rotted muck came up to a person's torso. After quarantine and cleanin', tha rot level was still visible on tha walls, like when a flood leaves a watermark from that particular flood... What came next was restoration and since tha rot was so intense tha walls hadda be repainted with a special paint, this hadda be done to cover up tha stench. Story goes, those walls have been painted a million times, and that stain keeps coming through tha coats. Numerous accounts state that people have smelled a stench of rot that floats through tha bottom level on a cold breeze... Now, before any excuses can be made this bottom level hasn't been used as a morgue since tha end of the civil war, therefore tha smell should be gone."

The storyteller allowed the group to speak amongst themselves then his stern voice filled the night once again. "After this facility closed as a hospital, it reopened as a rehabilitation center. All floors between top and bottom are used for tha rejuvenation of those who are injured or recoverin' from a terminal illness. Tha bottom level was closed off and tha top level, which is now also closed, was once a sanatorium ward for tha criminally insane."

Impatiently, a teenage girl near the center of the crowd eagerly pressed, "Why was it closed?"

"Well, an unusually high number of suicides happened up there. But here's tha catch, none of tha suicides were committed by patients, they were all committed by nurses and highly respected doctors. And tha longer this went on, tha more creative tha suicides became. There are documents statin' hospital officials overdosed, hung themselves, shot bubbles of air in their veins, slashed their wrists and throats, and lastly, threw themselves from tha top window to tha far left."

As soon as the words escaped his mouth, the specified room where people flung themselves from, became illuminated with a ghostly blue. The speaker didn't notice this action until a lady said over the gasping and mumbling crowd, "I thought you said the top floor was closed."

"It is," the guide confirmed then turned.

"Then why is there a light on up there?" A man badgered.

The tour guide removed his top hat and scratched his shaved head in confusion. Despite the many elaborations this man could have concocted or the reasonable excuses he could have spoken, he simply explained, "I have no idea why that light is on."

Near the center of the crowd a woman whispered,

"There's probably someone up there turning that light on at a certain time."

Although everyone heard the remark, the tour guide ignored the assumption. Before he started sweating bullets or had to answer questions that he couldn't find explanations to he said, "Well group, this is a fine example of tha unexplained and tha paranormal. There's a chance that tha top floor was reopened and there's an equal chance that there's somethin' lingerin' up there that will always remain unexplained. Although perhaps ya'll have questions, I have a question for ya'll. Don't ya think tha mystery is more excitin' than knowin'? Now with that question in mind, I hope ya'll all enjoyed tha tour and I hope ya'll have a safe travel."

Quickly, he tipped his top hat then turned away from the group and went about his business, lighting a cigarette on the way. After the tour group parted ways Tilbwa, Fish, and Janet remained standing outside the rehabilitation center. Tilbwa then asked, "The elevator doesn't go up to the top floor anymore, does it?"

"Even if it does, there isn't even any electricity up there," confirmed Fish.

"Well, someone's up there," said Janet, "anyone feel like an investigation?"

They fell silent then Fish noted, "We do have run of the hospital."

"I'm game," said Janet.

Even though Tilbwa was an atheist, she was the last to advance to the hospital. Surprisingly, her friends appeared eager with curiosity, unlike herself, who began feeling sick with weak nerves. Never before had she investigated, she had no reason to, ghosts didn't exist. Even as she walked, this unrelenting bitter sickness in her throat and stomach made her question skepticism.

They began up the brick stairs that treaded the hill to the rehabilitation center. On the walk up Janet suggested, "I have a flashlight on me, we can communicate with the spirits by light."

"How do we do that?" The rationalized medium believer, Fish questioned.

Janet pulled a flashlight from her pants pocket; it was the kind that would shine by twisting the end. "What we do is twist the end so that the flashlight is between on and off then we ask a question and if a ghost is in the room with us, the light will turn on by itself."

They approached the wooden front doors that were framed by an off color jade iron fixture, centered above the grand entrance was an engraved pineapple that welcomed its guests. Further up, beyond the pineapple was a hemisphere shaped window, which flickered lowly as if a candle had been set behind it.

Etched in the concrete, crowning the low lit window was the Greek inspired doctors' symbol, consisting of the Hermes staff. Wings flourished at the top of this pole, signifying the flight tools belonging to the ancient messenger of the Gods. Spiraling up from the bottom of this symbol were two intertwining serpents. Glairing the women in the face as it had many times previous, this specific instance made Tilbwa question if their fates would be in the hands of Hermes, after all not only was he a messenger of the Gods, he was a guide to the dead. Despite the eerie situation, Fish and Janet remained full of energy as they crossed the marble floor into the elevator. Behind the two thrill seekers, Tilbwa shuffled her feet at a hesitant speed then joined her friends in the antique structured carriage.

When the doors closed the three stared at the floor selection and although they knew to select the tenth floor they could only stare. Then, Janet extended her finger and pressed ten. Instead of the dead number illuminating orange and the elevator lifting up, the button marked, "B" glowed subtly then the elevator descended, its movement caused the stomach of all three women to flutter.

Before any of them could question what happened, the elevator sat at base level with its doors open and welcoming a never ending black ocean of despair. The waves of this ocean began to spill over into the threshold of the carriage, acting like hands grasping heinously at the feet of the interns.

Instead of exploring they stayed in the light. Tilbwa pressed the button for the top floor in repetition but it didn't change the situation. After not being delivered from the cold, dark hall where a breeze filled with rot met the women, Tilbwa began pressing the button labeled, "L" for ground level. Upon doing this hastily, she hoped the elevator would quickly lift them up as her skepticism subsided, causing her to feel that something menacing hid in the abandoned morgue.

Finally, a small luminance beamed into the blackness. Tilbwa turned to see the disturbance was caused by the light Janet held. Then, she noticed both women were shielding their noses from the rank that wafted in the unknown. "Let's check it out," suggested Fish, there are stories down here too, and it doesn't look like we're going anywhere."

"Yeah, but the doors could close, we could be stuck down here," Tilbwa argued.

Fish pulled out her cell phone, "We have service here. If we get trapped, I'll call the main office."

Tilbwa checked her phone to find she too had service and since they weren't going anywhere she said, "Okay, let's go."

Although Tilbwa had come this far, she acted her role of the fearless skeptic well, however, she felt horrified. When she spoke, "Okay, let's go," she intended to say, "let's get it over with, this place is scaring the Hell outta me."

As a child many elaborated visions frightened her, such as the monster in the closet and the creature in the bathroom. Despite what may have lurked in her bedroom or what hid in the bathroom, the dark had always struck the greatest chord in her heart. Even today, it embarrassed her to admit she didn't sleep or use the bathroom alone until she breached teenage years.

While standing in this mythical trap, all of her childhood fears attacked. Instead of causing a scene, she counseled that nothing supernatural existed. She had survived this long without a paranormal occurrence and she would continue living undisturbed. As childhood proved, nothing existed.

Before advancing the hall, she questioned that perhaps through practice she had conditioned herself to be an atheist, although perhaps something sinister awaited for her guard to go down. If this were so, all those nights of sleeping in the bed with her parents and using the bathroom with an open door only prolonged her fate, making her ripe for the picking to some ghastly thing.

Janet stepped forward, her light only strong enough to brighten a foot to two feet before them. The interns braved the level that had once been a biohazard. Once they had stepped far enough away from their transportation, the elevator doors dinged then began to close. Fish scrambled toward the sliding doors, gasping a blasphemous phrase.

Upon Fish's arrival at the threshold, she cursed as she had failed to prevent their entrapment. Feverishly, her index finger pounded against the up button only to result in the verification that they were stuck on the bottom level. "Don't worry," fearlessly reminded Janet, "we have service remember?"

"Yeah," grunted Fish, "let's go on and call."

"No," Janet argued, "if we're going to investigate we at least need an hour of peace."

Fish sighed as Tilbwa skeptically noted, "Come on, we don't have anything else to do, besides nothing bad will happen."

The tile they crept upon was cracked and in most places

broken in chunks. After moments of cautiously traveling the corridor, Janet shined her light to the right, granting visuals to the previously spoken haunted fact. "There's the level mark," she noted as the eyes of the interns acknowledged the lit area.

After squinting, Tilbwa and Fish noticed a line of fecal brown distinctly separate the white paint from where the flood of corpses had stained the halls. Tilbwa was further disturbed to find that even to this day, the stain bled through the attempts of repainting.

While acknowledging the discoloration, their walk continued until they arrived at the two oak double doors that pushed inward. Before adventuring the morgue Tilbwa breathed deep, still smelling the hint of decomposition accenting the chilled air. Suddenly, she felt the urge to discontinue and call for assistance; however, she remained acting strong and fearless.

Janet's hand touched the right oak door, her skin almost as white as chalk. She hesitated to push until Tilbwa instigated, "Let's see what the fuss is all about," she couldn't believe she was saying this as she began to feel breathless and nauseated. Although she wanted to cry out in defeat, she felt too prideful in skepticism to say she didn't want to investigate further.

Janet pushed forward and almost in unison, all three poured into the abandoned morgue. Before they could acknowledge the room, where rats scurried with sparkling red eyes, they broke into a coughing fit. The ripe odor they endured was an eye burning concoction of mold, ammonia, and most prominently liquefied corpses.

For only a second they could view this room and in that glimpse they saw dangling fixtures, overturned gurneys, and a few morgue drawers open. Instead of going further they quickly retreated from the room. Their eyes began to water and their nostrils stung with a burning similar to breathing Clorox. As Tilbwa's face grew crimson due to coughing, Fish stated, "I'm calling the office."

Once her phone entered her grasp, it lit her face blue. The expression Fish displayed explained trouble and her words confirmed the issue. "How in the Hell can you be powering down? You just had a full battery."

With that said, the phone's battery died. "Tilbwa, call help," Fish demanded.

Tilbwa followed instruction then looked to her phone in dismay, as her phone suddenly began to flash with low battery then terminate. "The spirits are draining the energy," Janet suggested, "maybe we should try to talk to them?"

Fish almost exploded at Janet due to the predicament that she had gotten them in. Before she began yelling and screaming at the instigator, she grabbed for a cigarette.

"Maybe if we talk to them the elevator will come back down, if not by chance then by fate," continued Janet.

Fish sighed with frustration, "We have nothing else left to lose." Her tone of voice indicated she wanted to claw someone's eyes out.

Janet was the only one of the bunch who sounded

perky, "Okay, why don't we sit by the elevator and I'll set the flashlight by the morgue doors."

With the believer chiming this, the flashlight was laid by the double door. Tilbwa and Fish advanced in the darkness, estimating where the elevator was, then sat Indian style with Fish grumbling, "How in the Hell did we get ourselves into this?"

"We were bored," Tilbwa answered.

At this time Janet joined the two, then instructed, "We have to open our minds and believe that there is the possibility that something wants to communicate."

"How do we start," Tilbwa asked, wanting less to communicate and desiring more to leave.

"We introduce ourselves and tell the spirit something personal. But, we shouldn't tell the spirit our last name."

"Why not?' Fish asked.

"Because, with a full name they can use information against us," Janet warned.

Silence lingered in the drafty corridor, "I'll start," eagerly blurted Janet, "my name is Janet and I am a nurse."

"My name is Fish; I like to read horror stories."

"My name is Tilbwa Quirk and I don't believe in ghosts."

"You weren't supposed to say you're last name," Janet warned.

"Maybe we'll contact a friendly ghost," Tilbwa joked to cover the accident. Instantly, a wave of heated fear caused her to feel belittled. With this emotion came the question to if she were now nothing more than a sitting duck. Trying to rationalize that everything would be fine and not to worry, Tilbwa recalled the reason why she forced herself into the shoes of an atheist. Once, a long time ago, she did believe and she had found in her skeptical conditioning that believing was scarier than not believing. Then her thoughts added the cherry to the cake, *Even if you don't believe in ghosts, they believe in you.* Suddenly, she wanted to call for help, but if she did her friends could tease her, and she was too vein to endure that.

The other two didn't find her bravery or humor amusing. Instead of being scolded or sided with, Tilbwa lingered in ignorance. "If there are any spirits here that would like to speak with us, please tap the flashlight at the morgue doors on," Janet encouraged.

Nothing happened just as Tilbwa hoped. In the following seconds or minute, Tilbwa wanted to scorn Janet's expectations. This urge to mock Janet was only for self-reassurance that nothing spiritual hid in the shadows. To bring upon this verbal abuse would not only relieve her own tension, but hearing herself explain that Janet was ignorant for expecting a reaction would help herself firmly understand once more that there was nothing, nowhere.

Instead of mocking her, Tilbwa remained cordial, biting her bottom lip. Despite the failure, Janet continued to coax, "Come on, and just tap it on. We aren't here to hurt you. We just want to speak to you. If you're here, please tap the flashlight on."

For seconds, they sat in blackness. *Nothing is going to*

happen, Tilbwa coaxed herself, *we might as well be here talking to a box of matches.*

"Come on and tap the light on if you're here, please."

"Janet get real, noth-" Tilbwa was silenced, her breath stolen. Suddenly, all by itself, this inanimate object flickered on.

Visually, the hall remained empty. Straining desperately for hope of seeing that a rat had bumped into the flashlight, Tilbwa saw that not even a rodent resided in the hall with them. In this tunnel of light that bleached the corridor, Tilbwa noticed they were truthfully alone and since the flashlight hadn't been tapped by a miniature pest, she advised that the flashlight was defected or rigged for joking purposes.

"Good, thank you," Janet praised, "now tap the light off please. Just tap it a little so that I know you understand how to communicate with me."

As requested the light flickered off. Janet encouraged, "Turn it on once more please."

This time, much more quickly than previous the light flashed on. In this luminosity, Tilbwa could see the joy mounted on Janet's face and the look of shock that Fish expressed. "Turn the light off if you're the only spirit here," Janet continued.

The shining remained prominent, "Turn the light off if there is ten or less."

The shine upon the women stayed lit, "Turn off the light if there are twenty or less."

With the cool hall remaining lit Janet asked, "Turn off

the light if there are fifty or less."

All three hoped the flashlight was broken, especially when Janet requested, "Turn off the flashlight if there are one hundred or less." With the light shining eerily Janet requested, "Turn the light off if you understand me." Immediately, the light extinguished, causing all that witnessed to feel shocked. At this request the black hall engulfed the three allowing whatever menacing things that hid amongst the shadows to creep closer.

Before simply concluding that the light WAS defected or that Janet WAS playing a prank, Tilbwa wanted to cry out that they needed to leave now. Despite the characteristics that an actual haunting was taking place, she tried to discard the evidence just so she could feel safe.

Elements such as the chill that brought the smell of a stagnated crypt had been blamed on being underground. Secondly, the light was defected. Finally, this malevolent emotion that drowned Tilbwa in the anxiety that some rancid specter stood only an inch away from her face was blamed on childish fears. Although reasonable excuses were given to each disturbing occurrence, the skeptic felt in indescribable words that something powerful and massive wanted to hurt her from the soul. Silently, she began to cry.

With hopes of regaining light, Tilbwa blurted, "Turn on the flashlight if there are 1,000 spirits or more."

Suddenly the light beamed on. In unison the three shared an unspeakable thrill, however, Tilbwa's thrill was opposite of her friends who seemed optimistic to the achieved contact.

"Flicker the light if any of you mean us harm," Janet instructed.

The light then jittered the same as Tinker Belle's actions in the Disney classic of Peter Pan. With this flicker, Tilbwa ran to the flashlight, seized it, and then declared, "It's time for us to leave! All you have is a defected light and I'm tired of this!"

***

At the end of her statement the morgue doors flew open, knocking Tilbwa to her hands and knees. The dropped flashlight spun. During its spin Fish and Janet noticed a decayed, naked body jolt from the historic room and seize her by the waist. This haunt was the entity that had broken free from the shell of a male body.

Splattered and torn indirectly upon this soldier was a collection of scars and discolored bruises. From the brief second they witnessed this long bearded, scraggily haired spirit, they noticed he was translucent and although he didn't fully exist as a whole but as a fog, he was tangible enough to render Tilbwa helpless.

Before creating further action, his attention was directed from the victim and set upon the shocked voyeurs. A sickening grin stretched upon his leathery face, exposing butter yellow teeth, revealing the malevolence or insanity, that he intended to inflict. His devilish, curled grin appeared just as violent as his existence and it defined the cruelty that he not only had in store for Tilbwa, but for her friends.

For Tilbwa, who believed nothing existed, released a crazed scream. Her eyes, once relaxed and knowledgeable emerged differently in the darkness. In this opaque that was interrupted by a white beam, her eyes seemed as wide and full as purgatory. Brazenly, she attempted tearing at the hands that restrained her, each time she failed as this invincible force had fantastical abilities that kept her bound.

The haunt cackled in a mixture of pleasure and dementia. With one sudden yank, the snarling ghost pulled her into the morgue. Her prolonged cry echoed then was cut short by a gurgled choke. Speechless, both women felt sickly remorseful that they had simply allowed the spirit to carry their friend into the unknown.

Following the gurgle a heavy flopping, thudded and thrashed against the morgue floor, a nerve shattering CRASH sounded and was figured to be a gurney falling onto its side. The tragic act drunkenly continued for seconds that seemed to be an eternity then abruptly ended.

Although still feeling as if they should have helped, they understood that once the flopping sound became silenced, that Tilbwa was dead. At any minute that room would spew out another gravely villain, if not the same one, to claim both of them for its lair. The women grew cold and clammy, their chattering teeth clicked in a hollowed echo that filled the corridor. Too afraid to think or move, they became possessed with bovine stupidity.

Both lacked the desire to investigate or rescue, Fish

turned to the elevator and pressed in repetition the button that should allow the carriage to retrieve them. Finally, Janet turned to her cell phone to see that she now lacked battery.

Attempting to find a way of escape, the two screamed in unison for rescue while clawing feverishly at the elevator doors. Soon, the very spirit that abducted and what sounded to be koshered their friend, would attack and maybe in his return a ghastly platoon would follow. Although they knew yelling was useless as the walls and floors were made of concrete, they continued crying for help. In the midst of their plea something witchy choired from the morgue in a legion of torturous mumbles, miserable cries, and banshee screams.

The two women clung to one another then the morgue doors flung open and expelled a river of liquefied rot. This wave of putrefaction roared like a raging sea. Its tide hurled up then crashed down, covering the flashlight and causing the corridor to eclipse black.

As the ghoulish river flooded closer, the elevator doors parted open. After jolting into the carriage, the florescent light from the ceiling allowed them to see six feet into the shadows. To their horror, the unspeakable was witnessed. From this approaching slime induced monster, animated skeletons clawed their way free from the biohazard to inflict death upon the interns.

The doors closed and Fish instantly pressed the button for ground level. On the outside of the elevator doors a series of bangs and slaps hit against the cool metal. When the elevator refused to uplift them from this desolation, Fish began no longer pushing one button. She began pounding on the keypad hoping for anything to trigger their ride to a safer level. Once the carriage refused movement, Fish hit the emergency button to find that too hadn't made a difference in their travel. They were now at the mercy of the ghosts.

"Do you think the light on the top floor was a trick," Janet asked, "like something down here was using it to lure us in?"

"I don't know," blurted Fish while fumbling with her dead cell phone. Angrily, she threw her device to the floor and screamed, "Dammit," as it shattered.

Following the tantrum, the doors budged inward as if they were a thin plastic and they squeaked as if a person walked on old wood. When the doors returned to a straightened structure the elevator dinged. Before the women had a chance to react, the doors cracked open a foot. Massively, the muck flooded in with the intensity of a fire hose, the waterpower knocked the women off their feet.

Both interns struggled to stand; however, the rotting river smothered them and continued flooding inward until the liquefaction filled the carriage. Once the elevator was filled to the brim the doors closed, then the ride up began.

***

It was the following morning when the hospital administrator, Henry Carlisle, received notification of a mysterious light shining from the top floor. The administrator took the lobby elevator to the ninth floor then walked the busy hall that was filled with nervous interns, overworked nurses and stressed doctors. Excusing his way through the chaos of another typical work day, he came to a door which only he maintained a key for.

Upon opening the door, he ventured upward on the staircase that brought him to the tenth floor. In this travel his pocket flashlight, which had been used uncountable times to gaze into the eyes of his patients, was apprehended to guide his way. Upon reaching the top floor, his feet began to swiftly walk the dusty, shadowed hall.

For him, this wild goose chase felt ignorant. The top floor had been shut off securely and no one but he had a key. This search felt useless; after all, the call had come from William, a pest who had repeatedly inquired to see the top floor due to historical accuracy for his paranormal tours. Each time this request had been asked, the opportunity had been denied by none other than Mr. Carlisle.

Even though Henry expected to find nothing in this search, he decided a quick look wouldn't hurt; after all there was a chance that a hobo nested in this respectable facility, no different than a rat.

When the fifty year old administrator arrived at the room that supposedly shined light the night before he gasped, "Oh God!"

In this particular room, three corpses decayed, the cause of death determined as nothing more than a suicide pact. To the far right of the room, Tilbwa Quirk sat slumped with blood staining the collar and chest of her shirt, in her right hand was a bloody shard of glass. From the ceiling fan hung Fish, below her swaying feet was an overturned chair. Finally, lying on her back was Janet with a syringe sticking from her vein like a porcupine quill.

The administrator turned against the room and attempted to gather his thoughts. Before he could even fathom how these women were able to break into the top level, his thoughts directed to the renovation of the facility.

Within the next year he had debated reopening the top and bottom levels to the hospital, however, after this grizzly display he decided the top level had too much of a bad reputation. Although he felt somewhat skeptical, this ungodly act was interpreted as a bad omen. Therefore, this floor would never house another patient; however, the bottom level was still good. With its odor aside, he was certain that reconstruction would make it suitable for residents again. As he selected his cell phone and called the coroner, he decided, yes this level would stay closed but within a year the bottom level would reopen. By doing this their space for patients would be plentiful.

EPILOGUE

Now that your imagination has been put to the test, we offer you the opportunity to stretch it even further. Though the stories you have read may be fiction, the places where these stories took place, though slightly embellished, are real. They are places in the South and Southwest of the United States that has had phenomenal events occur. Maybe these places have actual reports on sightings of apparitions or objects being moved around which would instill the possibility of some sort of entity. Perhaps some of these places merely have that certain eerie sensation you get when the hair on the nape of your neck stands up and there is that distinct feeling that you are not alone or you're being watched. Maybe some of these places have a natural occurrence that only science can explain but the explanation is beyond the comprehension of the average individual.

Whatever the reason, the places in this book have caused the locals to believe they are, in truth, haunted, and therefore fuel the fires of imagination. It does make you wonder though, if maybe, just maybe, some of these stories are real. After all, reality is a matter of opinion. It may very well be that we are nothing more than an illusion to them, but then, what would that make us? Indeed we certainly feel that we are not alone and if you find yourself in one of these places mentioned here, you too may encounter the spirits that walk among us.

J.L. Mulvihill

IMAGICOPTER

Imagicopter is a non-profit voluntary endeavor of authors and artists working together toward promoting their own publications while lending a hand to other writers and artists; a network system which offers authors and artists venues to promote their work via book signings, conventions, and other events.

Imagicopter is not an agency, not a publisher, not any kind of entity at all. Imagicopter is simply the umbrella name we call our network system. www.Imagicopter.com offers links to the artists and authors including those you see here in this book, so that you can purchase their books and art directly from them or their publishers. It also enables public awareness of the local talent in their area, and allows the capability to see who or what may be available for events by the links provided on the website.

Author Biographies

H. David Blalock - H. David Blalock writes speculative fiction. Since 1997 more than two dozen of his stories have appeared in print and online magazines. His novels include Ascendant and Emperor from Sam's Dot Publishing and Angelkiller from Seventh Star Press. In 2012 his work will appear in: Midnight Screaming Magazine, Call of Lovecraft anthology (Evil Jester Press), The Martian Wave magazine, Rogues in Hell anthology (Perseid Press), and the second novel of the Angelkiller Triad, Traitor Angel. David lives in the Memphis, Tennessee area.

To read more about H. David Blalock go to: www.thrankeep.com

William R. Eakin -William lives on a cliff above the Arkansas River with a beautiful and creative family, an aging cat and a large rock (in the living room), outside a town that features most of the elements included in his story. He is a professor of philosophy and art at the University of the Ozarks and a member of SFWA. Over the past twenty years he has sold some 100 stories, many award-winning or

Nebula-recommended. Since his first pro sale to F&SF, tales have appeared in Ellen Datlow's sci-fi.com, multiple times in Amazing Stories and more times in Realms of Fantasy (during its 15-year run) than just a handful of other authors. Recent stories appear in the Kindle version of Digital Science Fiction and in ParAbnormal. Sam's Dot has published a 4-book collection of his "Redgunk" stories, including his most recent book The Wild Women of Redgunk. Critics call Bill "shamanistic," a "brilliant storyteller" who creates a "genre all his own"; and have compared his series to "James Joyce on moonshine," something like "the National Enquirer meets the Bhagavad-Gita." Bill also has contributed to a number of nonfiction works, including books on the world religions after patriarchy and in relation to ecological sustainability. His work has appeared in translation from Amsterdam to Mumbai.

He loves to get feedback and his email can be found at the following website: www.sfwa.org/members/eakin/

 **Jason Hughes** - Jason grew up in Texas. He has been a lifelong fan of the Horror genre for thirty-five years and counting. He likes to keep his writing on a level of realism with everyday people that are placed in horrific situations. He graduated The Tom Savini's Special Effects Make- Up Program in 2004 and still does Special Effects today. Jason

is the Editor of the anthology Moral Horror, available now in stores everywhere. He is a contributing Writer for The Houston Examiner, Beyond the Dark Horizon and Writer/ Reviewer for www.Horrornews.net . His writings can be found in such anthologies as Nocturnal Illumination, Ladies and Gentlemen of Horror 2010, Bleed and They Will Come, Quakes & Storms along with the magazines Twisted Dreams and House of Horror. He is also a multi-published (and transferred to audio) Poet. Jason was chosen as one of the top ten best Horror Authors of 2009-2011. He has written screenplays for Mudd Miller Films/ Rebellious Cinema, Sick Flick Productions & American – International Pictures (released The Amityville Horror and much more) He is also a Drummer, t-shirt Printer, Sky Diver and avid Supporter of The West Memphis Three (www.wm3.org).

Visit Jason on-line at:
www.facebook.com/JasonHugheshorrorauthor

Windsong Levitch - Windsong is an Ojibwa Native American. She has a Bachelor's degree in Mythology, a Master's in Shakespearian Literature, a Master's in Elizabethan English, and is a Doctor of Zoology. Retired for many years, she began writing again. She has been writing since her early teens and is now seeing her lifetime of writing come to effluence. Windsong has traveled extensively, and she speaks many languages. Windsong's first book came out in the spring of 2009 titled The Lighter Side of Dark containing gothic and fantasy poems as well as short stories. Windsong also has a poem in Dragons Composed an anthology. The poem is titled "A Funeral for a Dragon" She and her husband currently live in the Memphis area with their many cats. As a polio survivor, she has accomplished a great deal, but if you ask Windsong what she feels is her greatest accomplishment she will simply smile and say, "I am a wife, mother, and grandmother." Her most recent story is featured in Clockwork Spells and Magical Bells an anthology. The poem is titled "Time."

Visit her at: www.facebook.com/authorwindsong. levitch

Angela Lucius - Angela is the Author of Hauntings in My Head, a collection of ghostly Southern poetry (under the pen name Angela L Burke) published in 2009 and Darkness Deep a collection of short stories & dark poetry published in 2011. She writes history and cemetery preservation articles for several online blog sights and is a member of The Association of Graveyard Rabbits Cemetery Bloggers. In 2007 she co-founded the Mississippi Society of Paranormal Investigators, where she is a History Researcher, Dark Literature Review Writer, and Website Editor. She likes to travel to haunted locations, loves old historical buildings and Civil War and Native American history. Angela is currently working on a Horror/ Ghost Fiction Novel with a Native American setting to be available in 2013.

Angela's books are available on Amazon.com and Createspace.com. Read Angela's blogs/articles at: www. headboardsofstone.blogspot.com and www.mississippi-spi. com

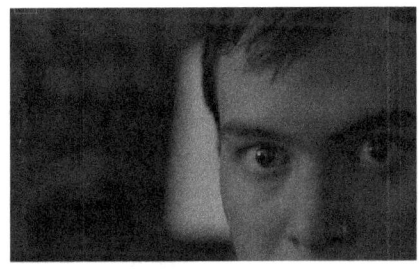 **L.S. Nadler -** Hailing from the wonderful White North of Canada, Lonnie Nadler is currently an Editor and Columnist at www. Bloody-Disgusting.com, where he covers horror-related news. Lonnie writes his own independent comics and has illustrated for various publications. During his undergraduate degree at McGill University, he received his B.A. in Philosophy and English Literature. When he is not writing or reading, Lonnie can be found watching films, biking, and searching for untold stories. He dislikes the sun and soft fabrics.

Visit him at: www.bloody-disgusting.com

 **Roland Mann** - Roland Mann is a writer, editor, speaker, and professor. As writer, he is best known for his work on Cat & Mouse, a comic which ran for nearly two years, garnered critical acclaim, and led Roland to other work. Some of his other work includes Miss Fury, Planet of the Apes: Blood of the Apes, and Rocket Ranger. As editor, Roland is best known for his work as a Malibu/Marvel Comics editor where he edited The Protectors line of comics and many Ultraverse titles. Roland also served as Editor and Publisher of Silverline, a line of independent comics that included such titles as Switchblade and The Scary Book. Roland earned an MFA in Writing from Spalding University, a MA in English from the University of North Alabama, and a BS in Creative Writing from the University of Southern Mississippi. Roland has been a newspaper editor, an advertising flunky, a college professor, and a speaker at writing workshops/conferences where many find his sessions encouraging. Roland's recent work includes his first novel, Buying Time, graphic novel adaptations of The Adventures of Huckleberry Finn and The Wonderful Wizard of Oz. Roland teaches Creative Writing for Entertainment at Full Sail University.

He occasionally blogs at: www.rolandmann.me.

Roman Merry - Roman is a horror enthusiast and an art photographer living in Jackson, Mississippi with his grumpy cat, Fickle Fae Vader. He writes poetry and short stories that pour from the shadows of his mind, culminating into mesmerizing verse. A creature of the night, his photography stirs your imagination and revives the childhood wonder of things that go bump in the night.

See his photography work at:
http://www.etsy.com/shop/entropystings

Check him out on Facebook:
https://www.facebook.com/roman.merry

Richard Parks -Richard lives in Mississippi with his wife and a varying number of cats. He collects Japanese woodblock prints but otherwise has no hobbies since he discovered that they all require time. His fiction has appeared in Asimov's SF, Realms of Fantasy, Lady Churchill's Rosebud Wristlet, Fantasy Magazine, Weird Tales, and numerous anthologies, including Year's Best Fantasy and Fantasy: The Best of the Year. He's been a finalist for both the World Fantasy Award and the Mythopoeic Award for Adult Literature.

He blogs at: www.richard-parks.com

 **Herika R. Raymer** – Herika grew up consuming books - first by eating them, later by reading them. Her mother taught her the value of focus and hard work while her father encouraged her love for literature and art; so she has been writing and doodling off and on for over 30 years. After much encouragement, Mrs. Raymer finally published a few short stories and has developed a taste for it. She continues to send submissions, sometimes with success, and currently has a collection of stories in the works. She is the Assistant Editor for a science fiction magazine and Lead Editor for a horror magazine. A participant of the voluntary writer/artists/musician cooperative known as Imagicopter, Herika R. Raymer is married with two children and a dog in West Tennessee, USA. Assistant Editor of Sam's Dot Publishing, Aoife's Kiss, Shelter of Daylight, Cover of Darkness Managing Editor, Imagyro Magazine (geekzine).

Her website is at: www.herikarraymer.webs.com

 **Kalila Smith** – Kalila was born and raised in New Orleans. She personally researched and wrote the material featured on Haunted History Tours. She is the author of New Orleans Ghosts, Voodoo, & Vampires, and Tales from the French Quarter, and the soon to be published, Miami's Dark Tales. She has been featured on and worked behind the scenes on television productions featured on A&E, Travel Channel, History Channel, BBC, and PBS. She appeared in the motion picture, The St. Francisville Experience. She wrote and directed Journey Into Darkness... The Trilogy," a video documentary, featured in segment in television broadcast in the US & UK. And worked on and appeared in the documentary for Sony's Playstation II game, Ghosthunter. She conducted all of the paranormal investigations for the local television show, "Haunted New Orleans." She was a producer in the PBS documentary "Southern Haunts" New Orleans episode produced by Sky Dive Films.

Websites: www.kalilasmith.com
www.neworleansghosts.com
www.hauntedhistorytours.com

M.R. Williamson - A writer never grows tired (or surprised) of hearing positive things from EDITORS— especially if it's constructive criticism. After retiring from 'Ma Bell' in the year 2000, Williamson seriously took to the pen. Through E-Bay and various bookstores, his novel collection, The Pragamore Chronicles, eventually reached more than eight countries.

Williamson's new book, 'I, Gnome — Rising of a Wizard' is about the life of Yenwolk Stonesmith, a young gnome born into the world of the normal. He is an old staunch character in my novels, 'Pragamore — A New Beginning' and 'Krypendorf — The Fourth Lesson'. His life is chronicled here from birth until about sixteen when he makes the most important decision of his life — becoming a wizard.

Williamson's poetry has won the Editor's Choice Awards from the International Library of Poetry in 1999, 2000, and 2002. Some of his poems have appeared in such anthologies as America at the Millennium, The Silence Remembers, and Endless Mysteries.

This is a good year (2012) for short stories. View from the Easley Place is on exhibition at Munford Library. Williamson's stories are published in such anthologies as Clockwork Spells and Magical Bells ('Quest for the Dragon Scale-Kerlak), ParAABnormal ('Spotter'-Sam's Dot), Stories in the Ether ('Shelled'-Nevermet), 'Unlikely Friend' (Sam's

Dot), 'Apprentice' (Sam's Dot), and... Well, you get the picture—a writer never stops.

Williamson is now on tour with a group of Writers, Artists, and Publishers in a group called Imagicopterwww. imagicopter.com.

-

 **Miguel Viscarra** - is a sociologist from Alamogordo, New Mexico. An alumnus of New Mexico State University, which is where he graduated with honors in the field of sociology, Miguel is currently pursuing a Master's Degree in the university's graduate program. The oldest of three children in a matriarchal and matrilineal family, Miguel has lived in the state of New Mexico for his entire life with his mother, grandparents, and two younger sisters. The author currently spends his time providing tutoring for the writing, sociology, and women's studies students of New Mexico State University's branch campus in Alamogordo, which is also where Miguel started his education by receiving an Associate of Arts Degree in Social Services.

Writing has long been one of Miguel's passions, whether it is a poem, song, story, or academic paper. Miguel is not merely your typical horror fan. Recent gendered ventures into the horror genre and academia prompted Miguel to study the classic horror theories of Julia Kristeva, Barbara Creed, Linda Williams, Carol J. Clover, and Sue Short. Alongside a handful of other writers and authors, he contemporarily continues to critically review many pieces of horror literature for a website dedicated to the genre. Inspired by

an affinity for the supernatural and an open-mind, the New Mexico native has sought-out, visited, and ventured into some of the state's many haunted attractions. You can find him at:

www.fearfiends.webs.com

His Facebook:

https://www.facebook.com/pages/Miguel-Viscarra/121038154645141

His Wordpress: http://miguelonastar.wordpress.com

 **Diane Ward** – As a rising young author, Diane writes short stories and poetry. She lives in Brandon, Mississippi and enjoys playing old-time music on her mandolin. Her science fiction short story "Doorknobs" will appear in The Best Teen Writing of 2012 presented by The Alliance for Young Artists and Writers.

About the Interior Illustrator

Robert K - Robert K.began his life in the arts at a young age and although mastered classes regarding the arts he was self-taught. His skills include sketching, painting and photography. He has spoken at numerous conventions regarding his artistic talent and has worked many commissions. His first published illustrations are in the very book you hold, Southern Haunts.

About the Editors

Alexander S. Brown – Alexander S. Brown is a Mississippi author who was published in 2008. His first book *Traumatized* is a short story collection that has received rave reviews from horror fans throughout America. Although, Brown began as a horror author, he has recently published two young adult steampunk tales, which can be found in the anthologies *Dreams of Steam 2: Brass and Bolts* and *Clockwork Spells and Magical Bells*. His poem, "Maters" was later published in the magazine *Midnight Screaming Volume 3 number 4*. Brown says there are more upcoming projects as he plans to write a series of novels chronicling the lives of residents in a town that is damned. Eventually, he will pen a fantasy/horror trilogy. He organizes author/artist events for Mississippi along with author, J.L. Mulvihill in the Magnolia Tower for Imagicopter. Keep updated on Alexander S. Brown at:

www.traumatizedsouls.com

J. L. Mulvihill - (Jen) is the author of the young adult fantasy novel, *The Lost Daughter of Easa*, published by Kerlak Publishing. Other stories J. L. has written and had published includes, "Chilled Meat", a steampunk thriller, found in the anthology, *Dreams of Steam II: Brass and Bolts*, and "The Leprechaun's Story", a steampunk urban fantasy found in the anthology, *Clockwork Spells & Magical Bells*. "A Real Dragon"

and "Magic in The Ozarks", are found in, *Memories and Dreams*, published by The Fine Arts Center of Hot Springs, AR. "Jen's Spicy Crawfish Bisque", is found in, *It's All about Food with a Mississippi Twist*, published through the Clinton Ink-Slingers; and "TheProud Oak", published through the Gulf Coast Writer's Association.

Jen has written several articles for Examiner.com as the Jackson Literature Examiner. She is also an events coordinator for the Mississippi Chapter of Imagicopter known as the Magnolia-Tower, a volunteer organization of authors and artists who promote their own publications while lending a hand to other writers and artists. J. L. Mulvihill is a member of the Society of Children's Book Writers and Illustrators (SCBWI), Gulf Coast Writers Association (GCWA), The Mississippi Writers Guild (MWG), as well as the Arts Council of Clinton, the Clinton Ink-Slingers Writing Group, and the Java Jotters.

Jen is currently working on her second novel, *Elsindai*, as well as her young adult steampunk series, Steel Roots. She also continues to write short stories in the fantasy, steampunk, horror, and sci/fi genre, as well as poetry inspired by her life in Mississippi. She has also been known to Karaoke from time to time when she thinks no one is looking.

Be sure to check out her webpage: www.elsielind.com/

Check out the following pages to see more from

 SEVENTH STAR PRESS

All Seventh Star Press titles available in print and an array
of specially priced eBook formats.

Visit www.seventhstarpress.com for further information

connect with Seventh Star Press at
www.seventhstarpress.com
seventhstarpress.blogspot.com
www.facebook.com/seventhstarpress
www.twitter.com/7thstarpress

Now available!   A Seventh Star Press Anthology from
editor **Michael West!**

eBook ISBN: 978-1-937929-69-5

Softcover ISBN: 978-1-937929-60-2

Vampires Don't Sparkle! poses the question: What would you do if you had unlimited power and eternal life?

Would you…go back to high school? Attend the same classes year after year, going through the pomp and circumstance of one graduation after another, until you found the perfect date to take to prom? Would you…spend your days moping and brooding, finding your only joy in a game of baseball on a stormy day? Or would you…do something else?

The authors of this collection have a few ideas; some fanciful, some humorous, and some as dark as an endless night. Join us, and discover what it truly means to be "vampyre."